PRAISE FOR ANNIE REED

"One of the best writers I've come across in years. Annie excels at whatever genre of fiction she chooses to write."

— KRISTINE KATHRYN RUSCH, AWARD-WINNING WRITER/EDITOR

"You can't go wrong with Annie Reed. Her deftly-crafted tales —with characters as memorable as the stories themselves— far surpass most of what's out there. She deserves a wide audience."

— MICHAEL J. TOTTEN, AUTHOR

"Annie's writing is magic, seriously."

— ROBERT J. MCCARTER, AUTHOR

"Annie Reed is considered by many to be one of the best new writers appearing in fiction."

— DEAN WESLEY SMITH, EDITOR *PULPHOUSE FICTION MAGAZINE*

ROAD OF NO RETURN

ANNIE REED

TV *Ink*
Thunder Valley

Road of No Return

Copyright © 2023 Annie Reed

ISBN: 978-1-954460-02-7

Published by Thunder Valley Ink

Cover art Copyright © DPimage/depositphotos.com

Cover and layout Copyright © 2023 Thunder Valley Ink

For more information on the author, go to anniereed.wordpress.com.

10 9 8 7 6 5 4 3 2 1

ROAD OF NO RETURN

1

———————

Nick James didn't expect the dumpster to yell at him.

Part of his job working nights at a strip club a few blocks away from the famous Las Vegas Strip was taking out the trash. He didn't mind. He spent most of his time behind the bar, mixing watered-down, over-priced drinks. Taking out the trash gave him a few minutes of relatively fresh nighttime air free of cigarette smoke, overbearing cologne, and the sweat stink of the customers, most of whom didn't care if anyone saw exactly how aroused they were.

Vegas had a well-earned reputation as Sin City, but these days it was in the midst of trying to upgrade its image. New casinos were being built at breakneck speed, all glitz and glamour, but some neighborhoods, like the one surrounding the strip club, still reeked of sleaze and backroom deals, especially at night when the glare from the Strip couldn't quite dispel the stark shadows of the city's past.

The strip club was the perfect place for a man like Nick to lose himself. Nobody paid attention to the bartender as long as the drinks kept coming. All eyes were on the dancers.

He took a deep breath, letting his ears recover from the same bump and grind music he heard every night. After midnight the air had a chill to it, something tourists didn't expect. Nick was warm enough thanks to the flannel shirts he wore at work over a plain black t-shirt. The boss kept the air conditioning in the club cranked up high to make the dancers more alluring, he said. Nick figured he was one of the few men in Vegas who wore flannel even during the height of the summer months.

Raucous cries and hoots and the sound of drivers leaning on their horns came from the direction of the Strip. Wedding party, or maybe a bachelor party, or possibly some other celebration fueled by too much alcohol and a lot of available credit left on someone's card.

When was the last time he'd been out drinking with a few buddies? Fifteen years ago? Maybe twenty? He'd never made any real friends here, just acquaintances. His choice but it still stung.

This was his life now. He thought he'd come to terms with it, but every now and then he longed for something different. Something in the same zip code as normal.

He was about to heave the heavy black garbage bag he'd lugged out the club's back door into the dumpster when a thin, yelping cry came from inside.

Not human, it was the sound of an animal in distress, and a young one at that, crying for help from a world that just didn't care.

Nick peered over the side of the battered dumpster.

In the middle of the mounds of trash that had baked to a stinking mess during the day sat a kitten. All big blue eyes—frightened eyes—that glittered in the light from the parking lot and fuzzy black fur that almost blended in with the black trash bags already in the dumpster. The only things that stood out were the patches of white fur around the kitten's nose and mouth. That mouth opened wide as it let out another yelp when it spotted him.

"How'd you get in there?" Nick muttered.

But he knew. Someone threw the kitten out just like trash. Didn't want the problem or the noise or just didn't give a fuck, and they figured what better place than a dumpster on the seedy side of the Strip.

Most people didn't seem to give a fuck anymore. He didn't want to think about the sort of person who could have done this. People who threw animals away were the kind of people who'd have no problem killing someone. Or watching while someone else did. Nick was well acquainted with the type.

He knew what he was going to do before he even hoisted himself up and over the side of the dumpster.

He wasn't a big man, average height and weight—a wiry little shit, the boss called him, but then again Chubs lived up to his name, and every guy who wasn't pushing two-fifty was a little shit in Chubs' book. Nick let himself down gently on the heaps of garbage inside the dumpster. At least most of the trash was in bags. He didn't let himself look too hard at the stuff that wasn't.

The dumpster stank to high heaven and made Nick glad he hadn't eaten dinner yet. He never did on nights he was working. In Vegas there was always someplace open where he could grab a bite to eat when three o'clock in the morning rolled around and he was out the door for the night.

He thought the kitten might run away from him, but it just sat on its garbage bag yelping at him. It was probably starving, but at least it had the good sense not to eat anything in the dumpster.

He picked it up with one hand. It fit neatly in his palm, its little kitten legs, claws out, hanging between his fingers and scrabbling for footing that wasn't there.

It was so thin. Nick could feel each of its tiny ribs as it shivered in his hand. He was no expert on cats, but it didn't look old enough to be away from its mother.

He brought the kitten close against his chest, cradling it with his other hand. It latched onto his shirt, claws sinking into the flannel as it climbed up the shirt until it burrowed its face against his neck, right below the scruffy not-quite-there beard that covered his chin. Its fur only smelled slightly of garbage. It couldn't have been in the dumpster all that long, just long enough to scare the crap out of it.

He stroked the back of the kitten's head with a gentle fingertip, and it quit crying and made a sound that wasn't quite a purr.

Getting out of the dumpster without dislodging the kitten wasn't easy—the bags of trash weren't exactly stable—but Nick managed. He kept the kitten cradled beneath his chin as he went in the back door of the club.

The kitten yelped at the sudden change in light and the music bellowing from the club's sound system. Nick murmured nonsense to it and the kitten quieted down. Probably had something to do with the way his voice vibrated in his chest. He sure as hell didn't think it could hear him above all the racket.

He kept some milk in the refrigerator behind the bar. One of the club's regulars, a fussy little man who carried a custom walking stick, always asked for a glass of milk along with a separate shot of Amaretto. The man tipped well, so Nick liked to keep him happy.

He found a clean ashtray, poured a little milk into it, and set in on the drain next to the small sink behind the bar. The club had an industrial sanitizer in the back, but Nick rinsed all the used glasses in the sink before they went in the back. The strip club might be a dive, but Chubs took cleanliness seriously. If he saw the kitten, he'd probably fire Nick on sight. Good thing Chubs had made himself scarce tonight.

Nick could always claim the kitten was his therapy cat. With the way he was living these days, he probably needed a therapy animal.

One of the waitresses—Janine—leaned over the bar. She was big breasted in a natural way with a flat tummy and the kind of shapely legs that made Nick think she might have done some serious track and field when she'd been in school. Unlike some of the dancers and a few of the other waitresses, she was clean—no drugs, no booze. If a customer wanted to buy her a drink, it was always soda water with a twist.

He didn't know exactly how old she was, but by the few lines at the corners of her eyes, he guessed she was early thirties. The smattering of freckles across her nose and high on her cheekbones made her look younger. Like all the waitresses, she wore pasties, a frilly little apron over a G-string, and a lace choker around her thin neck.

The apron had pockets for tips but left her ass hanging out in the air. Like all the other women who worked in the club, she didn't seem to care.

He didn't know her background, but he wouldn't have been surprised if she told him she'd worked as a showgirl for one of the casinos until the grind became too much. She owned a variety of wigs that she wore to work, all long and curly and made of real hair, not cheap synthetic stuff in wild colors. Beneath the wigs, she kept her auburn hair short.

Of all the club's female employees, Janine was the nicest and most down-to-earth. He supposed it was no surprise that she was the closest thing to a friend he had these days.

"Whatcha got there?" she asked, leaning further over the bar to see.

Nick didn't say anything. He was too busy watching the kitten go to town on the milk.

"You know you're history if Chubs sees you," she said.

Nobody called the boss Chubs when he was around. Stu Larraldi was three-hundred fifty pounds of flab with a meat hook of a fist that could pound you flat before he had the bouncer kick your sorry ass to the curb. Chubs acted like a Jersey wiseguy, but as far as Nick knew, he wasn't connected.

Nick grinned at Janine. "He can kiss my ass."

Janine laughed. "You say that now like you've already made the rent."

Making the rent was the barometer everyone who worked in the club lived by. If you were making the rent, you were doing okay. It made putting up with the bullshit from Chubs and the bouncers and the customers seem worthwhile.

Nick had worked enough dead-end jobs over the last fifteen years that he knew another dead-end job was just around the corner. The strip club was just a place to stop for a while. He joked about making the rent just to blend in, but truth be told, he could walk away tonight and never look back.

Except for Janine. He'd actually miss her, and he never missed anybody. He'd made it a practice never to care about anyone. That's how a man like Nick stayed alive, carrying for nobody and nothing.

So what the hell was he doing with this kitten?

Good question.

He filled Janine's drink order while the kitten was finishing off the milk, then he fixed a Bloody Mary for an overweight man at the bar dressed in tourist casual. He'd been one of Nick's steadiest customers all evening. If the man noticed the kitten, he didn't mention it.

After the kitten licked up the last of the milk, it stumbled around beneath the bar on unsteady legs. It sniffed at the sink and then batted the soap bubbles with one tiny paw. Nick folded up one of the unused bar towels and put it on the counter next to the sink, and pretty soon the kitten curled up on the makeshift bed and went to sleep.

"Adaptable little shit, aren't you," Nick murmured, resisting the urge to pet its tiny head.

He lucked out. Chubs stayed noticeably absent for the remainder of Nick's shift. The dancers worked the pole and then they worked the customers, and Nick mixed drinks with the skill of a long-time pro while the bump-and-grind music ate away at his brain.

When his shift was over, Nick picked up the sleeping kitten, towel and all. It chirped a meow once and burrowed against Nick's shirt, its eyes still closed.

The relief bartender, a college student at UNLV who worked the slow late night/early morning shift so he could study, only gave the kitten a cursory glance. He was more concerned about how tips had been.

Janine stopped Nick on his way out the back door. She'd changed into street clothes—faded jeans, tennis shoes, and an oversized t-shirt—and she'd ditched the night's wig. Her short hair curled around her ears and her forehead, giving her face an elfin look accentuated by her impish grin.

"Looks like you've got yourself a pet," she said.

Did he want a pet? He hadn't planned on letting anyone—or anything—get close to him ever again. But the kitten had attached itself to him. He was surprised just how good that made him feel.

He returned Janine's grin with a seldom used one of his own. "Yeah," he said. "I guess I do."

2

—————

Most nights after Nick got off work, he picked up a couple of street tacos from a food truck that specialized in Mexican food. The truck always staked out the same spot in the back parking lot of a fast-food restaurant that closed up at midnight. The truck had food that was good and cheap, and it stayed open until five in the morning.

Nick was usually their only non-Hispanic customer. The cook spoke just enough English and Nick spoke just enough Spanish to get by. The best part was the food truck's regular spot was on Nick's route back to his apartment.

He'd gotten used to walking everywhere when he'd been a kid back in Jersey. People who lived in downtown Vegas walked places, and the tourists walked up and down the Strip. Everywhere else? People drove.

Vegas was the desert version of urban sprawl. Suburbs complete with strip malls and shopping centers and clusters of professional offices filled the desert. The city had bus service and a monorail circled around the Strip, and there were taxis and car services and limousines for those who felt flush. But out west people had cars. Call it western independence.

Nick had a car of his own, an old beater that got him places he needed to go, but he preferred to walk to work. His car was safer in the parking lot behind his apartment building than it would be parked in the club's lot, and his apartment was within easy walking distance.

Walking through the neighborhood between the club and his apartment after midnight wasn't recommended for the tourist crowd. Gentrification hadn't reached this part of the city yet, and the neighborhood was filled with darkened strip malls and auto repair shops and rundown houses and apartment buildings.

He'd learned long ago to give off a *don't fuck with me and I won't fuck with you* vibe whenever he was out walking in almost any part of Vegas, especially at night. His unkempt hair that insisted on falling over his eyes and his full mustache, combined with the scruffy, two-day-old beard only added to that vibe.

Unlike a lot of wannabe hard cases, Nick had the skills to back up the attitude, and he didn't much care if he got hurt delivering the message. He usually only had to deliver that message once or twice for word to get around. By now, the neighborhood toughs knew him and they left him alone.

He wouldn't be hitting the taco joint tonight. The truck wouldn't have anything the kitten should eat. Nick could survive on street tacos and spicy burritos. The kitten would need real food.

His usual route home took him by a twenty-four-hour convenience store. The few times he'd been inside, he hadn't paid attention to the pet food section, but he guessed they might have something he could feed the kitten besides milk. He also had a vague idea he'd need a litter box and something to fill it.

"You're worse than a fucking kid," he muttered at the kitten as he walked, his boots clocking a steady rhythm on the sidewalk. There was no malice in his voice, just gentle amusement at himself.

The kitten squirmed a little inside the towel, but it never let go of its grip on his shirt. Its face had the kind of innocence he hadn't seen in a long, long time. It didn't escape him that it was now relying on him to keep it safe. And he didn't resent it. The world made baby animals adorable for a reason, he guessed.

The convenience store was an island of bright white light at the end of a strip mall. The rest of the shops were closed for the night, and that part of the parking lot empty. A couple of cars were parked in front of the convenience store's plate glass windows—a mid-size sedan in no better shape than his beater car and a black Hummer that looked like it had just been driven off a car dealer's showroom floor.

The Hummer was definitely out of place. It bore Nevada plates, which made Nick think it was a rental. Some tourist from out of town, no doubt. A local would know better than to drive a car like that in this neighborhood.

He only saw a couple of customers inside the store. A worn-down middle-aged woman was at the counter counting out bills while the clerk, a kid in his twenties with stooped shoulders and lanky brown hair, waited behind the counter. A well-dressed couple, the man in his sixties, the woman in her mid-twenties, perused the selection of overpriced booze off to one side of the store. No doubt they were the people who belonged to the Hummer.

The clerk barely acknowledged Nick when he came in the front door. The door had a sign saying no pets except service animals, but the clerk didn't seem to notice the kitten at all.

Nick found the pet food section near the back of the store and scanned the shelves, looking for something the kitten might eat.

The well-dressed couple passed down the aisle behind him, looking in the cold cases. The man was carrying a bottle of whiskey and he grabbed two plastic bottles of Diet Coke from the racks of cold sodas. They must have seen the store on the way back to their hotel from whatever party or show they'd been to and decided convenience store booze would be cheaper than anything they could get at their hotel.

The woman noticed the kitten. "Ooo, isn't she sweet?" she cooed. "She's just a baby."

Up close, Nick could see the layers of makeup the woman had

applied to her face in an attempt to look older. He revised his estimate of her age to be somewhere in her late teens, twenty at the most.

Given her top-heavy shape and the perfect coif of her hair and all that makeup, she was well on her way to becoming one of the plastic people who frequented the Strip—artificially perfect bodies shoved into skintight designer fashions that all looked the same despite the attempt at individuality. Most of all the forced vapid personality that practically shouted *take me home and I'll be your perfect Stepford girlfriend.*

In ten years she'd be working the pole at a strip club on the seedy side of the city, or if she was lucky, at an upscale gentlemen's club where the tips were better but the work was the same. In twenty, she'd be all used up.

Or what did he know. She could be happy right where she was.

"You know," she said to Nick, "if you can't find kitten food, try a jar of baby food. Something meat. It's better than milk."

The old guy she was with shot her a look, and she shrugged.

"My mom used to foster kittens," she said to him. "It was fun to have them around the house."

"You're fun to have around the house," the old guy said. He gave her the kind of look Nick didn't see all that often anymore—genuine affection.

Nick revised his opinion of the couple. Working at the club had left him jaded.

The couple made their way toward the snack food aisle near the front of the store. Nick found the baby products further down the aisle, close to the self-serve soda and coffee machines and a soft-serve ice cream machine. The ice cream machine had a hand-printed sign saying it was out of order.

Jars of baby food, which were far more plentiful than canned cat food, shared shelf space with baby shampoo, baby powder, and an alarming variety of disposable diapers and baby wipes. He barely glanced up as the electronic chime on the store's front door sounded as another customer came in.

He selected two jars of baby food, one chicken and one turkey.

The store didn't have any cat litter, or anything to put it in, for that matter. He supposed he could wash out the plastic container from the spaghetti dinner he'd finished off before he'd walked to work. The container was still in his kitchen trashcan. The kitten could probably get in and out of the shallow, round container.

"You do know how to use a litter box, right?" he murmured to the kitten.

He didn't have anything to put in the box for litter. He guessed he could make due with ripped up newspaper. The store had a stand out front with freebie classified ad papers. He could pick up one of those on his way out, then later today, after he got some sleep and before he was scheduled back at the club, he'd find a pet store and pick up proper supplies.

"Don't worry," he told the kitten. "I've got you covered."

He was so preoccupied with planning what he needed to do that he almost didn't feel the sudden tension in the air.

Almost.

Old instincts made him glance at a round security mirror mounted on the ceiling at the far end of his aisle. The security mirror gave him a good look at the clerk's back and the new customer at the counter. Nick went very still at what he saw.

The middle-aged woman had left. The guy at the counter now was a rough-looking man, white, thin-faced with a dark, patchy beard. He was wearing a stained zip-front hoodie, and he held a pistol aimed at the clerk.

Convenience store robbery in the dead of night. At least the asshole was keeping it quiet. It wouldn't stay that way for long.

The robber wasn't wearing anything to disguise his face. That was always a bad sign. Either the guy was so high he didn't realize his face was hanging out for everyone to see, or he didn't plan to leave anyone around who could identify him later.

Were the store's security cameras even working? Some store owners cut costs by cutting security. Nick wouldn't be surprised if that was the case with this store.

The mirror gave Nick a semi-decent view of the rest of the store.

He could just see the couple who'd stopped in for booze. They were still in the snack food aisle, apparently trying to decide what chips went with the whiskey and Coke. They seemed oblivious to the drama taking place at the counter. Nick hoped they stayed that way. It just might be the only thing that would keep them alive.

The robber wasn't a meth head. He didn't have that twitchy, skeletal look about him. If he was a gang member, he was in one Nick hadn't run across, and he didn't appear to be wearing gang colors. If he was just out for some quick cash, things might not escalate, but Nick wasn't about to bank on that.

He hadn't witnessed a crime in a long time, if he didn't count the over-priced, watered-down drinks at the club. He should just leave things alone. Get ready to defend himself if he had to. He could do that. His skills might be rusty, but he could do that.

Except he liked the well-dressed couple. The woman had been kind to him when she didn't have to be, and the old guy seemed okay.

They just had to stay where they were for a little while longer. Stay oblivious.

He set the jars of baby food back on the shelf. He peeled the sleepy kitten's claws from his shirt and wrapped the bar towel more securely around her. She squirmed a little but didn't yelp. Good kitty.

He stroked her forehead with his fingertip until her eyes began to close, then he put her in an empty spot on a shelf next to plastic bottles of baby shampoo and baby oil.

Everything will be okay, he promised.

He wasn't sure who he made the promise to—himself or the kitten.

He hoped it was a promise he'd be able to keep.

3

Nick didn't like to fight. Not because he wasn't any good at it, but because there'd been a time in his life when he couldn't make himself stop.

Long ago, in another lifetime it seemed, his dad had taken him to a neighborhood gym. Not the kind of gym that catered to businessmen who wanted to work the machines or lift free weights to keep themselves in shape after sitting at a desk all day.

This gym catered to boxers.

Nick's dad had introduced him to the grizzled old hardcase who ran the place. The hardcase had been a corner man for a few welterweights at one time, a trainer for a few others before that. He'd quit the circuit because, as he put it, he couldn't stomach what gambling had done to the sport.

"Gives boxers a swell head when all that money's on them," he'd told Nick during the first boxing lesson his father had paid for. "You got a swell head on you, boy?"

Nick did at the time.

He'd been in more than a few fights in school, and he'd won every single one of them. At fifteen he'd still been a beanpole, but what he lacked in size and pure muscular strength, he more than made up for in ferociousness.

His last fight in school had been against a kid who outweighed Nick by a good forty pounds. The fight had ended when Nick sent the boy to the hospital with two broken ribs and a broken jaw. The kid had thought he could push little Nicky around. Nick had taken exception to that.

Nick had the fight won, the other kid down on the ground with his hands held out in front of him, but Nick couldn't stop. Punch after punch after wild, frenzied punch. He kept swinging away even though his own hands were busted up, the knuckles swollen and bleeding. It had taken two other kids, both a couple years older and far bigger than Nick, along with the football coach, to break up the fight.

His dad hadn't been furious, and he hadn't given Nick a beating of his own, which Nick had expected. Instead he'd calmly explained the financial repercussions of the fight. How his parents would have to pay the boy's hospital bills, and how the entire family would have to tighten their belts because money like that didn't grow on trees.

That quiet conversation, the first time his dad had treated fifteen-year-old Nick like an adult, had been infinitely worse than any punishment his dad could have doled out.

Afterward, he'd taken Nick to the gym.

"If you're going to fight," he'd said, "learn how to do it right."

The only gym Nick had ever been in before that was the one at his middle school, a little room filled with free-weight machines and exercise bikes that was the domain of football players who were twice his size. This gym was nothing like that.

The hardcase's gym had been filled with the sounds of men working heavy bags and the speed bag and sparring in the ring. The smell of leather mixed with the stench of sweat, but it was sweat from good, hard exercise, not from fear and certainly not from sex, which Nick had only experienced once in his life at that point.

At least he'd had the good sense not to brag to the hardcase about how many fights he'd won.

At least he'd had the good sense to know the man wouldn't have been impressed.

The hardcase had wrapped Nick's scabbed-over knuckles with white tape and fitted him with a pair of boxing gloves. The things made his hands look like cartoon fists. They were heavier than he'd thought, big and awkward, but just wearing them made him feel dangerous.

The first few punches he threw at the heavy bag had been pathetic. The gloves deadened his blows, and the bag barely moved. But the old hardcase must have seen something in him because he'd told Nick's dad he'd teach Nick how to box for only half his usual fee.

"For a half-size boy," he'd said.

Nick had overheard, and he'd hated the hardcase for that. He'd always been small for his age, and by the time he turned fifteen, he'd been good and tired of being teased about it, but he'd kept his mouth shut.

Only later, after he'd learned all the old hardcase was willing to teach him, did he figure out that the man had been testing him. He'd wanted to see if Nick was a hothead. Hotheads, he said, couldn't be trained because they wouldn't listen.

"Don't fight when you're mad, boy," he told Nick over and over again. "The hardest battle you're going to have is with your own self. You keep yourself in check, and you'll be a dangerous man."

Dangerous men, he'd said, went into a fight knowing they'd get hurt. They just didn't care.

All dangerous men cared about was that the other guy went down and stayed there. Dangerous men didn't have to keep wailing on a guy just to prove how tough they were. They already knew they were the toughest guy in the room.

Nick never fought an actual bout in the ring that mattered, but he didn't care. He loved boxing for the discipline of the sport. How it channeled his energy into the pure rhythm of making a speed bag sing. How it toned his body not with mere exercise, but exercise with a purpose.

He imagined that's how football players felt. He'd always been too small for football. For any kind of team sport, for that matter. But with boxing, he wasn't too small and the only person he had to rely on was himself.

By the time he turned seventeen, he'd grown a few inches and put on muscle. More important than that, he'd finally gotten his emotions under control, something his dad attributed to maturity. But Nick knew that came from the self-confidence boxing gave him. He didn't need to prove himself to anybody. He didn't need to be the toughest kid in school anymore because he knew he was the most dangerous kid in school, period. Even the bullies gave him a wide berth. He was no longer easy pickings.

That attitude translated well to the street. What didn't translate well to street life were boxing's rules.

Street fights had no rules.

He'd learned that lesson the hard way.

It was a lesson he'd teach the robber, if he had to.

He wasn't about to cower at the back of the store in the hope that the robber wouldn't see him and just leave. He gave the kitten one last gentle rub on the top of her head and started walking slowly, quietly, toward the front of the store.

As he made his way up the aisle, Nick kept track of the robber in the round security mirror. The robber still had his gun trained on the clerk, who was busy pulling bills out of the register.

The mirror reflected movement a couple of aisles away. The well-dressed couple from the Hummer were heading toward the front of the store as well, a bag of chips added to their party stash. They still seemed oblivious to the fact that the store was being robbed, and they were closer to the counter than he was.

Not good.

Nick needed to create a diversion. All he had in the way of weapons were his fists and a small pocketknife. The robber already had his gun out. Nick was good, but a gun at the ready beat fists and a knife any day.

The baby products had been at the back end of Nick's aisle. The shelves next to him now were filled with cooking supplies. The convenience store didn't have any utensils—no kitchen knives or anything with heft that he could smash down on the robber's head to knock him out. The small bottles of cooking oil and vinegar were plastic and useless.

Then he saw the flour. The store had small bags of flour, smaller than the five-pound bags his mom had bought to bake with. These bags were small enough to fit in his hand, and the bags themselves were made out of thick paper that would be easy to rip.

As diversions went, it wasn't as good as a flash-bang grenade SWAT guys used or tear gas, but it would have to do.

He took a bag of flour off the shelf and stabbed one side with his pocketknife, creating a slit nearly the width of the bag. He double-checked the mirror, but the robber still seemed to be focused on the clerk. He was holding the gun in one hand and stuffing cash into his pockets with the other.

An experienced robber would have kept checking the security mirror to see if anyone was sneaking up behind him. Hell, an experience robber would have been wearing a mask. This guy was an amateur.

An amateur with a gun was unpredictable. Dangerous. Almost more dangerous than a long-time gang member.

Nick slipped his knife back in his pocket. He gathered himself, ready to make a run for the robber.

That's when a woman's scream cut through the store.

The woman from the Hummer must have seen the gun. Figured out what was going down. Knew in some part of her brain that this quick stop at a convenience store might be the last thing she ever did in this life.

The robber turned toward the couple, gun pointed right at them. The woman screamed again, and the old guy shoved her behind him.

The couple were less than ten feet away from the robber. If he fired, they were as good as dead. Even an amateur couldn't miss at that distance.

Nick didn't hesitate. He ran toward the front of the store, no longer concerned about keeping quiet. He wanted to make noise.

Make the robber turn his attention away from the couple. Nick deliberately knocked boxes of crackers off the shelves with his shoulder. The robber flinched as the boxes clattered to the floor.

He lifted the ripped bag of flour in one hand and yelled, "Hey, asshole!"

He got lucky. The robber hesitated a split second. Customers weren't supposed to fight back. He was probably wondering if the guy he hadn't even known was in the store was coming at him with a gun. In this day and age, lots of people carried guns.

That split second was all Nick needed. When the robber swung around toward Nick, he threw the bag of flour right at the robber's face.

The robber shouted something that could have been a curse and flung his gun arm up to protect his face. Just what Nick had hoped he'd do.

The bag exploded in a cloud of white dust as it hit the robber's arm.

The robber started firing blindly. Nick dropped to the floor and scrambled forward through the cloud of dusty flour that still hung in the air until he collided with the robber's legs. He grabbed the man's legs and wrenched his feet out from under him.

The robber went down hard on his back, smacking his head on the stained linoleum floor. His gun went off again. Nick held one of the man's legs in an iron grip and twisted the leg while he punched hard against the side of the man's knee.

The robber screamed as his knee gave way. But he still had the gun.

Grappling for the gun while they were both on the floor would get somebody killed. All Nick had done so far was blow out the man's knee. If he gave the robber time to work through the first wave of pain, the guy might actually start aiming at what he wanted to hit.

Like Nick.

So Nick did what he did best. What he'd always done best.

He went to work on the robber with his fists.

The robber was stronger than he'd looked beneath that hoodie, but he didn't stand a chance. He got off one more shot. The bullet missed Nick's head by less than an inch, but the important thing was that it missed.

As he registered how close that shot had come to blowing his brains out, something clicked in Nick's mind. A fuse that he'd controlled for so long just blew. He didn't see red exactly like he had when he'd been a boy, but a kind of cold black fury overtook him.

All he'd wanted was some food for the kitten, and this asshole had decided to fuck up everyone's night. The nice couple who'd just stopped for booze and snacks. The poor, freaked out clerk who was probably cowering behind the counter and pissing in his pants. They hadn't done a damn thing to deserve what this asshole was dishing out.

With his head still ringing from the sound of the gun going off right next to him, Nick yelled something incoherent and ripped the gun out of the robber's hand, not caring that he probably broke a couple of the man's fingers in the process. He tossed the gun behind himself and started throwing punch after punch at the man's face.

A gout of blood erupted from the man's nose. A cut opened over one of his eyes. Blood streaked through the flour on his face and made a muddy paste that stuck to Nick's hands and mixed with his own blood as the skin on his knuckles gave way from the force of his blows.

The muscles in Nick's shoulders bunched and sang with the need for more, more, more, just to keep going. Teach this asshole a lesson. Nobody but nobody would ever bully Nick again. Not ever. He was done with that shit. Done and over it and he'd damn well never—

The kitten yelped.

Even through the ringing in his ears, he heard the kitten's scared, sharp baby yelps.

That stopped him cold in mid swing.

The robber was out. His face was a mess, streaked with blood and flour. Both of his eyes were swollen shut, his nose clearly broken. He wasn't going to hurt anyone anytime soon.

Nick pushed himself off the man. He was breathing hard and

covered in enough flour that he looked like someone who'd been out fighting a wildfire.

Before he could brush himself off, he realized the kitten wasn't the only one crying.

The woman from the Hummer was on her knees on the dirty stained floor. The old guy she was with was flat on his back beside her. Her expensive dress was ripped and bloody. She was shrieking. She didn't appear to be injured, but there was a growing pool of blood surrounding her, soaking into her dress.

The blood wasn't hers. It came from the old guy.

One of the stray bullets from the robber's gun must have caught him in the chest. He'd dropped the bottle of whiskey he'd been carrying, and it had shattered, spraying alcohol across the floor.

He'd shoved the woman behind him, and the robber had shot him.

Now he was bleeding out on the floor of a convenience store where he never should have been in the first place.

Nick had tried to stop this very thing from happening, but it had happened anyway. The old anger flared up again, sharp a vicious. He gave the unconscious robber a savage kick in the ribs, but only one.

The robber wasn't going anywhere, but there was still time to save the old guy.

There just had to be.

4

Nick had seen gunshot victims before, but that had been part of his old life. In this new, anonymous life he'd created for himself, he'd managed to avoid gun battles and firefights. He hadn't fired a gun once since he'd left that old life behind. He hadn't even touched one, not until he'd ripped the gun out of the robber's hand.

But all the training from his old life had never left him. Just like learning to ride a bicycle, once learned, the old skills remained.

The convenience store clerk had just started to get to his feet from behind the counter. He didn't appear to be hurt, but he had the slack-jawed look of someone in shock.

Nick pointed at him. "You. Call 9-1-1!"

"What about...?" The clerk was staring wide-eyed at the battered robber.

"He's not moving anytime soon," Nick said. "Make the call! Tell them we need an ambulance here right away!"

The clerk nodded, jerky movements that made him look like someone just getting used to the fact he had muscles he could control.

Nick didn't have time to make sure the clerk did what he was told.

The old guy didn't have that kind of time. Nick needed to slow the bleeding or the guy would bleed out right there on the floor next to his date.

Nick found a small package of sanitary pads. He ripped open the package and dropped to his knees next to the old guy.

The bullet had caught man in the upper chest right below his collarbone. Nick pressed a sanitary pad against the wound. Given the size of the ever-growing pool of blood, the bullet must have gone straight through, blowing a larger exit wound in the old guy's back. Just stopping the bleeding on the entrance wound wasn't going to cut it.

"Hold this," he said to the woman.

She'd stopped screaming, but the look in her eyes told him she wasn't all there.

He grabbed her hand, grateful she didn't try to snatch it away. He put her hand flat against the sanitary pad. "Hold this," he said again. "Keep pressure on the wound. Got it?"

She nodded, jittery little shakes of her head no better than the clerk's had been, but Nick would take it.

He ripped open another pad. Trying not to jostle the old guy too much, Nick lifted his shoulder off the floor and shoved the pad beneath him. The man was out cold, and his face had a waxy pallor. The pads would help slow the bleeding, but he needed proper medical care.

"I need duct tape," Nick shouted at the clerk. "You have any?"

"Yeah. Some." The clerk was still holding a cell phone against his ear. The 9-1-1 operator had probably told him to stay on the line.

"Get it," he said.

The clerk just stared at him.

Nick didn't have time for this. "Put the phone on speaker and get me the damn tape!"

The clerk jerked like he'd been slapped, then he ran out from behind the counter and disappeared down an aisle. It took him a minute before he came back with a baby roll of duct tape—pink with red hearts, of all things. At least he'd had the foresight to take the plastic wrap off the tape and get the end started.

Nick used the tape to secure the pads to the old guy's shoulder, front and back. When that was done, he taped the unconscious robber's wrists together. A determined man could still break the tape apart. Nick had done that himself—part of the training from his old life—and this printed tape wasn't the heavy-duty kind. But the robber was still out cold. Nick hoped the tape would do for now.

He couldn't do anything else for the old guy who'd been shot. The way the robber had sprayed bullets around the store, it was a miracle no one else had taken a bullet. Nick wiped his bloody hands on his jeans and went back to the baby food aisle for the kitten.

She was still yelping. Nick's head was just starting to throb with what promised to be a hell of a headache and his ears were still ringing. Aftereffects of adrenaline compounded with the gunshot next to his ear. The kitten's yelps were like icepicks to the brain, but when he picked her up and snuggled her in the hollow of his neck, she rubbed her fuzzy head against him. The tension he'd felt since he'd seen the robber in the security mirror began to drain away.

He murmured nonsense to the kitten, like he'd seen some women do with babies, and she started to purr.

He'd never done anything remotely like this before, not even in his prior life—especially not in his prior life.

Even when he'd been a kid, back when his life had been somewhat normal, he'd never been around pets. His parents never had a dog or a cat or even a damn goldfish.

Maybe he should just take the kitten to an animal shelter. Wouldn't she be better off with someone who had the temperament to really love a cat?

Wouldn't she be better off with someone whose life wasn't a dumpster fire?

Hell, he hadn't even known what to feed her.

All these thoughts went through his head while he waited for the police to arrive. He could hear sirens now and knew it wouldn't be long.

He could just leave—should leave—but he needed to buy food for the kitten and the clerk was in no shape to ring up a sale. Even if Nick decided to take the kitten to a shelter later, she needed to eat now.

He grabbed a jar of baby food off the shelf and opened it. He used a finger to scoop a little food onto the lid, then put the kitten down in the same empty spot on the shelf where he'd hidden her. She cried at him, but once he pushed the lid toward her, the kitten dove into the baby food with the gusto of a half-starved man at an all-you-can-eat buffet.

"You're really going to town there," he said.

The kitten was just digging into a second helping of pureed beef when the police and the ambulance arrived, almost simultaneously. Nick stayed where he was. The paramedics didn't need his help and the police would find him when they secured the store. He didn't have to go to them.

It didn't take long for one of the police officers to hit his aisle. The female officer looked far too young for the job. Her face didn't have the guarded expression he'd seen on so many cops' faces, but she had sharp, hard eyes. The kind that didn't miss any details.

She took in the dried blood on Nick's knuckles. The flour on his clothes. She put one hand on the butt of her gun as she walked down the aisle toward him.

"You the guy that did that?" she asked, gesturing with her head toward the front of the store.

No sense denying it. Hell, the clerk had probably told the cops what Nick had done.

"Yes," he said.

"We're going to need a statement from you. And you might want the paramedics to look at your hands."

Nick shook his head. "They need to work on the old guy."

"He's being taken care of," she said. "We called for a second rig for the suspect, but he can wait."

Nick didn't comment about the state of the robber, nor that the cop had called him a suspect. That was just how cops talked, something Nick knew well.

As for his hands, he'd been hurt worse before. Back in his old life. All he needed was some soap and water for his hands and enough Ibuprofen to knock the swelling in his knuckles down and lower the intensity of his headache a few notches.

The officer watched him pet the kitten.

"You going to have a problem filling out a statement if I bring one back to you?" she asked. "Your hands be able to handle that?"

She was talking about filling out a witness form in the store. She wasn't going to put him in the back seat of her shop and transport him to the station to give a formal statement. That told him they weren't going to book him for beating the living shit out of the robber.

The cops here must have a decent amount of discretion about who they arrested and who they let off with a warning. This particular cop was willing to let him off with a warning, provided he gave a statement about the robbery. The supervising officer on scene would have to agree with that, but the female officer made it sound like it wouldn't be a problem.

A siren whooped into life right outside the convenience store. That would be the paramedics leaving with the old guy. Nick hoped he'd make it.

"Don't worry about it," he said to the officer. "My hands still work fine."

He'd been able to grip the baby food jar enough to twist the lid off. His knuckles might not be in such great shape in the morning, but he had ice in his apartment to keep the swelling down.

The officer gave him a curt nod. "I'll get the clipboard. Stay here. You don't need to come up front." She glanced at the kitten. "Cute cat. It yours?"

The kitten was apparently done with her meal. She was sitting on the shelf washing her face. She must have been around her mother at least long enough to learn how to do that. Or was it instinctual? Nick had no idea.

What he did know was there'd be no shelter in this little kitten's future. No cage where she would be locked away to grow up unloved and unwanted.

For better or worse, he had a pet.

"Yes," he said. "She's mine."

5

The old guy died. The robber didn't.

Nick caught the story on a local news show the following afternoon. He had a little cast-off television he'd found three months ago on a neighborhood sidewalk with a hand-printed sign that read *Free. Works.*

He'd taken the set back to his apartment and futzed with it until he managed to pick up a couple of local channels. The picture had a faint line running down the center and the speakers were crap, but whenever he wanted the sound of a human voice to keep him company, he turned it on. The crappy little TV was good for that.

He'd been dozing on the couch with the kitten, the television tuned to some black and white Western. The kitten had fallen asleep on his chest after a hearty meal of pureed turkey from a jar with a smiling baby on the label.

The kitten was cuter than the baby on the jar as far as Nick was concerned. He didn't want to disturb her, which meant he'd halfway decided to blow off work and just spend the rest of the day inside.

He was tired, his ears were still ringing, and his headache was a dull presence at the base of his skull. He'd iced his knuckles last night, but they were still swollen. At least the scrapes had scabbed over. A couple of butterfly bandages had closed the cut on his forehead. The other scrapes on his face from the robber's knuckles were little more than scratches with only light bruises underneath. His shirt covered the more serious bruises on his ribs, and he'd taken a couple of ibuprofen to dull the pain from his aching muscles.

The fights he'd gotten into as a boy—hell, the fights he'd gotten into in his twenties—hadn't taken this much out of him. But forty-two wasn't twenty-two, not by a long shot.

Chubs would probably fire him if he didn't show up, but so what? Nick could always find another job. He'd miss Janine. She was good people, one of the few he'd met since he came to this town, but she'd get along just fine without someone like him in her life.

He barely registered when the Western on TV got over and the early edition of a local news show came on. The lead story was something about an eight-car pile-up on I-15. Not surprising. Drivers got impatient in the Vegas heat, and the early May afternoon had been a scorcher. The steering wheel in his car had been almost too hot to handle when he'd gone out earlier in the day to get supplies for the kitten. The best thing his car had going for it was a working air conditioner, which was also the best thing about his tiny apartment.

His eyes were starting to drift shut again when the news anchor, a pert graduate of the school of happy news who hadn't quite mastered the art of conveying serious stories in an appropriate manner, announced the death of a man in a local convenience store robbery.

The sixty-nine-year-old man, whose name is being withheld pending notification of his next of kin, was shot during the robbery of Lucky Bucks on...

Nick pushed himself up, dislodging the kitten and causing his head to give a warning throb. The kitten gave him a sleepy mew, but he kept her cradled against his chest and she settled down again.

A daylight photo of the convenience store appeared in an inset over the pert blonde's shoulder as she continued reading the story off a teleprompter.

One suspect was arrested at the scene and taken to a local hospital for treatment. No other injuries were reported. The police have not yet released the name of the man taken into custody. We'll have more information on this developing story during our nightly news at 6:30.

In other local news...

Nick leaned back on the couch.

No other injuries were reported, she'd said. That meant the media didn't know about him. They would have if he'd allowed the paramedics to treat him.

One of the paramedics from the second ambulance, the one the cops had called for the suspect, had tried to talk Nick into getting himself checked out. He didn't remember getting the cut on his forehead. That used to happen to him in fights. He'd end up with injuries and have no idea how he got them. The paramedic told him he'd need stitches, but he'd made do with the butterfly bandages.

The last thing he wanted was to create any more of a paper trail than he already had. He hadn't really had a choice about the witness statement. If he'd refused to give a statement to the cops, that would have sent up a big red flag. As long as he agreed to give them his personal information, they'd seemed willing enough to overlook the fact that he'd beaten the robber unconscious. They might not have been so cooperative if he'd given them any reason to be suspicious.

He felt bad for the old guy who'd been killed. He'd seemed like a decent sort, and he'd been protective of his date.

Nick leaned back on the couch, the kitten purring against his chest as he stroked her head with one finger, and thought about his situation.

He'd spent a lot of years perfecting the art of being invisible. He'd grown his hair out until it brushed the collar of his shirts, not because he liked his hair long, but because it was messy enough that people tended not to notice his face. If they did, they just saw a middle-aged man with blue eyes, a mustache he could shave off if he needed to, and a scruffy, barely there beard.

While he was at work at the club, he slicked his hair back. When he wasn't, he let it fall around his face. It was long enough to cover the butterfly bandage on his forehead and sometimes got in his eyes, but it covered their brilliant blue. Those eyes were his most distinctive feature, but there wasn't a lot he could do about that unless he wanted to wear colored contact lenses, which he didn't.

He had no obvious scars and no tattoos. His clothes came from secondhand stores. He didn't own a cell phone and he had no social media accounts. He didn't even own a computer. He worked the kind of jobs where references weren't required. His I.D. didn't list his real name, and it was the best identification the federal government could provide.

The people who might still be interested in him had no idea who and where he was, and he wanted to keep it that way. The address he'd listed on the police report had been for an apartment he'd lived in the year before. A determined search could probably still find him. He wasn't exactly unknown in the neighborhood.

That could be a problem.

"Think it's about time to pack up and move on," he murmured to the kitten.

Not that he had a lot to pack. All the possessions he cared about would fit in a duffel bag he'd picked up at Goodwill, and most of those were the things he'd just bought for the kitten. The furniture came with the apartment. He'd lose the security deposit if he just took off with no notice, but he had money stashed away and he had a car. He'd survive. So would the kitten. He'd make sure of that.

He just had to stay invisible. Things had a way of snowballing out of control. The trick was to never let the snowball get any traction.

If he could do that, he'd be just fine. They both would.

The knock on his door that night took him by surprise.

No one knocked on Nick's door unless they were delivering food. That didn't happen all that often, and certainly not tonight. He'd bought takeout for himself on the way back to the apartment after picking up supplies for the kitten. He wasn't late on the rent—he was never late on the rent—so there was no reason for the manager to come see him.

As for his neighbors, they didn't bother him and he didn't bother them. Sometimes he heard them through the apartment's thin walls or he smelled a particularly pungent meal, but that was it.

He'd decided to stay in for the night and leave in the morning. That way he could turn his key in to the manager and give her some story about an out-of-town relative whose health had taken a sudden turn for the worse. She might remember him if someone asked or she might not, but she'd sure as hell remember him—and not fondly—if he skipped out in the middle of the night.

His apartment was on the second floor of a square block of a building, three stories tall, built around a central courtyard containing a miniscule swimming pool and a building with a few coin-operated washers and dryers that mostly worked. Tenant parking surrounded the building on the three sides that didn't face the street. His apartment was in the back. The only windows were in his bedroom and a high, narrow window in his bathroom. The apartment came furnished, which meant he had a bed, a dresser, the couch, and a kitchen table with two mismatched chairs, all of which looked like discount store rejects.

The apartment's front door opened directly into the living room, which was why he'd positioned the couch off to the side where it couldn't easily be seen if anyone kicked in the door. It wouldn't take much. The door only had a single flimsy lock.

Most days he slept on the couch, and he planned to do the same thing tonight. The couch was actually more comfortable than the bed, and the living room was cooler than his bedroom with its south-facing window. Besides, since the living room had no windows, it was also dark during the day, an important consideration for a man who worked nights.

After he caught the news story about the robbery, he'd packed up his few belongings—mostly clothes—and ate the extra burger he'd put in the fridge. He added cans of kitten food to the duffel. He left out the one frivolous thing he'd bought for her, a felt mouse with feathers for a tail. The toy was almost as big as she was.

He'd debated whether he needed some sort of carrier for her, and in the end he'd bought a soft carrier he could strap on like a backpack. The carrier had mesh panels so she could see out and was ridiculously oversized for a kitten, but he figured she'd grow into it.

He'd put the thing on the floor with the front unzipped so she could check it out, and after she started playing with the mouse, he put the toy inside just to get her used to being inside the backpack. She'd be living in it for a day or two until he found a new place for the both of them to live.

It was nearly eleven and he was thinking about whether he might actually be able to fall asleep this early when someone knocked on his front door. He still had the television on, the volume turned low, and the knock was so soft he almost didn't hear it.

The kitten was curled up next to him on the couch, a fuzzy black furball. She didn't move when he got up. So far she seemed to alternate between being a ball of clumsy energy and the sleepiest animal on the planet. At least she knew how to use the small litterbox he'd purchased for her.

Nick didn't look through the peephole in his front door. Old habits died hard. Even now after all these years, he never stood directly in front of a closed door. Instead he stood off to the side. If he decided to open the door the length of the security chain, he'd be able to see who was in the hallway and slam the door shut if he needed to before they realized he wasn't behind the door.

He started to reach for the knob, then pulled his hand away. He stood with his back to the wall and listened.

The robbery and the news story had put him on edge. He shouldn't have gotten involved, wouldn't have gotten involved, but he'd liked the couple. The robber would have shot them both dead. Probably would have tried to kill Nick too. At least the woman had survived, but a death was a death, and it brought back memories of the former life he'd left behind.

After a minute, the soft knock sounded again. The only other sound in his apartment came from the television. It wasn't much, but the walls in his apartment were thin. Whoever was knocking probably heard the television and knew he was home.

"C'mon, Nick," came a soft female voice from the other side of the door. "I know you're in there."

He recognized the voice. Janine, the only person he really talked to at the strip club.

Janine, who was supposed to be working tonight.

Janine, who'd never been to his apartment.

He didn't open the door. How the hell did she know where he lived?

"I wouldn't have come if it wasn't important," she said. "And if you had a damn cell phone like the rest of the civilized world."

It was the frustration in her voice that decided him. That was quintessential Janine.

He opened the door.

She was in her street clothes—jeans and scuffed-up tennis shoes and a faded t-shirt that was two sizes too big. She still had on the makeup she wore at the club—dark eyeshadow and thick false eyelashes that made her eyes look deep and smokey—and her short auburn hair was flat and messy.

She'd been at work and had left in a hurry. Most nights when her shift got over, she removed her heavy makeup and replaced it with subtle makeup that made her look five years younger and a whole lot more innocent. Then she'd fluff up her hair, giving herself a wind-blown look before she hit the street. Tonight she hadn't done either.

"Let me in," she said when he didn't move away from the door. "I'm not sure if anyone followed me."

That made his pulse kick up a notch. He moved out of the way to let her inside.

"What do you mean?" he asked as he shut the door after her and threw the flimsy lock and replaced the chain. "Why would you think someone was following you?"

"Not me," she said. "You."

She took in the small apartment, the new backpack carrier for the kitten, and most of all his packed duffel bag, which he'd left on the floor next to the couch, ready to go in the morning.

She put her hands on her hips. "But it looks like you already know that," she said.

Then her glance moved upward and her expression softened. His hair must not be doing such a great job of covering the butterfly bandage on his forehead after all.

"Looks like you got yourself into a mess of some kind," she said. Her hands dropped away from her hips, and for a moment he thought she was going to touch his arm.

Instead she shook her head, exasperated. "Well, since I'm probably getting my ass fired for trying to help you out," she said, "you feel like telling me what the hell is going on?"

7

Nick didn't drink coffee except when he was at work. One of the few perks Chubs offered his bartenders was free coffee from the pot behind the bar. The college student who bartended the early morning shift drank coffee like water, but Nick only had a cup every now and then. He'd never gotten into the habit.

He certainly didn't have any coffee in his apartment, or any way to brew it, for that matter. He didn't have any soda either, not even a can of beer. About the best he could offer Janine was a glass of water. At least he had a couple of plastic cups he'd saved from convenience store sodas, which he'd washed out and reused like water glasses, and his refrigerator had an ice maker.

He brought two cups of ice water into the living room. Janine was sitting on his couch with the kitten on her lap, and the little black fuzzball was mock-fighting with her hand.

"Careful," he said. "She's got razor blades for claws."

"All kittens do," Janine said. "Hey, you called her 'she' not 'it.' You figured out she's a she?"

He hadn't really noticed that he'd given the kitten a gender. He'd just started thinking of her as female. Probably the next step would be to give her a name.

"I guess so," he said. "Is that right?"

Janine peered beneath the kitten's tail. "Pretty sure it is. It's been a while since I've done this sort of thing." She gave him a steady glance. "And I don't mean just figuring out if a stray kitten is a boy or a girl."

There was no mistaking her meaning. She expected some sort of explanation. Depending on what had happened to send her running out to find him—and how the hell had she found him in the first place anyway?—he might actually owe her one.

The couch was the only place to sit in his living room. Sitting next to her on the place where he usually slept felt too intimate, so he pulled one of his mismatched kitchen chairs over in front of the couch and turned it around. He sat down across from her, straddling the chair.

"I'll tell you what I can," he said, "but first, you want to tell me why you're here?"

She took a sip of water before she started talking. Nick recognized it for what it was—taking a drink gave her just enough time to get her thoughts in order. In his old life, he'd seen people do that often enough. Sometimes they did it to give themselves time to think up a lie. He hoped that wasn't was she was doing.

When she did start talking, she kept her eyes on the kitten instead of him. Another warning sign, not looking him in the eye.

"I always got the feeling that you were just biding your time at the club," she said. "Some of the girls, they think you're gay because you're not interested in them, but that's not the vibe I get from you." She shrugged. "It's like you've got this big secret, so you keep to yourself, never getting too close or opening up. Which I understand. It's not like all of us aren't pretending to be something we're not, you know? It's safer that way."

She gave him a quick, almost apologetic glance.

He shouldn't be surprised that she'd made such an accurate assessment of his situation. He'd worked in a bunch of strip clubs not only in Vegas but in other cities he'd passed through after he'd been let off his official leash. One thing he'd noticed about most of the women who worked places like that, whether they called themselves exotic dancers or strippers or they just waited tables, like Janine—they were quick studies of human nature. Janine was one of the best.

She leaned forward and put the glass down on the floor. The kitten climbed down her jeans to investigate, her little razor-sharp claws snapping the denim as she scaled down Janine's leg.

Janine winced. "You're right. Her claws are super sharp."

He didn't say anything. He wanted her to get to the point, but she'd get there faster if he just let her talk. He'd learned that back in his old life too. Interrogating people never worked as well as just sitting back and letting them tell their stories in their own time.

She leaned forward and rested her elbows on her knees. Now she did look at him, but he couldn't quite read her expression.

"You know, Chubs was pissed when you didn't show tonight," she said. "He actually had to work the bar." She gave him a quick grin that had no real humor in it. "Can you image Chubs mixing drinks?"

Nick couldn't. The man might be able to open a bottle of beer, but mixing an actual drink took the kind of skill Chubs didn't possess.

"He had Celia come help him out," Janine said, and her smile warmed up a bit. Celia was everyone's favorite, a barely legal brunette with a sweet face.

Janine had told Nick once that Celia'd had a rough childhood, but it didn't show in her disposition, only in the few faint scars across her back. When she was on stage, no one looked at her back.

Janine gave a little shake of her head, like she was trying to get herself on track, and her smile faded.

"Anyway, I was waiting for a drink order at the bar when these guys came in. They came straight to the bar, didn't look much at any of the dancers, just asked for you. Slick-looking guys, three of them. One of them older than the other two. Nice suits hiding a lot of muscle. Probably other stuff too."

She paused for a moment, pulling in her lower lip and catching it between her teeth.

"You see a lot of guys like that in this town," she said. "Not so much in the club, but when I worked the casinos? There was being nice to the customers, and then there was being *nice*. I learned pretty fast to give guys like that the bare minimum of nice."

The kitten must have decided the cup of ice water on the floor was boring. She bounced over to Nick on legs that seemed to be made of springs. He gave her a gentle scratch along her spine, and the kitten rolled on her back and batted at his fingers.

"I wouldn't have touched any of these guys if you paid me," she said. "When one of them realized I was watching them, he says to me, 'You should mind your own business. This has nothing to do with you.' I started to tell him I was just waiting on drinks, but the way he looked at me, I knew he was the kind of guy who'd slit my throat and not lose a minute's sleep over it."

Nick went very still. He might not know the guys she described, but he knew the type. He knew the type only too well. As far as he knew, he hadn't pissed off anyone like that in Vegas, but he'd had run-ins with a lot of guys like that in his former life. He'd even caused some of them serious trouble. Unforgivable trouble.

This was more than bad. This was bug-the-hell-out-now bad. Do not pass Go, do not wait for morning. Leave now bad.

"Did they ask for me by name?"

She took a moment to think. "I can't remember." A frown creased her forehead as she concentrated. "The music was too loud, and they'd made it clear they didn't want me listening in on their business." She gave her head a little shake. "Whatever it was, Chubs said he never heard of the guy. Then one of them described you. Chubs told them they were a day late and a hundred bucks short. Told them you didn't show up for work and your good-for-nothing ass was fired. Only that's not the word he used."

What name had they asked about? Nick had only been known by two names in his life. One his parents had given him when he was born. The other name, the one he used now, he'd been given by the government.

Very few people knew him by both names, and all of them were supposed to be working for the government. Not that any of his old government contacts would go looking for him at the club. They'd cut ties with him long ago after he'd outlived his usefulness.

Only one other person would care enough to track him down and then screw up and call Nick by his real name. He was supposed to be in prison, but what if he wasn't? What if he'd been released for good behavior? Or because he'd called in a favor or two, or threatened the right people? It wasn't outside the realm of possibility.

Nick's blood ran cold. This was worse than bad.

"They tried to stare Chubs down," Janine was saying. "But you know Chubs, he won't back down for anybody. He told them to either buy drinks or get the hell out of his club. There for a minute I thought somebody was going to pull a gun. Then the older guy threw a card on the bar, told Chubs that if he knew what's good for him, he'd get in touch if he saw you again. Then all three of them left."

Nick stood up. He had to get a move on. He didn't have a weapon other than his pocketknife and his fists. He might be able to take out one or two of the guys Janine had seen, but not all three at once.

"Thank you," he said. "You didn't have to come warn me but you did, and I appreciate it more than you'll ever know. But you need to go. Now."

If the men were who he thought they were—and he was pretty sure he was right—they'd somehow figured out where he worked. And if they could do that, they could find out where he lived. He didn't want to be in his apartment, much less have Janine still in his apartment, when they got there.

She stood up with the fluid grace of someone who made a living being physically fit. "You're in trouble, aren't you," she said. It wasn't a question. "Because those guys looked mobbed up.

He gave her a grim smile. "Don't worry. I'll be fine. I've had a lot of practice at this."

She put a hand on his arm. Another delaying tactic? In any other circumstances, with anyone else, the move should have raised alarm bells. With Janine, it didn't. Maybe it should have, but it didn't.

"This is goodbye, right?" she asked.

He didn't answer. She already knew it was goodbye, he could see it in her eyes.

"You taking the kitten?" she asked.

He glanced at the ball of fuzzy black floof playing with the over-sized toy he'd bought her that day. It wouldn't be smart to take her. Maybe he should leave her with Janine, but he couldn't. He'd already become attached, something he'd sworn never to do.

"Yeah," he said. "I guess I am."

Janine's gaze softened, and for a moment he thought she might kiss him. Instead she gave his arm a gentle squeeze and went to open the door.

Nick stopped her.

The doorknob was moving.

He hadn't heard a thing from the other side of the door, but it was clear that the men had, in fact, followed Janine to his apartment building. He didn't have his name on the door, but somehow they'd found him anyway.

Delays were over.

It was time to run.

8

Nick never rented ground floor apartments.

Apartments in low-rent districts like this one had flimsy doors and even flimsier locks. That made them easy targets for smash-and-grab robberies. Second floor apartments took more work, and the getaway time was longer.

The down side was that second-floor apartments didn't have a back exit unless you wanted to jump out a window and take a chance that you wouldn't break something vital when you hit the ground.

It was a trade-off, but a trade-off Nick had prepared for.

After he'd moved in, he'd purchased a length of heavy-duty rope and anchored it to his bedframe. Then he'd coiled the whole thing up and stuffed it beneath the bed.

Even though he hadn't boxed in years, he worked out in his apartment on a regular basis to keep his upper body strength. All the walking he did kept his legs in shape. If he absolutely had to, he'd kick out the bedroom window. A quick throw of the rope out the window, and he'd rappel down the side of the building. Then a sprint to his car, which he kept parked only a few spaces away from the back of his apartment, and he'd be gone.

He'd just never planned on taking a kitten and the closest thing he had to a friend out the window with him.

Janine had seen the doorknob move a split second after he had. She froze, her hand hovering just a few inches from the door. All the color had drained from her face, making the smattering of freckles across her nose and cheeks stand out in sharp relief.

He pressed a finger to his lips and backed away from the door. She followed him without a word.

When he thought they were far enough away from the door, he leaned in close to her ear. "We're leaving," he said, his voice barely audible. "Out the back."

She gave him a startled look. "You have a back door?" she asked, her voice as low as his.

"Not exactly." He pointed at the kitten's backpack. "Grab that for me."

The kitten was still playing with the feathered toy. Nick scooped up the kitten and her toy in one hand. Janine held out the backpack, and he put the kitten inside and zipped it up. He slipped the straps over his shoulders as he headed toward the bedroom.

He'd never be able to carry both the kitten and his duffel and rappel down the side of the building at the same time. Everything inside the duffel was replaceable. The kitten wasn't.

He left the duffel behind.

He always kept his wallet and car keys and what little cash he had on hand in his pockets. Besides the kitten and her toy, he'd have to make do with what he had on him.

Janine followed him into the bedroom and he shut the door behind them. He grabbed the rope from beneath the bed and crossed the narrow distance to the window.

Unlike a lot of apartments he'd lived in, the windows in this building actually opened. The cheap aluminum frame on his bedroom window leaked on the few occasions Vegas got a serious thunderstorm and rattled when it got windy, which was practically every night. Nick didn't much care since he didn't sleep in the bedroom, but now he thanked his lucky stars that the window was the kind that slid open to the side instead of cranked open. It meant he wouldn't have to break the glass.

He opened the window as far as it would go and knocked off the screen. It fell to the asphalt below with a faint clatter.

The opening was narrow, but Nick wasn't a big guy. He could fit through just fine, and Janine was narrower in the hips and shoulders than he was.

He threw the coiled rope through the open window.

"This is your back door?" she asked. "You sure that's going to hold us?" She jerked her head toward the bed where he'd anchored the rope.

"I'm sure the bed won't fit through the window, and we're not going to be on the rope long enough for the frame to break." He gestured with his head toward the open window. "You first. Go out with your—"

"I got this," she said, interrupting him.

She wrapped the rope around herself, mountain-climbing style. She backed out of the window, turning her shoulders sideways to get through the narrow opening, then anchored the rope while she braced her feet on the outside of the window frame.

The bedframe creaked under her weight, but the bed didn't move.

So far, so good.

"Give me the kitten," she said. "You're never going to make it through with the backpack. You're not that skinny."

She was right. After he'd moved in, he'd made sure he could fit his shoulders through the window, but he'd had to twist to the side and he hadn't been wearing a backpack.

He was surprised how reluctant he was to slip the backpack off and hand the kitten over.

She must have read his expression. "Don't worry," she said. "I got this."

He held the rope while she slipped one of the backpack's straps over one shoulder. The kitten yelped once, but then Janine was lowering herself down, controlling her slow descent with ease even though the backpack put her off balance.

Nick had planned to let her reach the ground before he started down, but then he heard a crash in the living room.

His uninvited guests had given up on the lock and decided to simply smash in the door.

He couldn't wait.

He gripped the rope and went out the window.

The extra weight was too much for the bed. The tension on the rope abruptly went slack as the bed slid across the floor, dropping Nick down the side of the building much faster than he was prepared for. He slammed into the side of the building when the bed hit the wall and the rope jerked to a sudden stop.

He spared a glance down at Janine. She was only a few feet off the ground, still letting herself down the rope steadily hand over hand, the kitten's backpack on her shoulder. If the sudden descent and abrupt stop had bothered her, she wasn't showing it.

With the two of them on the same rope, Nick couldn't rappel down as quickly as he'd originally planned when he set up this exit strategy. He had to lower himself down hand over hand without anchoring himself with his legs. By the time he felt it was safe enough to jump off the rope, his shoulders and arms were screaming at him, and the rope was burning his palms.

Janine had settled the backpack fully on her back, both arms through the straps, when he hit the ground. His ankles protested the impact. It was another stark reminder that walking to and from work every day wasn't the same as jumping rope for what felt like hours on end at the gym until the old hardcase told him it was time to stop.

"This way," he told Janine as he sprinted toward his car.

For the first time since he'd bought the car, he wished for a key fob that unlocked the doors and started the engine with the press of a button. It took precious seconds to get the doors open, but at least the engine in his old beater caught on the first try.

He'd backed into his usual parking spot, a habit he'd picked up along the way. He put the car in gear, and as he pulled out of the parking lot, he spared a glance at his bedroom window.

His apartment building might have been in a low-rent district in

Vegas, but the parking lot was well lit. Not as bright as the Strip, but bright enough and with enough security cameras mounted on the light posts to dissuade car burglaries or worse crimes. Nick had always figured the cameras were just for show, but sometimes just for show was good enough.

The lights gave him a decent look at the man silhouetted in his open bedroom window. The men who'd broken into his apartment had turned on the lights in his bedroom, but the back lighting wasn't enough to obscure the man's face.

Even at night, even with Nick speeding out of the parking lot— even fifteen years later—Nick recognized the man who'd come after him.

Oscar O'Dell.

The man who'd tried to kill him and had very nearly succeeded.

9

———

Nick drove away from his apartment without a destination in mind other than to get away from his apartment and the unexpected apparition from his past. He took back streets and side streets and doubled back on his tracks more than once, all the while checking his rearview and sideview mirrors.

Oscar O'Dell.

Oscar Fucking O'Dell.

Of all the nightmares that might have come true, O'Dell was the worst. Nick had lived the life of a paranoid recluse, half-expecting that O'Dell or one of his buddies would come after him someday, but maybe he hadn't been paranoid enough.

O'Dell had found him.

So far Janine had just been sitting quietly in the passenger seat. If she realized he was driving in circles, she hadn't said anything. She'd taken off the backpack when she slid in the car and now she had it on her lap. The kitten had yelped off and on, and Janine was petting the backpack almost like she was petting the kitten.

He'd never meant to drag her into this, and he certainly didn't mean to frighten the kitten, but he needed time to think and he couldn't stay still while he did it. At least no cars had followed him out of the parking lot and he hadn't spotted a tail so far, which he took as good signs.

A bad sign was that he had less than a hundred dollars cash in his wallet. He had another three hundred in tens and twenties stashed under the spare tire in the trunk. He actually had some money in the bank, just like a regular person. He'd gotten complacent enough to open an account to stash away some rainy day money just in case, but he couldn't get to that money now.

Sure, he might be able to get away with using his debit card once to withdraw as much money as the card would let him, but ATM withdrawals had limits. And using the card would create an electronic fingerprint. Back in the day, O'Dell knew guys who'd been good at reading electronic fingerprints. Nick didn't doubt O'Dell had the same kind of connections now. That was the kind of guy he was.

Somehow O'Dell had gotten ahold of Nick's new name, the one the government had given him. He probably already knew that Nick had a bank account in that name. All O'Dell had to do was wait for Nick to make a withdrawal, and that would be just as good as sending up a balloon that read *Here I Am, Come Get Me.*

So scratch the idea that he could even use his debit card once. The money he'd socked away might as well be in the First National Bank of the Moon.

He'd lived too long in one place. Held the same job for too many months in a row. For the first time in a long time, he'd earned more money than he needed to live on, and thought the money would be safer in the bank than squirreled away in his apartment.

He'd been stupid. If he wasn't careful now, his stupidity might get them both killed, and the kitten along with them. O'Dell didn't value human life, and he certainly wouldn't value the kitten's.

After driving the backstreets and one-way streets for another ten minutes, Nick still didn't see an obvious tail. Vegas never slept, not even out in the backstreets, so there was always some traffic. None of it seemed to be following him.

He finally pulled into an alley that ran behind a strip mall. All the shops in the mall were closed. Dumpsters for the shops lined the alley along with a short stack of empty pallets. Garbage drifted down the alley in a light breeze, the bits of paper trash barely visible after he switched the car's headlights off. Just to be on the safe side, he left the car running.

He'd have to find someplace to hole up. Someplace that O'Dell wouldn't expect. Vegas was a big city, but O'Dell would put the word out. A man like O'Dell had connections, or at least he had when Nick had known him.

Why the hell was O'Dell in Vegas anyway? O'Dell still should have been in prison, but even before then, he'd been strictly an east of the Mississippi guy. A Jersey guy.

"Think it's safe to take me home?" Janine asked, interrupting his thoughts.

Nick considered the question. Had O'Dell gotten a good look at her in the parking lot?

Not that it would matter if they'd followed her from the club to his apartment. At least one of them had gotten a good look at her at the club. Even though she'd ditched the long-haired wig she wore at work, he'd recognize her face. They'd know where to get her home address—the same place they'd tried to get his. Chubs might have said no the first time. That didn't mean he'd say no again. O'Dell knew how to persuade people to do things they didn't want to do. Even a guy like Chubs would eventually cave.

If they'd followed her. She hadn't seen anyone following her, but unless you had experience with that sort of thing, or unless the guys were sloppy—something Nick doubted—she wouldn't have seen a tail. O'Dell had always been good at tailing people. It was one of the things that made Nick so paranoid.

Instead of answering her question, he asked, "How soon after Chubs kicked those guys out did you leave work?"

"Five minutes," she said. "Ten tops."

"You just walked out?"

"I told Chubs I was sick. That I was gonna puke all over the bar if he didn't let me go home."

That would have done it.

The only people Chubs actually respected were the guys from the city health department, and that was only because they could shut his business down. Cleanliness wasn't next to godliness in Chubs' book, but it was pretty damn close. He could deal with customers puking in the restrooms—he had guys to take care of that—but a waitress puking on the bar? It was the one thing Janine could have said that would have made Chubs actually let her leave before her shift was over.

"How'd you figure out where I lived?" he asked.

"I looked in your file." She said it matter-of-factly, without any embarrassment at doing something she shouldn't. "Chubs was stuck behind the bar, so I knew he wouldn't catch me. It's not like he ever locks his office door when he's around. He figures we're all so scared of him, no one would dare go in his office."

A week after Nick had started working at the club, Chubs had shoved a piece of yellow lined paper and a pen under Nick's nose while he was mixing drinks and demanded he write down his address and phone number.

Nick had told Chubs he didn't have a phone number. Chubs hadn't even blinked. Apparently he had experience with employees who were one step above the vagrants who lived in the storm drains and drainage canals that ran beneath the city. But he'd been adamant about an address.

A real one.

"I pay you by cash," Chubs had said. "No FICA, no Medicare, none of that bullshit. No vacation pay, no sick pay."

Nick had figured as much. Chubs had only glanced at his I.D. when he gave Nick the job, and he hadn't made Nick fill out any tax forms. Working at the club—at least in Nick's case—was strictly a cash deal, and one that Chubs didn't have to report.

"This piece of paper stays locked away," Chubs had said when Nick hesitated to pick up the pen. "Just between you and me, but I gotta have something on you if you're gonna work here. And if you lie about it, you're out the door. I'm gonna check it out, understand?"

Nick got the message. Give the man what he wanted or it was job over, just like that.

So Nick had written down his name and his real address. At the time, he'd thought it wouldn't matter. He always moved after a few weeks anyway.

Except he hadn't moved. He'd gotten complacent. The apartment suited him, and working at the club suited him. He started to think of himself as just another anonymous guy in a glitz and glitter city surrounded by unforgiving desert, secure in the knowledge that no one would ever see what he'd written down because Chubs had assured him the information would stay locked away.

Apparently, it hadn't been locked away enough.

Janine had been openly interested in the conversation O'Dell and his pals had with Chubs at the club. That put her on O'Dell's radar. When they saw her leave the club not that long after they got the brushoff from Chubs, that would have peaked their interest. Especially if she'd acted all furtive or worried.

Nick doubted that they'd been specifically waiting outside the club for her. Chubs was the bigger target, no pun intended. He'd insulted them, and O'Dell didn't take insults lightly. They might have decided to work Chubs over right there in the parking lot. Break a few of the big man's fingers until he caved. Janine had just given them a different target—a target that would be far easier than Chubs to control.

So they'd followed her, probably thinking she'd head to her apartment. A woman alone in an apartment would be far easier to convince. They could rough her up in the privacy of her own place until she told them whatever she knew about him. Afterward, she'd become just another disposable person. A potential witness that needed to be taken care of.

Nick decided to lay it out for her. To let her figure out for herself whether it was safe to go home.

"I don't think they planned on you," he said. "I think they were waiting for Chubs. To rough him up and teach him a lesson. When they saw you leave, they decided to follow you instead."

She pulled her bottom lip in between her teeth. The hand holding the backpack tightened until her knuckles turned white. Most people would have been scared, but Janine was angry.

"Sonofabitch," she said. "Those bastards were going to hurt me, weren't they?"

Nick wasn't going to lie to her. "Yes," he said.

She turned her head to look out the window. "Was I right, are they mob?" she asked. "Is that what you're running from?"

"Running?" He'd never thought of what he was doing as running, maybe because it hadn't started out that way.

She snorted. "That's what we're doing right now, hot shot."

He'd give her that. "Point taken," he said.

The alley was deserted except for the two of them. Not even a cat or a stray dog was out nosing around the dumpsters. No homeless were camped out here. No cops on patrol. In his past life, Nick used to roust homeless from spots like this. That had been in a different city, but there were always spots like this.

"You didn't answer my question," she said. "Those guys looked mobbed up."

Convinced that no one had tailed them, he decided it was time to keep moving. He inched the car forward toward the end of the alley. Looked both ways before he switched on the headlights.

"Not mob," he said. "At least, not what people think of when they say mob."

Or at least O'Dell hadn't been when Nick had known him before. He couldn't be one hundred percent certain of the two men O'Dell had been with at the club and in the apartment.

"So then what are they?" she asked.

He shouldn't tell her. He should keep her out of this, but wasn't it already too late? She was already on O'Dell's radar. O'Dell was many things, but stupid wasn't one of them. He'd assume the two of them were together and that she knew everything Nick knew.

He'd deliberately kept people out of his life so something like this wouldn't happen, but it was too late now for Janine. Keeping things to himself wouldn't save her. It might just get her killed.

And he owed her. He'd be dead now if she hadn't warned him they were looking for him.

"The guy who's after me, his name is Oscar O'Dell," Nick said. "He was one of the guys in my apartment, so I'm guessing he's one of the guys who went to see Chubs."

"And he's what exactly, if he isn't mob?" she asked.

That was the million-dollar question.

"He used to be a cop," Nick said. "A dirty cop. I'm the one who turned him in."

The best day of Nick's life had been the day he graduated from the police academy.

His parents had attended the graduation ceremony, both of them beaming from the second row. For a kid who'd had anger management issues most of his life and who was sure his parents were somewhat ashamed of him, the realization that they were actually proud of him was both astonishing and unexpected.

"I always knew you would be a good man," his dad had told him when the ceremony was over and the new graduates were being congratulated by their friends and family. "I know you're going to be a good police officer."

His mom had simply smiled at him and hugged him, a little too tightly, just like she had ever since he'd announced he wanted to be a cop. She'd only made him promise once to be careful, but he could see in her eyes the worry that someday he wouldn't be careful enough.

Rookie hazing had been as bad as he'd expected it would be, but he managed to hold his temper. He spent extra hours in the gym working the heavy bag and the speed bag until sweat ran down his body like rain. He survived the hazing and along the way he learned how to navigate life on the street as a cop instead of a civilian. He learned how to handle people on the worst days of their lives, and how his brothers in blue protected each other.

"You have a second family now," the chief of police had told Nick's rookie class before they rolled out for the first time with their training officers. "You watch your partner's back and they watch yours."

Those words came back to haunt him not long after his rookie year was over.

Nick's first real partner after he'd completed his training was a family man with two kids and a third on the way. He'd been tough but fair, a good cop by Nick's estimation, and he'd taken a bullet when they rolled on a domestic disturbance call.

The call had come from a woman who said her ex had broken into her apartment and was waving a gun around. She'd locked herself in the bathroom. By the time Nick and his partner got there, everything was quiet. The woman, still locked in the bathroom, said her ex had left when he realized she'd called the cops.

Only he hadn't. He'd been hiding on a fire escape just outside the kitchen window. Nick hadn't checked the fire escape, just the kitchen, and had told his partner the room was clear.

Nick's partner had sent him to tell the woman it was safe to come out of the bathroom when her ex fired three shots through the open kitchen window. Two shots hit Nick's partner in the back. The third shot went wild, punching through the refrigerator and burying the bullet in a support beam on the other side..

Before the ex had taken more than a few steps into the kitchen, Nick had shot back, wounding the ex in the shoulder. But instead of just taking the man's gun away and cuffing him, Nick went to work on him.

All the guilt and anger at making such a stupid mistake had consumed him. Nick had beaten the man unconscious. The guy had ended up in the same hospital as Nick's partner.

Nick had been called up on review because of it.

In the end, he'd been cleared of any wrongdoing. The man had shot a cop, after all. The boys in blue protected their own.

"Don't let me see your name on another report," the internal affairs officer who'd caught Nick's case had said.

He'd promised the officer—and himself—that it was one and done. That he'd learned his lesson. His partner was going to pull through, although he had a long recovery ahead of him. Nick still wanted to be a good police officer, and not only because he wanted to be the kind of cop who would make his parents proud. He owed it to his partner.

Then he met Oscar O'Dell.

Nick found out later that O'Dell had only noticed a newly minted cop like Nick because he'd heard that Nick had beaten the crap out of the man who'd shot his partner.

O'Dell had been on the force for ten years, a big city cop with a big attitude and a bigger mouth. O'Dell had no illusions that he'd ever make detective, nor did he want to. He had his beat, mostly made up of immigrant neighborhoods and family-run small businesses. He had a partner who looked the other way when O'Dell got free lunches and free coffee and the occasional envelope with tickets to a basketball game or a football game or a couple hundred in cash.

When his partner got transferred to a different precinct, O'Dell called in a couple of favors, and Nick was assigned as his new partner.

O'Dell was a hard man, half a head taller than Nick and every bit as in shape. He wore his hair buzz-cut short, his uniform crisp, his shoes shined, and he took no shit from anyone. On their first day together, O'Dell told Nick how life really was in the department.

"You got one strike on you already, kid," he'd said. "I can make it two. I can make it three and you're out. Or I can make sure you never get that second strike. Understand?"

Nick understood. He'd seen men like O'Dell in the gym. Guys who came in with an attitude a mile wide who thought they were king of the world. Guys who'd get in your face, push you to make you think you had something to prove. Nick ignored most of them, and the ones who didn't get the message, he beat up in the ring.

He couldn't ignore O'Dell, and he sure as hell couldn't beat the ever-loving shit out of him. This was the side of police work that his dad wouldn't be proud of, but as long as he was partnered with O'Dell, Nick would have to put up with it.

So Nick looked the other way when O'Dell got his freebies. He didn't cringe when O'Dell slapped him on the back and called him a good sport. Nick soothed his conscience by telling himself that for the most part, he was still doing good police work. Still protecting people, still doing the job.

Then O'Dell started taking money from a local drug dealer to look the other way. Serious cash by the size of the envelopes O'Dell came away with.

"Strike two," O'Dell had said, waving the envelope in Nick's face the first time O'Dell had taken the drug dealer's money. "I got your balls in a wringer, don't you ever forget that."

O'Dell had offered to cut Nick in on the take, and he'd laughed at Nick when he'd refused.

"Think just because you don't take the money, you're clean? Life don't work that way." O'Dell's clap on Nick's shoulder that time had been harder than usual. "I go down, I take you with me, and that's a promise."

Nick had started hitting the gym more often after that, especially on those nights when he couldn't sleep.

His brothers in blue were his family, but O'Dell was corrupt, plain and simple, and no one seemed inclined to do anything about it. Especially not O'Dell's cronies, long-time cops all, and pretty much all on the take just like O'Dell. And who'd listen to Nick anyway? By that point he was only a few years out of the academy and he'd already been in trouble once. Who'd believe him if he did decide to turn O'Dell in?

So Nick held his tongue and worked out his aggression on the heavy bag. He stopped visiting his parents as often because he was sure they'd see the guilt in his eyes. He certainly saw it there every time he looked in the mirror.

Then the drug dealer had shot a kid right in front of Nick and O'Dell.

And O'Dell covered it up.

The kid was just a fifteen-year-old screw-up, just like Nick had been a screw-up at that age. He'd come up short on one of his deliveries. Probably not even his fault, but the drug dealer had pulled out a piece and shot him dead like he was just human garbage.

O'Dell had cursed up a blue streak, called the drug dealer every name in the book. The dealer had just smiled at him. O'Dell was bought and paid for.

"Take care of this for me," the dealer had told O'Dell. "They be a little something extra in your envelope if you do." His gaze had hardened. "They be something a little extra in your face if you don't."

O'Dell had taken the gun the dealer had used to kill the kid and thrown it in the river on their way back to the station at shift end.

"Strike two," O'Dell had said to Nick. "Don't you forget it."

The kid's body had ended up in an alleyway halfway across the city. He'd just been a street kid. The cops in that precinct would open a file, maybe do a little digging, but no one would put any real effort into it.

Nick couldn't sleep. He couldn't eat. Every time he closed his eyes, he saw the kid's eyes right before the dealer shot him. Saw the terror there.

He hadn't served and protected that kid. No one had.

Be a good cop, Nick's dad had told him. Keeping quiet, was that being a good cop? Letting that kid's killer walk around like he owned the cops, like he owned *Nick,* was that being a good cop?

He couldn't keep that kind of secret to himself, but who the hell did he have to talk to? He wasn't a religious man. Neither were his parents. Their family had been the only ones on the block who didn't go to church on Sunday mornings. Confessing his sins to a priest wasn't an option.

He couldn't talk to his parents about this. Not only would the disappointment he'd see in their eyes kill him, sharing that kind of information with them would put them in actual physical danger.

He certainly didn't know who he could trust at the precinct. The internal affairs officer wasn't his friend, and for all Nick knew, internal affairs had only let him off the hook because O'Dell wanted him for a partner.

In the end, he'd decided there was only one person he could talk to—the grizzled old hardcase who ran the gym. The old man was walking with a cane by then, but he still ran the gym with an iron fist, even if the knuckles on that fist were swollen with arthritis.

After a workout that left Nick drenched with sweat, he sat in the man's office with the door closed and told him about the kid the drug dealer had killed, and how Nick's partner had covered it up. The old man listened without interruption, taking it all in like it didn't faze him at all.

"It's making me sick," Nick said.

The old man grunted. "I don't doubt it."

He sat quiet for so long, just tapping his cane on the concrete floor, that the silence grew uncomfortable. Beyond the closed door, Nick could hear one of the old man's proteges wailing away on the speed bag, faster than Nick could ever hope to hit the thing. He wondered if the old man was training the kid for actual competition. Maybe even grooming the kid for a championship bout.

"I know somebody," the old man had finally said. "I think it best you tell this story to him."

Two days later Nick did.

Two weeks after that, his life imploded.

11

As Nick told Janine the story of who he'd been and how his life back then had ended, he drove through blocks far rougher than the neighborhood around the strip club. The traffic was non-existent in this part of the city compared to the streets around the Strip. He could count the number of people he saw out walking on the fingers of one hand. Vegas wasn't a 24/7 town everywhere.

Janine sat quiet in the front passenger seat, one hand idly stroking the kitten's carrier. The kitten was curled up inside, fast asleep.

"A dirty cop," she said at last. "I guess that rules out calling the cops about the guys chasing us."

"Wouldn't be my first choice," he said.

It wouldn't even be his second. He didn't know the cops in Vegas and didn't want to. Too much to explain to people who had no clue who he was. They'd take their damn sweet time trying to verify his story. He would have, back when he'd been one of them.

"I never liked the cops out here," she said. "Guess I know why."

"Not from here," Nick said. "Back east. New Jersey."

She blinked at him. "You're a Jersey boy? You don't have the accent. Not even a trace."

"I worked hard to get rid of it." Just like he'd worked hard to get rid of everything else, anything and everything that would tie him to his old life.

Even his parents. The feds who'd set him up with his new identity made it clear. He had to cut all ties or chances were he'd end up floating face down in the Hudson.

"We can't guarantee your safety," they'd told him. "You have to do your part to protect yourself. Don't be stupid."

Back then he'd been their star witness against O'Dell. The fact that the feds had been that blunt with him told Nick exactly how deep the corruption ran. It didn't end with O'Dell. Nick's partner was just the tip of the iceberg.

Saying goodbye to his parents had been the hardest thing Nick had ever done in his life.

"So let me get this straight," Janine said. "This guy—this dirty cop —he followed you all the way to Vegas? He must have a real hard on for you."

Nick shook his head. O'Dell definitely had a hard on for him, but there was no way he could have known Nick was in Vegas.

"Last I heard, he was on his way to prison. That was a long time ago."

O'Dell had ended up taking a plea deal. He hadn't flipped on anyone further up the food chain, and there had to be someone further up the food chain. Someone who'd been protecting O'Dell all along. The plea deal guaranteed that O'Dell would still be spending serious time in prison, although he'd be getting some concessions on the inside aimed at keeping him alive. Former cops weren't the most popular cons among their fellow prisoners.

Janine snorted. "Long time ago. Listen to you. Just how old are you, anyway?"

"Depends on whether you're asking in years or how old I feel."

She didn't say anything, just gave him a look that clearly said she wasn't in the mood to take any of his bullshit.

He sighed. "Forty-two. All this went down fifteen years ago, give or take."

"I imagine you know the exact date, no give or take involved," she said.

True. He knew the exact day, the exact time right down to the minute, when he first met with the federal investigator who spent his evenings working out on a heavy bag in the old hardcase's gym.

"You were still a baby cop when you decided to stand up to a corrupt partner," she said.

He hadn't quite been a baby cop. At twenty-seven, he'd survived the streets for a number of years at that point, which had made him feel older and more experienced than he was.

Janine was looking at him like she didn't think he was quite real. "Most people I've met in my life would never even think about taking a stand against something like that. Too dumb or too scared." She sighed. "Then again, I shouldn't expect anything less. Not after what you did last night."

He shot her a look. "What I..."

"The robbery?" she said, making it sound like he might be a little on the dumb side after all. "I saw you on TV this afternoon before my shift started."

Nick's hands tightened on the steering wheel. There hadn't been any video on the local news he'd been watching, but that wasn't the only local station in Vegas that had an early news show.

"What exactly did you see?" he asked.

"A video," she said. "Something somebody took with a cell phone. It wasn't a great picture, but I recognized you. Especially since you were holding the kitten."

Crap.

"What did they say about me?" he asked. "Did they mention my name?"

"No. I don't think so. The report just said an unidentified local man assisted in apprehending the suspect." She said it like she was almost repeating it word for word from the broadcast. "But the video was playing in the background, and there you were, talking to some cop."

By the time Nick had left the convenience store the night before, all the activity with the cops and the emergency personnel had drawn a few lookie loos, even at that time of night. A couple of them had cell phones.

He hadn't thought much about it at the time. It seemed everyone had a cell phone these days—except him—and he'd been too busy after he'd turned in his written statement declining medical attention. One of those lookie loos must have figured out they could make a quick buck by selling their cell phone video to a local news show.

"I'm not the only one who saw you, am I?" Janine said.

No, no she wasn't.

That must have been how O'Dell figured out Nick was in Vegas.

He should have known that a man like O'Dell wouldn't stay in prison for long. He wasn't just a corrupt ex-cop. He was a smart corrupt ex-cop. If he didn't already have the right kind of connections to keep himself alive in prison, he would have made new alliances. Gotten himself paroled early for good behavior, or maybe his case had been transferred to a sympathetic judge. Or a judge who owed him a favor.

Whatever the reason, O'Dell was back out on the street and just happened to be in Vegas at the right—or the incredibly wrong—time. Either he'd caught the video of Nick or one of his minions who knew the whole story had.

As to how the man had known to look for Nick at the strip club, there was only one explanation.

Nick had screwed up.

Oh, he'd been smart enough to not put his current address on the witness statement. Instead he'd written down an old address from two years ago. But he'd been beyond tired by that point. The adrenaline from the fight had worn off, leaving him shaky, and his head had been pounding. When he got to the blank on the witness statement form where he was supposed to fill in a phone number, he'd written down the number for the strip club. It was the only phone number he knew by heart.

Once he realized what he'd done, he'd considered scratching the number out but decided that would look suspicious. The cops could have arrested him for beating the crap out of the robber, but they'd made the decision to let him walk, at least for now. If he'd given them any reason to be suspicious of him, to think that he might disappear into the woodwork, they could have rethought that decision on the spot.

If they'd arrested him, they would have called Animal Services to come get the kitten. He might never see her again, and by that point, he'd done something he'd sworn he would never do. Not in this new life.

He'd let her become important to him.

So he'd decided to leave his fuckup alone. He needed to look like a good, upstanding citizen. The detectives assigned to the case might try to reach out to him, or the public defender assigned to the case might want to talk to him, but only if it looked like the case was actually going to trial. Otherwise, the prosecutor would rely on the clerk's testimony. Chances were no one would ever try to call him.

It was actually not a half bad call. It would have worked, too, except for O'Dell.

Whatever had brought O'Dell to Vegas, he must have cultivated a connection inside the local police department, and a damn good one at that. The local news shows came on late in the afternoon. O'Dell had been a beat cop. He would have recognized what Nick was doing in the video—handing over his witness statement to the cops. So O'Dell had called his connection—maybe even called in a favor—and he'd gotten a copy of all the witness statements for the robbery, including Nick's

A witness statement that included Nick's new name.

If O'Dell had gone to the home address Nick had put on the report, it wouldn't have taken long to figure out the address was bogus. So he'd called the phone number, probably expecting that to be bogus too.

Nobody at the club actually answered the phone. The number rang to an automated answering service. Press 1 for hours, press 2 for location, that kind of thing. Finding the address for the club had been as simple as pressing 2. Then O'Dell and two of his minions had shown up at club and tried to intimidate Chubs, only they'd spooked Janine instead.

Then they'd followed her to Nick's apartment. They hadn't immediately kicked in his door. They'd given her time to tell him that someone was after him. Let him get scared. Let him know they had him cornered.

That would be O'Dell's style. To let Nick know that strike three had come and gone, and O'Dell was ready to take Nick out of the game for good.

He'd make Nick sweat. Just killing him wasn't O'Dell's style. Besides, he'd already tried that.

This time, O'Dell would make Nick pay.

He wouldn't be satisfied with anything less.

12

Nick slowed the car down as the motel he was aiming for came into sight.

The motel wasn't quite a dump. It had probably been new a handful of decades ago, which was ancient by the Vegas standards of today. But the motel was cheap and clean and rented rooms by the night, not the hour.

Located off one side of the freeway between Vegas and Los Angeles, the motel got the kind of business Strip hotels didn't. Travelers who were looking for a place to get off the road for the night. Travelers who weren't awed by the glitz and glamour and neon of the Strip or the Fremont Street Experience. Families with kids who came to Vegas for something other than gambling and drinking and all the other vices America's adult playland had to offer.

The motel was tucked behind one of those 24/7 chain restaurants that served the same crappy food no matter what city you happened to be in. A combination gas station and minimart took up the corner of the block on the other side of the restaurant's parking lot. A banner hanging over the pumps advertised Loose Slots.

That was Nevada. Even the laundromats had slot machines, and they certainly weren't loose. The convenience store where Nick had interrupted a robbery in progress had two slot machines tucked away in a corner next to an old-style video arcade machine.

Nick drove through the restaurant's parking lot and stopped in front of the motel's registration window.

Janine eyed the motel and wrinkled her nose. "Runners can't be choosers," she said. "I'm guessing we're staying for the night?"

"We need to get off the road." And he needed time to think about what to do next. He could hit the road with the kitten tonight and never look back, but Janine had a life here. She was in danger now thanks to him, and he couldn't just leave her alone to fend for herself. He wasn't built that way.

He took a couple of bills from his wallet and held them out to Janine.

"Why don't you get us a room," he said. "I need to grab some food for the kitten."

All the food he'd bought for her was in the duffel bag he'd abandoned in his apartment. He was pretty sure the gas station's minimart would have some kind of baby food. Of course, that's what had started this whole mess in the first place—buying baby food at a convenience store—but Nick decided not to think about that.

She waved off the money. "Keep it," she said. "Tonight was a good tip night."

"I got you into this," he said. "I'm not about to make you pay for a crappy motel room."

"You're not 'making' me do anything," she said. "I earn a hell of a lot more than you do. Or I did, but that doesn't matter." She gestured at the carrier. "You have a kid to feed, and I wouldn't mind a sandwich myself."

She effectively ended the conversation by getting out of the car. Before she shut the door, she put the kitten's backpack on the floorboard where it would be out of sight.

Smart woman.

The minimart was all bright fluorescent lights and sad-looking junk food. Hot dogs that might have been fresh a week ago turned on hot rollers, and trays of tortilla chips and congealed cheese sauce sat in a plastic display case that might have held cookies or donuts in a previous life. At least the soda machines looked like they all worked, and the aroma surrounding the self-serve coffee machine made Nick think the coffee might actually be drinkable.

A place like this didn't cater to babies. He had a choice of pureed turkey or strained carrots.

"Turkey it is," he muttered, and took two jars off the shelf.

He grabbed a sad-looking salad from a cold case merely because the plastic container was the right size for the kitten to use as a litter box. He added two cheap sandwiches on deli rolls that were more bread than meat, one for himself and one for Janine. He thought about buying a couple of bottles of water, then decided water from the tap would have to do. Like she'd said, he had a kid to feed and his money wouldn't last forever.

The clerk behind the counter eyed the salad. He was a skinny, slow-eyed kid in his early twenties who looked half-stoned. "Our salads suck ass," he said as he rang up Nick's sale.

"Just want the bowl," Nick said.

The kid raised one eyebrow, then squinted at the butterfly bandage on Nick's forehead and the scratches on his face. "Dude, you must be into some freaky shit."

Nick handed over one of the bills he'd offered Janine. "You have no idea."

The kid put Nick's purchases in a plastic sack and handed back a few singles in change. Nick picked up a freebie newspaper from a rack next to the door and added it to the sack. The newspaper advertised all sorts of awesome apartments in the greater Las Vegas area that he'd never be able to afford. Even if he wasn't running, once again, from the bastard who'd been his partner on the force.

The fluorescents over the gas pumps lit the entire corner of the street with brilliant blue-white light. It was after midnight now and only one car was at the pumps, an older model SUV caked with dust from a recent drive through the desert. A rumpled, weary looking middle-aged man stood next to the car, watching half his paycheck ring up on the pump.

One of the interior lights was on in the SUV. Nick could see two kids in the back seat, one of them slumped against the window, eyes closed—sleeping, no doubt—and the other was peering at a tablet. A middle-aged woman sat in the front passenger seat. She looked as tired as the guy pumping gas.

Welcome to Vegas. Not the spot Nick would choose for a family vacation with the kids. Not that he'd thought much about having kids of his own the last fifteen years or so.

Had he ever wanted kids? Maybe, back when he'd been a newly minted cop and his parents were still proud of him. That was the kind of life he'd been programmed to want. Marriage. A family. A couple of kids and a dog and a pension at the end of a twenty-year career.

What did he have now?

Nothing except a kitten, which in itself was no small thing.

A woman he'd ripped from her normal life just because she'd done him a solid.

And O'Dell. Couldn't forget O'Dell, his psychotic former partner. Nick had done the right thing getting him off the force, but sometimes the right thing turned out to be the exact wrong thing. Or at least it looked that way in hindsight.

Life would have been so much simpler if he'd just kept on looking the other way. Simpler but probably shorter. Nick wasn't sure how long he could have lived like that before he ate his gun. Looking the other way wasn't in his genetic makeup. Yes, he'd been a hothead, but he'd been a hothead for a good reason. In his book, taking down bullies was the best reason, and O'Dell was a grownup version of the bullies Nick had hated when he'd been a kid.

Seeing the family at the pumps made him realize just how much he missed his own parents. They'd never gone on a family vacation like that when he'd been a kid. His dad was too busy working—both his parents were—but that didn't mean they didn't have good times together.

Every now and then Nick went to a library to use one of their computers. He'd search for any mention of his parents, dreading the day he'd see their names in an obituary. They'd be in their late sixties now. Sometimes when he was trying to get to sleep in his solitary apartment, hearing the sounds of other people's lives filter through the apartment's walls, the ache to reconnect with his family was so strong he would almost get up to go find a pay phone and call them.

If he'd had his own phone, even a burner cell, he might have actually done it.

Called his parents just to hear their voices. To let them know he was still alive. That he hadn't forgotten them. Let them know that he still loved them.

That would have signed their death warrants. The fact that O'Dell was chasing him now only proved that fact. No doubt O'Dell and his cronies had his parents' phone bugged. Surveillance might have slackened over the years, but now it would pick up again.

Now that O'Dell knew Nick was still alive.

He couldn't even call his parents to hear their voices one last time, just in case things went south.

As he walked through the restaurant's parking lot to the motel, the plastic bag of supplies in hand, his mind wasn't in Vegas. He was still thinking about his parents and the good times they'd had when he'd been a kid. So when he glanced up at the front of the motel, it took him a moment to process that something was wrong.

Something was missing.

His car—and the kitten—were gone.

13

The motel was a long, skinny, two-story building with parking in the front and back, and the office in the center. Two sets of concrete steps led up to a second-floor walkway that wrapped around the building. The metal rails along the walkway had been painted turquoise—faded now—that matched the faded paint on the doors.

Lights were on in half a dozen rooms on the first and second floors, with cars parked in the spaces in front of the rooms.

Nick's car wasn't among them.

He patted the pocket of his jeans just to reassure himself that he still had the key to his car. It had only taken him ten minutes at most to walk to the minimart and buy the few things in his bag.

More than enough time for someone to steal his car. Not that his beater car would be on the top of any car thief's most wanted list. But then where was Janine? And where the hell was the kitten?

He hadn't locked the car. He'd expected Janine to wait for him in the car after she paid for the room. The office was behind a walk-up window fitted with bulletproof glass. Registering in a place like this was just a matter of paying the clerk who sat on the other side of the bulletproof glass and getting the key. Janine would have seen if anyone had slid in the driver's seat and hotwired the car while she was registering.

He could care less about the car. He'd miss the money hidden in the trunk, but money could be replaced. So could the car.

He cared about the kitten.

He stood in front of the office, heart hammering in his chest, trying to think of what to do next, when he heard a low whistle.

Janine stood at the far corner of the building. She held the kitten's backpack in one hand. A room key dangled from the other.

He gritted his teeth and strolled toward her, trying to keep his temper under control.

"You scared the hell out of me," he said when he got close to her.

"I got us a room around back," she said. "That guy who's chasing you, he knows what your car looks like. I didn't want to leave it sitting out front and you weren't back yet." She shrugged. "So I moved it."

"I didn't leave the key."

She gave him a look like he might be the dumbest person on the planet. He was starting to get used to that look.

"I had a rough childhood, let's just leave it at that," she said. "It left me with more assets than a big chest and a winning way with drunks who like to look at naked women."

She'd hotwired his car, and she'd done it fast. He was impressed in spite of himself.

When he'd been a cop, he'd learned that car thieves could break into a car and hotwire it practically before he could blink. That trick wouldn't work with newer models—thieves needed specialized equipment to lift a car that needed a fob to work—but hotwiring would do the trick on his old beater.

Janine led the way around back to the room she'd rented. The only thing wrong with it was that it was on the first floor. An air-conditioning unit crouched below the window, and the drapes were closed. His car was parked two spaces over, in front of the room next door.

Like he would have done. He was beginning to wonder just how rough her childhood had been.

He took the room key from her and opened the door, switched on the light.

The room had two double beds, a counter that held a television, a telephone, and a single-cup coffee maker, and a foldout luggage rack. The bathroom at the back was tiny, just barely big enough for the shower stall, toilet, and sink. The room had no closet. Instead a thick dowel hung beneath a high shelf on the wall outside the bathroom. If the dowel had come equipped with clothes hangers, they were long gone now. The shelf above the dowel held two bath towels and two washcloths, both rough, industrial grade white terrycloth.

A nightstand between the two beds held a cheap digital alarm clock and a lamp that was bolted down. The television was bolted down as well. The coffee maker wasn't. They probably figured no one would steal anything like that.

Nick set the bag of groceries from the minimart on the counter and opened the jar of baby food for the kitten. She looked up at him with big blue eyes when he took her from the backpack. She meowed at him—no scared baby yelps this time, which he took as a good sign. She dug into the strained turkey like she hadn't eaten in years, burying her face in the jar deep enough that she ended up with strained turkey on her whiskers.

Janine took the lid from the baby food jar into the bathroom. He heard her turn on the tap in the sink, and a minute later she brought the lid back, now filled with lukewarm water for the kitten.

After she put the lid down next to the kitten, she poked around in the bag. "I don't see any soda," she said.

He managed a small smile. Watching the kitten eat with so much baby enthusiasm had leached away his anger. He had to admit that Janine had done well. He didn't like the ground floor room, but in this case, quick access to his car wasn't a bad thing. It wasn't like he had a rope to rappel out a second-story window. Plus she'd set up a nice little misdirection with the car when she'd parked it in front of the room next door. Close enough to get to in a hurry, but not an obvious sign pointing to their room. Anyone who recognized his car would think he'd be in the room next door.

"Water's free," he said. "You reminded me I have another mouth to feed."

"A mouth connected to a butt that will need to pee and poop."

He took out the salad and popped off the clear plastic lid. "Litter-box." Then he took out the freebie newspaper. "Litter."

"Resourceful," she said. "You sure you've never had a cat before?"

One of his buddies back in school had had a cat. The cat belong to his buddy's mom, but his buddy had been in charge of cleaning the litter box, a chore he'd absolutely hated. Everything Nick knew about taking care of a cat, he'd learned thanks to his buddy's bitching.

While he ripped the newspaper to shreds, Janine sat on the bed and poked at the salad, her nose wrinkling at the wilted lettuce and anemic tomatoes.

"If I'm going on the run with you," she said, "we're going to have to have a talk about the menu."

He tossed one of the sandwiches to her. "Comes with its own packet of mayonnaise and mustard."

The little packets were wrapped up at the bottom of the sandwich, along with packets of salt and pepper.

"Uptown," she said. "You sure know how to treat a girl."

He almost told her he was out of practice, but she probably already knew that.

She unwrapped one end of the sandwich, ripped open the mustard packet, and squeezed the contents on the paper-thin slice of roast beef inside. She took a bite, then opened the sandwich and added some of the wilted lettuce from the salad.

"Almost edible," she said. She stared at the kitten for a moment. "I guess I should ask what the plan is here, sport."

The plan. He didn't really have much of a plan except to get them both out of sight tonight.

The problem was he'd never thought much beyond bugging out at the first sign of trouble. That was the advantage of being totally on his own. When you cared about nothing and had no one to think of other than yourself, that was the only plan you needed. Pick up and go.

Even with the kitten, he could still just pick up and go.

He couldn't do that to Janine. Sure, it looked like she had the kind of survival skills that would help her get by, but he wasn't about to abandon her. Maybe he'd been a cop just long enough that serve and protect had become ingrained. Or maybe it was the other way around. He'd become a cop because it was in his nature to serve and protect people who couldn't protect themselves.

That was probably why he'd always been so quick to anger when someone figured they could take advantage of him just because he was smaller and they thought he was weak. An easy target.

He'd never run away from a fight back then.

So why was he running now?

Because the feds had convinced him O'Dell was a powerfully dangerous man. At the time, the feds had a vested interest in keeping Nick alive, and they needed his cooperation to do that.

So they'd hammered into him that if O'Dell or any of his people ever found Nick, they'd kill him. They needed him to agree to go into witness protection, and they'd painted such a bleak picture, Nick had agreed. What else could he do? Testifying against the man was the right thing.

The feds had given him a new name in a new location and enough pocket money to help him land on his feet. The way they'd whisked him away, almost without enough time to say goodbye to his parents and no time at all to say goodbye to his friends, they'd set him up for a life on the run. They'd made him believe that O'Dell was far more powerful than Nick had initially thought.

But what if he wasn't?

What if O'Dell was just another crooked cop with a few connections here and there? What if he was in town not because he was somebody important in some nebulous organization, but because he was a working stiff? He could be working a security job for all Nick knew. Lots of retired cops he'd known in Jersey went into security work.

And that was the problem. He knew what O'Dell had been, but he had no idea who O'Dell was now. He could be just some guy with a couple of goons who owed him favors, goons who like to imagine they were like some slick mob guys down here in the desert.

Janine was still waiting for an answer to her question. What was the plan?

"We have a couple of options," Nick said. "I can make a call to a guy I haven't talked to in fifteen years. Tell him my new name's blown, but he'll probably tell me to go pound sand."

Once the government hadn't needed him, they'd basically cut him loose to live or die on his own. The agent assigned to him had been a real peach, especially after he'd learned that Nick had gone along with O'Dell before ratting the man out. A call to that guy would just be a waste of time and money.

If the guy was even still in that job. He could be retired now too. Fifteen years was a long time.

"Not a local guy, I imagine," she said. "A state guy?"

He gave a nearly imperceptible shake of his head.

"Federal?"

This time he just stared at her.

Her eyes widened at the implication. "That means you're in wit—"

"I was," he said. "Till they didn't need me anymore and they cut me loose."

"They'd ignore you? Even with that guy after you, the one they were supposed to protect you from?"

"They don't need me anymore," he said again.

He'd given the feds a videotaped statement under oath. They would have only needed him if the case had gone to trial, but O'Dell had entered into a plea deal, which meant no trial.

"Bastards." She put the sandwich down on its wrapper, blew out a breath that puffed out her cheeks. "So that option's really no option. I'm guessing the second is we keep on running until we land someplace new."

Until he did. He'd give her his car and tell her to keep on going. O'Dell was after him, not her. If O'Dell was tracking them somehow,

Nick wanted the man to find him first. He'd make sure of it. He didn't want O'Dell to ever find Janine again.

She was staring at him. "If the look on your face is anything to go by, I don't think you much like option number two either."

He turned away from her to look at the kitten. She was batting at the water in the lid, touching the surface just enough to get her paw wet, then she'd back away and shake the water off. A few moments later, she pranced toward the lid and started the whole thing all over again.

No, he didn't like option two. Running and hiding and starting a new life, then doing it all over again the next time O'Dell found him. Nick didn't like that option at all.

"So what's option three?" she asked.

The only option left.

The option he'd been avoiding for years

"I fight back," he said.

14

The gym where Nick learned to box had a strict No Kids Allowed policy.

The old hardcase hadn't considered fifteen-year-olds like Nick kids. But he didn't tolerate anyone bringing little kids with them to the gym to work out.

"Not no goddamn babysitter," he'd told one thirty-something man who'd come in one day toting a baby in a carrier.

The man had argued with the hardcase. Said he paid his gym fees and his wife was out of town and he couldn't get anyone to watch the baby.

The argument fell on deaf ears.

"When you come to fight," the hardcase had said, "you give your total concentration to what your body's doing. Can't do that with a baby hanging around in the background. With you wondering if it needs your attention." He'd paused and pointed a finger at the man. "You can't give your work a hundred percent attention, I don't want you in my place."

Nick had watched the whole thing, fascinated. Some of his buddies had baby brothers or sisters, but he was an only child. He'd never given much thought about how much work babies were. How much attention they needed.

He thought about that conversation now. He'd seen enough of the world to know the hardcase had been right. Babies had no place around men who were about to go toe to toe.

Neither did kittens.

O'Dell wouldn't see any value in the kitten's life. Hell, the kitten had probably been thrown in the dumpster by a someone like O'Dell. If he caught a clue that the kitten was important to Nick, he'd wring her neck out of spite.

He couldn't keep her.

The realization made him heartsick and stole what little appetite he had left.

Janine had made an early morning run to the minimart and brought back two breakfast sandwiches she'd heated in the minimart's microwave. The greasy sausage and dry biscuit was only marginally better than the sandwiches Nick had bought the night before, but it was cheap and filling.

She'd also brought back two coffees and a fresh freebie newspaper to shred for the makeshift litter box. Nick didn't have the heart to tell her that he wasn't all that fond of coffee, so he'd been sipping it as he ate. His knuckles were still swollen, the middle two on his right hand in particular, and the heat leaching through the coffee's cheap container make them feel better.

As for the shredded paper, it didn't do that great a job compared to the actual litter Nick had to leave behind in his apartment. Who knew a little kitten could pee that much?

Janine was sitting cross-legged on the bed. Nick's back had been barking at him that morning, so he'd claimed the room's lone chair. He'd brought it over to the counter so he could ride herd on the kitten. He'd put her on the counter so she could eat, and now he was watching her play with her feather toy while he ate. She was trying to rabbit punch her toy with her hind legs and only being partly successful.

He put the rest of his sandwich down. Janine noticed.

"What's up?" she said.

Exhaustion had finally won out the night before and he'd gone to sleep before trying to map out what to do next. Whatever he ended up doing, he might very well end up getting bloody before this mess was over, but he'd make sure O'Dell wouldn't come away unscathed either. Only he wouldn't be able to give a hundred percent of his attention do the job ahead if he was worried about the kitten.

And unlike the boxing ring, if he didn't give his all to getting out of this mess once and for all, he'd end up more than bloody. He'd end up dead.

Nick sighed. "I can't fight back if I'm worried about her."

He rubbed the knuckles of his left hand against his chin. His left hadn't taken as much of a pounding as his right hand, but when he used to box he'd always relied more on his right than his left to deliver the goods. He'd still cut up his knuckles pretty good. The cuts had scabbed over, and the scruff of his beard caught on the scabs.

Janine watched him while she sipped her own coffee. She'd taken a shower that morning. All the heavy makeup she'd worn at the club was gone, and she looked fresh-faced and girl-next-door pretty, sitting there in her oversized t-shirt and jeans. If the circumstances had been different, Nick would have enjoyed waking up in a motel room with her. He would have enjoyed the night before a whole lot more.

"What you need is a cat sitter," she said. "And before you ask, I'm not volunteering. I think she's cute, but I'm going to be a little busy."

He raised a questioning eyebrow at her.

"Helping you," she said.

He started to protest—this was his fight, not hers—but she held up a hand to cut him off.

"The way I see it," she said, "I've got as much to lose as you do. If this O'Dell finds me, he might try to use me as leverage." She wrapped both hands around the cardboard cup again as if she was cold. The room was actually stuffy. The air conditioner hadn't been doing much to fight off the morning heat. "Call me crazy, but I don't like the idea of some dickhead using me as a punching bag—or worse—just to get to you."

She had a point. He didn't want to admit it, but she had a point.

"You can't take her to any of your friends," she said. "He might be able to find your friends, and then they'd be in the same boat I am."

He didn't want to tell her that she was the closest thing he had to a friend. He didn't even have any acquaintances he could ask to kitten-sit.

"We live in a big city," she said. "Probably not as big as where you came from, but big enough. I don't think he can find all *my* friends."

A slow smile stole across her features. Without makeup, she looked a good ten years younger, what with the freckles across her nose and cheekbones. The smile made her look the kind of innocent a woman who worked in a strip club couldn't be.

Nick couldn't help himself. He smiled back.

He'd run out on his life with nothing except a kitten, a car, and whatever he carried in his pockets. A deranged ex-cop with revenge on his mind was chasing him, and he'd just spent the night hiding out in a low-rent motel room. By most accounts, his life was at a particularly low point, and the prospects of it getting better anytime soon were somewhere between slim and no way in hell.

And yet, here he was smiling.

"You have something in mind?" he asked.

She finished her coffee, crumpled the cardboard cup, and tossed it at the trash can next to the counter where Nick sat. It landed dead center in the can. Nothing but net.

"How do you feel about a trip to Boulder?" she asked.

15

Boulder City was a twenty-minute drive to the southeast. While Janine checked out of the motel, which consisted of throwing the room key in a receptacle by the check-in window, Nick spent a chunk of the remaining cash in his pocket filling up the car.

Janine bought two large bottles of water from the mini-mart. With the kitten safely asleep in her carrier, they headed out of Vegas into a part of the desert Nick had never explored.

Boulder City was the closest town to Boulder Dam. It looked like any other mid-size desert community in the southwest that had been skirted by a major freeway bypass. A proliferation of half-dead strip malls shared the main drag through town with gas stations, convenience stores, auto repair shops, and motels that made the place they'd stayed the night before look like the Hilton.

Once they hit the city proper, Janine gave him directions to a mobile home park not far from the commercial district. The park had little in the way of greenery, just a few desultory palm trees here and there, with asphalt lanes that snaked through spaces occupied primarily by double-wide manufactured homes, all with big air-conditioning units churning away. The residents' cars were parked beneath aluminum carports that might protect them from the sun but did little to keep them cool.

Janine had him pull behind a classic Volkswagen Beetle parked beneath a carport attached to an older single-wide. The Bug was sporting a recent paintjob that rendered it a bilious neon green. A miniature rainbow flag was attached to the top of the Bug's antennae, and the license plate holder was encrusted with pink glitter.

"Leon works at the erotica museum," Janine said, as if that explained everything.

Maybe it did. Nick had driven by the Erotic Heritage Museum once or twice, but he'd never been inside. He'd heard customers at the strip club talk about it from time to time, and never in a good way. He supposed men who liked watching naked women dance weren't much interested in spending time learning the history of all things erotic.

"They inherited this place from their grandmother," Janine said as the two of them got out of the car. "It's a bit of a commute, but as housing costs go around here, they can't beat it."

Nick took note of the deliberate pronoun. Leon preferred they. He'd have to remember that.

He retrieved the kitten's carrier from the back seat. The kitten was still curled up inside, but she was awake now and looking out at the world with wide eyes. She didn't cry or yelp when Nick moved the carrier. In fact, she'd been pretty quiet for the whole car ride. Maybe she was getting used to life on the run. With any luck, this wouldn't be her life from now on.

"You sure this is okay?" he asked. Janine hadn't called her friend Leon to let them know company was coming, or that she was hoping they'd agree to cat sit for however long it took Nick to deal with O'Dell.

Come to think of it, he hadn't seen her use a cell phone at all, not even to check for messages. She could have done that while he was in the shower. He'd assumed she had her phone in the pocket of her jeans. What with her oversized t-shirt, he couldn't tell.

Most of the dancers at the club stashed their phones behind the bar. When Chubs wasn't around, they'd sneak a look to check for messages. Janine never did. She apparently wasn't someone overly attached to her phone.

If she even owned one.

She was grinning at him now. "Just wait. You'll see."

The trailer had a small wooden front porch decorated with flowerpots holding a variety of plastic flowers, some bleached by the sun but others shiny bright and obviously new. Rainbow pinwheels and small whirligigs were anchored in still other pots. The day's breeze hadn't kicked up yet, and Nick could see cracks in the plastic petals of the pinwheels. The Nevada desert took a toll on everything, even plastic cheer.

Janine climbed the four steps up to the porch and knocked on the door.

The curtains in a window to the side of the door twitched back just enough to let whoever was inside see who was knocking. Nick stayed at the base of the steps holding the kitten's carrier in case this turned out badly.

He needn't have worried. The front door flew open, and a big black man filled the doorway.

"Janie!" the man said as they enveloped Janine in a bear hug that seemed to swallow her whole. "What in the world are you doing out in middle of nowhere, girlfriend?"

Janie?

Janine laughed and gave Leon an enthusiastic hug in return. "Burning my lily white skin in the sun standing on your porch," she said. "You going to invite us inside?"

"Us?" Leon seemed to see Nick for the first time. "You brought a visitor with you?" The big man raised a mostly shaved eyebrow as they scrutinized the cut and scratches on Nick's face, then traveled down the rest of him, clearly giving Nick the once over. "Is that a gift for..."

They trailed off as their eyes shifted to the carrier and the little ball of fluff inside.

The big man squealed.

"Is that what I think it is?" Leon said, letting Janine go. They stepped away from the door, one hand fluttering in Janine's direction. "You brought the price of admission, girlfriend." They shot Nick a warning look. "I'm trusting you're not trouble, am I right?"

No, not exactly trouble. With any luck, O'Dell would never find out about Leon or the kitten.

"We're hoping you can watch this little girl for a short time," Janine said, deftly bypassing Leon's question. She introduced Nick. "He bartends at the club. He just lost his apartment."

Well, that was one way to put it, Nick supposed. Better than telling Leon the truth.

He tried his best to look non-threatening. It must have worked because Leon's semi-suspicious gaze softened, and they shook their head and clucked their condolences. "Landlords are the bastards of the universe, that's for sure."

Nick shrugged in agreement.

The stairs creaked as he climbed the wooden steps, and the porch itself felt unsteady as he followed Janine through the mobile home's front door.

And into a surprisingly cozy living room.

Leon had a modern, overstuffed loveseat that was obviously their favorite place to sit. A low bookcase on the wall next to the loveseat was filled to overflowing with well-read paperbacks, and a smartphone docking station sat on the top shelf between two small speakers. A mid-size flatscreen television was mounted to the wood-paneled wall, and the loveseat was angled just enough to give Leon the perfect viewing angle. A rainbow-patterned area rug covered the trailer's ancient gold shag carpeting, and a rainbow bead curtain separated the living room from a hallway that led to the back half of the trailer.

A recent theatrical release was playing on the television, the sound turned down low enough that Nick figured Leon just had the movie on in the background. Whatever Leon did for a living—and Nick didn't think it was just working at the museum—they made enough to afford a new paint job for their car and pay-per-view movies.

But the movie wasn't the thing that really caught Nick's attention.

An elaborate carpeted cat tree took up most of a corner of the living room formed by a breakfast bar that separated the living room from the kitchen. A large ginger cat lounged in the bed at the top of the cat tree, staring at the visitors with sleepy golden eyes. Another cat, this one a long-haired gray tabby with white paws and white around its eyes and mouth, lay sprawled across a platform one level below the ginger cat.

Cat toys were scattered across the rainbow rug. Throw pillows on a small chair off to the side of the cat tree featured art deco cats, as did two of the prints on the wall next to the television.

So did the sequined dress Leon wore in framed photographs on the narrow wall between the trailer's front door and the window next to Leon's loveseat.

Leon was a drag queen.

Nick had been right. The museum gig was just Leon's day job. The big man's real passion was drag. Leon's joy practically radiated from each of the photographs.

And these weren't just any old publicity shots. A wide variety of celebrities were featured in most of them. Leon standing next to an entertainer who'd had a successful residence show at one of the Strip casinos for months on end. Another photograph had Leon's muscular arms draped around two well-known sports personalities.

But the photograph that caught Nick's attention was the one where Leon was flanked by a pretty young woman on one side and an older man on the other. All three had wide, happy smiles.

Nick had seen the couple before.

They'd belonged to the Hummer parked in front of the convenience store two nights ago.

And now one of them was dead.

16

———————

Nick had never been a big believer in coincidences.

Coincidences were fine for movies and television shows. Coincidences put the good guys in peril from unexpected sources. Coincidences also helped the good guys win and the bad guys lose, all in the span of an hour or two.

Real life wasn't supposed to be one damn big coincidence after another. *His* life wasn't supposed to be that way.

All he'd done was rescue a kitten.

Because he'd decided to take the kitten home with him, he'd gone to a convenience store that was on his way back to his apartment. A convenience store he'd passed by about a million times before on his walk home. Nothing bad had ever happened on any of those times.

Even when the neighborhood roughs were still hassling him, in the days before word hit the street that he wasn't someone to fuck with, none of those confrontations had happened anywhere near the convenience store.

But because he'd gone into the store this *one damn* time, he happened to run into the exact same couple in the photograph on Leon's wall. At the exact same time a robbery went down, and the damn robber shot and killed the man.

And because Nick had stuck around to fill out a witness statement like a good citizen, he'd ended up in the background of a video shot by a bystander with a cell phone.

And because of *that,* O'Dell knew he was alive and well and living in Las Vegas. Where O'Dell just happened to be.

The old hardcase who'd trained Nick to box all those years ago wouldn't have called them coincidences.

He would have called them consequences of the choice Nick had made.

"Choices," the old hardcase had told him more than once, "we all make choices, and you ain't no different. What you got to learn is how to live with the choices you make, even if they're stupid-ass choices."

Like beating up a bully in school because the kid deserved it.

Or turning in a crooked cop because the man had covered up the murder of a teenager just to protect a drug dealer.

Or rescuing a kitten some asshole had thrown away like trash.

"Who are they?" Nick asked Leon, indicating the picture of Leon with the couple from the Hummer.

The big man was on his hands and knees on the floor playing with the kitten and the feathery toy that had been in her carrier. They looked up at Nick, a big grin still on their face.

"Those two?" Leon cocked their head to one side, trying to remember. "I think he was an investor, or maybe a developer. Maybe he was both, but I know he was someone who got his fingers in a lot of projects down here. What was his name..." They trailed off, eyes on the picture but not really looking at it. "It's an old movie star name. It'll come to me."

Janine shot Nick a one-eyebrow-raised look. He shook his head, a barely there gesture meant to convey that now was not the time to talk about why he was so interested in this particular couple.

"Gregory Peck!" Leon said. "That was it. I remember now. I was joking with him about that name, and he said he had it first, but I told him 'honey, you're aren't nearly that old.' Made him laugh. And that's his wife. Stacy, she said her name was." Leon shook his head. "Mmmm, mmmm. You look at those two and think she's just after his money and he's an old fool, but that's not the vibe I got. There was some real love there."

That was the same feeling Nick had gotten.

Janine blinked and a barely there frown creased her forehead for a quick moment before it was gone and her expression returned to polite interest. Did she know the names? It was possible. It seemed that Janine knew a lot more people in this town than Nick would have suspected just a couple of days ago.

"Where was the picture taken?" he asked Leon.

"Some big new resort up on Mount Charleston. Me and the girls put on a show for their grand opening. That I remember." Leon chuckled. "I'm not sure those old white men knew what hit them, but we sure had fun."

"It looks like Mr. Peck did too," Janine said. "Did you do 'Black Cat Boogie'?"

"For that crowd?" Leon said. "Oh, honey, my Cajun version would have blown their little minds." They fanned a hand in front of their face. "We stuck to the standards. Streisand, a little Celine, you know. When you're big, black, and beautiful, you learn fast how to read the room."

The kitten chose that moment to let out a loud meow, and now they all laughed.

"Looks like she's learning how to read a room too," Janine said. "Will you be all right watching her for a day or two? Your other cats won't mind?"

"Oh, they might hiss at her if she gets too annoying," Leon said, "but she'll be fine. There's a reason nature made babies cute." They looked at Nick. "You never told me her name."

Janine stared at Nick with an expression that clearly said, "Well?" She knew the kitten didn't have a name yet, but did Nick really want to tell a man who loved cats that he hadn't bothered naming the kitten?

He thought about all the coincidences over the last couple of days. How they'd all started with the kitten, one coincidence snowballing into another until here he was, arranging for a pet sitter, of all things. And a good-hearted pet sitter at that. One of the first things Nick had done was offer Leon money for food and litter, which the big man had flat out refused.

Nick couldn't name the kitten One Big Fucking Coincidence After Another, but that made him think of something else.

The first girl he'd had a serious crush on back in high school. A girl so far out of his league it wasn't even funny. A pretty girl with striking blue eyes and brown hair so dark it was almost black.

A girl who hadn't even known he existed.

After all these years, after all the women and the lives he'd led since then, he still remembered her name: Connie.

He'd thought, in the way that kids did when they first fell in love, that when the two of them grew up they'd get married, have a couple of kids and a house of their own and maybe a dog. Cats had never been part of his daydreams about the love of his life, his Connie.

That had been a long time ago, but thinking about her now, he could still remember the bittersweet ache of first love, unrequited. Would it be bad luck to name the kitten after someone who'd never known she'd broken his heart?

He didn't care. Connie had always had a special place in his heart, and that was reason enough.

"Connie," he said, nodding toward the kitten. She was sniffing around the base of the cat tree while Leon's cats were studiously ignoring her from their perches overhead.

"Huh." Leon repeated the name, then said, "I'm guessing she'd be your first cat?"

Nick scratched the back of his head and gave Leon a rueful smile. "You can tell?"

"No, it's not that bad," Leon said, but Nick could tell that it was.

He glanced at Janine, but she just shrugged her shoulders and said, "Don't look at me. I never had a cat. Or a dog, for that matter."

He tried to remember the name of the cat his buddy's mom had had, but that was a lot of years and miles ago, and the cat hadn't seemed all that important at the time. "Connie," he said again. "Unless I think of something else, I guess."

"Oh, honey, don't think of it like that," Leon said. "Cats have a way of letting you know their names. They also pick their people, and it looks like this one picked you."

Had she? She was just a baby, but she'd certainly latched onto him like he was her lifeline. He only hoped he deserved that kind of a bond after years of having none at all.

"And I'm always happy to welcome a new member to the club," Leon said.

"Cat Lovers Anonymous?" Janine said. "That the club?"

Leon chuckled. "Not so anonymous, honey." They got to their feet. "Now I don't mean to be rude, but I need my beauty sleep. I have a show tonight." They sashayed their hips and gave Nick a coquettish grin. "Say your so-longs to your precious little girl Connie, and then head out to do whatever it is that you're going to do. That I don't want to know a thing about."

That last was said with a pointed look first at Nick and then at Janine.

Nick crouched down to give the kitten a scritch beneath her chin. The tight feeling in his chest at the idea of leaving her behind took him by surprise. Yes, he'd most definitely become attached.

"I'll be back for you," he murmured, the promise for her ears only.

She rewarded him with a swat of her paw, baby kitty claws extended. Nature might have made baby animals cute, but nature gave this one razor blades for fingernails. A bead of blood blossomed on his skin.

"Feisty," Leon said. "Don't you worry about her none. I think she's gonna do just fine."

Nick didn't doubt it.

On his way out the door, he spared another look at the picture of Leon posing with Gregory Peck, the investor (or maybe developer), and his wife Stacy.

A man who had his hand in a lot of Vegas deals.

Who'd come to the grand opening of at least one of those deals.

Wouldn't a man like that know better than to stop at a convenience store in a bad neighborhood in the middle of the night? He wasn't a tourist. He was doing business in this city. Apparently a lot of business. If he was a developer, and Nick figured that Leon had meant that Peck was a real estate developer, wouldn't he know which neighborhoods to avoid?

The only reason Nick had set foot inside that convenience store was to get food for the kitten. It was just one of those random things that happened that no one could plan for, so the fact that he was there the same time as Peck and his wife was a true coincidence.

But why the hell were they there in the first place?

And why was Peck the only one who'd died?

17

———

Nick had been a cop for what seemed like a lifetime before he'd finally had enough of O'Dell's brand of corruption. By that time he'd developed a pretty accurate bullshit meter. Whether you called it a gut feeling or intuition or reading the room, cops who were any good at their jobs got a sense of when things just weren't right.

Right now Nick's bullshit meter was telling him the convenience store robbery wasn't what it appeared to be.

Given who they were, Peck and his wife shouldn't have been in that store, that was a given. But that wasn't the only thing bothering Nick.

The robber had been all kinds of wrong too.

At the time, Nick had thought the robber was an amateur. He wasn't a gang member out to prove himself by knocking over a convenience store. No gang colors, and Nick had never seen him out on the streets, so he wasn't a neighborhood tough guy.

He wasn't a tweaker either. Not a meth head looking for some fast cash to finance his next buy. Alcoholic or gambling addict? Maybe, but Nick didn't think so.

The biggest problem Nick had was that the robber hadn't acted like a robber. Like a shooter, yes, but not a robber. He hadn't worn anything to cover his face, which meant witnesses could identify him. A robber who could be identified would walk in shooting so no witnesses would be left behind. A robber like that would take out store security too, but this guy hadn't even checked the security mirror to see if anyone was in the back of the store. Peck and his wife were visible through the store's plate glass windows, but if the robber had checked the security mirror, he would have known Nick was not only in the back row, but was sneaking up on him.

And once the shooting did start, the only person hit was Peck.

Why?

Because Peck had been the robber's real target all along and the robbery was just a cover?

Nick unlocked the passenger door for Janine and then went around to get in the driver's seat. His car was already sweltering inside. He still had on the flannel shirt he'd been wearing the night before. He'd been dressed for the club last night—black t-shirt under the flannel shirt—and hadn't bothered to change when he'd decided to blow off work. All his lightweight shirts, what few he owned, were packed away in the duffel bag in his apartment.

He'd put the flannel shirt back on that morning out of habit. He certainly didn't need it now. He stripped it off and tossed it in the back seat. His black t-shirt wouldn't be much better on a hot sunny Vegas day, but it was all he had. At some point he was going to have to find something else to wear if he didn't want to roast.

Maybe his brain was already fried. Here he was, concocting conspiracies to try to explain coincidences. He had enough on his plate with O'Dell's sudden reappearance in his life. He didn't need to get distracted by anything else.

Still, he couldn't stop thinking about Peck's wife. She'd been kind to Nick when she didn't need to be. He could still see her screaming over her husband's body, his blood on her hands and soaking into her clothes.

The last straw in Nick's law enforcement career had been O'Dell's coverup of the street kid's murder. Was that why this was bothering him now? Peck had been killed right in front of his face. The cops would write it off as a random act of violence—wrong place, wrong time. They had the shooter in custody, end of story.

But what if it hadn't been random? It wasn't outside the realm of possibility that a man like Peck might have the kind of enemies who took care of things with a gun. Hell, the robber could have been someone who'd been evicted from his home to make way for a new development. Enough of that had been going on in Vegas lately, what with all the renovations under way. Whole neighborhoods had been bulldozed to bare earth.

In the heat of a place like Vegas, it didn't take much for some people to go off the deep end.

Nick tried to poke holes in his suspicions. Logistics was the first problem. Unless Peck was in the habit of stopping at that convenience store at that time of night, which Nick doubted, someone would have had to put a tracker on the Hummer to know where the Pecks were going and where they stopped. Tailing someone in Vegas traffic could be done, which was why Nick had been so worried about losing O'Dell the night before, but it wasn't easy, even at night.

Or maybe he was overthinking the whole thing. Road rage wasn't out of the question. Vegas could be a violent town, just like any other big city. Pull up next to the Hummer and take a shot at the guy who cut you off. He doubted the Hummer's windows were bulletproof.

Only a better opportunity came along when Peck parked the Hummer and went into the convenience store. Peck and his wife were already inside the store when Nick got there, and they stayed in the store the entire time Nick had been trying to pick out food and something that would work as a litterbox for the kitten. That would have been more than enough time for an angry guy to park a block away and make his way into the store.

Except the guy hadn't walked in the store and shot Peck right away. He'd tried to rob the place.

Which didn't make sense if it was road rage. But it also didn't make sense as a robbery. So what was it?

A hit disguised as a different crime?

Nick still liked that scenario best. Hell, the shooter might have been hired to take out Peck on the road and make it seem like road rage. He'd wouldn't have needed a mask for that. When the situation changed and the shooter decided to improvise and make the hit look like a robbery gone wrong, he didn't have a mask because he hadn't expected to need one. The killing would still have looked like a random act of violence, especially if everyone in the store had been killed during the robbery.

So who was the man—or woman, Nick reminded himself—behind the whole thing? The robber? Nick didn't think so. If the man's beef with Peck had been personal, he would have fought harder to keep Nick from stealing his opportunity to get even for whatever wrong Peck had done to him.

Nick had pummeled the robber, yes, but a determined man fueled by fury could have out-punched him. Nick hadn't used his fists like that in years. Muscle memory was good, but muscle memory wasn't fast. The man had given up too soon. He'd fired his gun wildly, Nick was sure of it, and he'd just gotten lucky that one of the shots had hit Peck.

Janine cleared her throat, interrupting his thoughts. By the way she was staring at him, he must have been sitting in the car for a lot longer than he'd planned while he turned everything over in his mind. He hadn't even started the car yet.

"You've got some serious thinking going on in that skull of yours," she said. "Want to let me in on it?"

He gave her a quick smile that was more than a little on the grim side. He wasn't ready to share his theories about Peck and the shooting, not just yet. None of that had anything to do with O'Dell. Nick's thoughts were just an echo left over from his previous life. A need to protect the innocent and see that the guilty were brought to justice for their crimes.

He had to remember that he wasn't that person anymore. The shooting had happened, and he couldn't do anything for Peck or his widow. He might not be able to do anything about O'Dell either, but he sure as hell was going to try.

"I need to see what I can find out about O'Dell," he said. "Why he's in Vegas."

That little frown built back between her eyebrows. "You don't think he's here because he tracked you down? I thought you said you're the one who turned him in. I didn't catch much of a look at him last night, but I'm pretty sure he hates your guts."

"Oh, he hates my guts all right," Nick said. "But I don't think that's why he's here. Finding out I'm here's just a bonus."

Figuring out why O'Dell was in Vegas would be the first step in fighting back. It might be futile, but Nick was really sick and tired of running. He couldn't fight back if he didn't know how to find O'Dell.

"I need a library," he said. "Internet access." He met her gaze. "I think that's what we do next."

She settled back in the passenger seat. "Library it is then."

Nick spared one more glance at Leon's trailer as he backed the car out of the spot next to Leon's green Bug with its rainbow flag and pink glitter license plate frame. He could almost imagine the kitten getting to know Leon's two cats. She'd probably charm those two cats just like she'd charmed her way into Nick's heart.

He only hoped that when all this was over, he'd be able to keep his promise to her. That he'd be able to come get her and they could drive off into a new life.

A safe life.

A life without Oscar O'Dell.

18

Before Oscar O'Dell snared Nick in his network of corruption, Nick had set his sights on making detective.

Most of his police academy graduating class had the same goal. Detectives did important work, not grunt work. Detectives worked the clues and worked the witnesses and did more than hand out speeding tickets, roust drunks, and break up domestic disputes.

The closest patrol officers got to an actual investigation was canvassing neighborhoods after a crime had been committed. Patrol officers didn't get to see an investigation through to completion.

It was that lack of follow-through that bothered Nick the most. He didn't like walking away from something that wasn't finished. Detectives got to keep working the case.

Most of his police academy class wanted a shiny gold detective badge for the prestige and the bump in pay. Nick wanted it because to him, detectives did the real work of law enforcement. They caught the bad guys.

O'Dell had never wanted to be a detective. He gave Nick shit because Nick spent all his free time studying for the detective's exam when he wasn't working out at the gym.

"What, you think you're some smart guy?" had been one of

O'Dell's favorite jabs. "You ain't going nowhere, smart guy" had been another.

At first, Nick thought all the verbal abuse was just part of O'Dell generally being a dick. That O'Dell was one of those older cops who hated detectives—hated anyone, really—who thought they were better than beat cops just because they wore a suit to work instead of a uniform.

After Nick learned the true depth of O'Dell's corruption, and this was long before O'Dell covered up the drug dealer's murder of the teenage runner, Nick had attempted to get his career plan back on track.

He'd put in for a transfer.

He told his captain he would take any assignment at any precinct. He hadn't mentioned the real reason he wanted the transfer—to get out from under O'Dell's thumb—but simply said he wanted to work with a partner who had the same career goals that he did.

The captain had seen right through Nick's line of bullshit. In retrospect, it probably hadn't been all that hard to do.

"You know how it works," the captain had said. "You fill out the paperwork for a transfer for any open spot you think you're qualified for. Then they get to decide if they want you." He'd grinned at Nick, but the humor behind it was at Nick's expense. "Since the request's not coming from me, they got the final say so, understand? It's only automatic if it's coming from higher up the food chain. The kind of transfer you're after is discretionary."

The captain had leaned back in his chair. His office was strictly utilitarian. Gray steel desk, two gray hardback visitor chairs, gray steel filing cabinet that remained locked even when the captain was in his office. The only thing that could be deemed a luxury was the captain's chair. Padded black leather with a million levers and hydraulics that would support a man twice the size of the captain's trim body.

The chair belonged in the office of the CEO of a multi-billion dollar company, not the office of a Jersey precinct captain.

"So the first thing they'll do is look up your record," the captain said. "Then they'll ask for my opinion. Ask me whether you'd be a good fit."

The captain had just stared at Nick without saying anything else. That was fine. Nick got the point.

The captain was telling him it was common knowledge O'Dell was dirty. Not only at Nick's precinct, but at other precincts throughout the city. Even if the other precincts didn't know for certain, they would have heard the rumors. And because Nick was O'Dell's partner, they'd assume Nick was just as dirty.

No other precinct would want him, and even if they did, his own captain wouldn't give him a good recommendation.

Nick was stuck right where he was. O'Dell wasn't about to let him go, and his captain wasn't about to give him a way out. Without actually saying the words, the captain had made it clear that he wouldn't take something away that O'Dell wanted.

For the first time, Nick had an idea just how far the corruption had spread. Why the captain had been able to afford such a fancy office chair. No way in hell would the department have sprung for a chair like that. Nick just hadn't thought about it before. Hadn't put the pieces together. Some detective he would have made.

The captain must have been getting a percentage of the money O'Dell collected. Payment to look the other way.

Most men would have given up their dreams then and there, but Nick wasn't most men. While his high school buddies were out getting into trouble, Nick had been in the gym working the speed bag. Learning how to move his feet, how to throw a punch like he meant it, and how to follow through in a way that protected his body instead of leaving himself open for more damage than he'd dished out.

He'd done that because he wanted to learn how to fight the right way. How to excel at something that would keep his temper in check. He wasn't about to give up on the idea of making detective someday.

So he kept right on studying for all the exams he'd have to take to move up the ladder within the police department, he just never told O'Dell about it. But he did more than that. He paid attention whenever he overheard detectives talking in the squad room. Whenever he got the chance, he'd watch how they went about their jobs, trying to learn as much as he could without coming right out and telling them that's what he was doing.

What he'd discovered early on was that detective work was all about research. Not just going out to interview witnesses and follow up leads, but the kind of research that put the detective's butt in a chair looking up information in computerized databases.

Nick didn't have access these days to the law enforcement databases the detectives had used. But the detectives used public databases too, sifting through records that anyone could use if they only knew where and how to look.

In the fifteen years he'd been living his new life, Nick had kept up the research skills he'd learned back then. Every now and then he'd go to a local library on his day off. When he wasn't reading a book he'd picked up off the shelves, he'd use the library's computers to research some random topic. Sometimes he'd pick a year, find a significant event that happened in that year, and research the hell out of it. Other times he'd simply find an article from one of the local newspapers the library kept on hand and see if he could expand on whatever the article discussed.

On rare occasions he read court opinions. It didn't happen often, but sometimes he'd find an opinion that made him chuckle. Some judges had a biting sense of humor, and they'd bury that sense of humor in an otherwise dry bit of legal writing.

In all that time, Nick had never researched O'Dell.

When the feds had relocated him and given him his new name, they'd warned him to steer clear of any sort of contact with his old life. Even computer searches.

"Don't let your curiosity get you noticed," the feds had told him. "Assume someone's always looking for you. Because they are."

Now it didn't matter. O'Dell already knew that Nick was in Vegas. He'd probably be doing his own research, trying to figure out where Nick was, so what the hell. Turnabout was fair play.

Boulder City had a public library, but Nick didn't want to do anything that could lead O'Dell to Boulder City. Especially not if a computer search at the public library could be traced to the Boulder City branch.

Leon was doing Nick a solid, as the college kid who worked the early morning shift at the strip club would have said. You didn't repay that kind of selflessness by pointing the bad guys—and O'Dell was one of the worst—right at their door.

Instead, Nick decided to use a branch in Vegas that was halfway across the city from the strip club. He'd been there a few times, back when he was new to the city and still trying to get his bearings. The library was a small place in an older section of the city. From the outside it looked like just another bland, years-out-of-date building, but inside it had a bank of fairly recent computers available for public use.

Nick sat down at the last computer in the row, in a spot where he could sit with his back to the wall and see the front door over the top of the monitor. Janine wandered off to find the ladies room and maybe a good paperback book.

"Mysteries," she said. "I like mysteries."

Probably why she was still hanging around him. Not that he had all that many mysteries left for her to discover. He'd told her far more about his life than he'd told anyone in years.

Nick sat and just stared at the computer as sweat beaded up on the back of his neck. The sweat had nothing to do with the hot day outside. The library actually had decent air conditioning, but it couldn't stand up to the sick heat Nick felt as he was about to break one of his cardinal rules.

Entering Oscar O'Dell's name into a search engine would be the first real step on the road of no return.

It was one thing to sit in a motel room and decide to fight back. It was another to actually start the fight.

Sure, he could tell himself that O'Dell had started the fight when he'd come to the club looking for Nick. He could even tell himself that the fight had started long before that, when O'Dell had first made Nick an unwilling participant in his protection racket.

That had been only the tip of the rotten iceberg of corruption known as Oscar O'Dell.

Until the robbery, Nick hadn't actually been in a fight in years. He couldn't remember the last time he'd hit a heavy bag or worked a speed bag until it sang. Would the old hardcase be disappointed in what Nick had become?

Would his parents?

He'd been surviving for the last fifteen years, but he hadn't really been living. It was long past time he started. If he was really about to jump with both feet onto a path he couldn't return from, at least he'd be headed somewhere. Better than standing in place, looking over his shoulder for the rest of his life.

He rested his fingers on the keyboard and began to type.

19

Search engines were tricky things. Years of practice researching random topics had taught Nick a few tricks, like how to narrow a general search that returned way too much irrelevant information.

Like how many people had the name Oscar O'Dell.

Just typing in the man's name gave Nick articles on an Oscar O'Dell who'd pulled a drowning kid out of a lake in Wisconsin (not the Oscar O'Dell he was looking for) and another who'd just been appointed deacon at a church in Atlanta (definitely not the right man). He narrowed the search to Oscar O'Dells in New Jersey, but there were still too many. Like the deli owner in Elizabeth who sponsored a neighborhood softball team to keep the kids off the street. Not something the man Nick was looking for ever think of doing.

Then he added the words "arrest" and "custody" to his search string.

The third result down was a newspaper headline about a local cop who'd been taken into custody in connection with the death of a missing teenager.

Bingo.

Nick clicked on the link, expecting a popup telling him he'd hit a newspaper paywall and to continue he'd need to create an account. He wasn't about to give any newspaper—or any other site on the web —his debit card number. He was surprised when the link led him directly to the article.

The article was on the site of a small local newspaper. Nick dimly remembered seeing the paper in racks in Mom-and-Pop grocery stores back in Jersey next to heftier editions of *The Times* and the *Wall Street Journal.*

This particular article was sketchy on the details of O'Dell's arrest, merely stating that federal authorities had taken a veteran police officer into custody on undisclosed charges in connection with the death of a missing teenage boy. It filled in what scant facts the reporter had been able to obtain with the kind of information about O'Dell's years of service in the police department that would normally appear in a community service puff piece.

The thing that gave Nick a start was the picture of O'Dell that ran with the article.

The picture was a police department publicity shot taken when O'Dell hit ten years on the force. Nick had walked past that photograph countless times on the way to rollcall, but he hadn't been prepared to see it now.

O'Dell's photograph, along with the photographs of other officers who'd hit milestones within the department, had hung in the hallway between the locker room and rollcall. Not quite ready for public consumption, the running joke had been about those photographs. Most of them were little better than snapshots, or better yet, mugshots taken up against a blank wall. Unliked the professional portraits of the captain and the police commissioner that hung in the precinct's lobby.

Also unlike the professional portraits of the captain and the police commissioner, which exuded strength and confidence along with an Officer Friendly smile, O'Dell's photograph showed an officer who'd never be any civilian's friend. His expression in the photo was as dull and bland and emotionless as a department store mannequin.

Except for his eyes.

O'Dell's eyes looked flat and mean and absolutely deadly, like what Nick imagined looking into the eyes of a shark must be like.

He stared at the picture on the computer screen for a long moment. This was the man who'd screwed up Nick's life completely. O'Dell had done it because he could. He'd done it because he'd thought Nick couldn't fight back without implicating himself. He'd thought he'd backed Nick into a corner he wouldn't be able to get himself out of.

Well, Nick had fought back once. He'd refused to keep going along. He'd finally done the right thing. He could do it again.

The newspaper must have hired a few halfway decent IT and website design people. The paper's website included an easy to find search feature that actually worked the way all search engines should. Nick typed O'Dell's name into the search window along with the name of the reporter on the article's byline.

That search returned of over thirty additional articles. Not bad for a newspaper published only twice a week.

The articles were sorted by date. He skimmed through the first few, which were pretty much just a rehash of what little factual information on O'Dell's arrest was in the first article. From there, the articles devolved into simple one or two paragraph reports on court appearances on "multiple charges" relating to the teenager's death, although Nick did find it interesting that apparently O'Dell hadn't been able to make bail.

Nick didn't hit paydirt until he pulled up an article dated two days before the six long weeks he'd spent in the safe house the feds had stashed him in came to an abrupt end.

The reporter who'd written the piece had clearly known far more facts than he could include in his article, probably from an off-the-record discussion he'd had with a source familiar with the feds' case against O'Dell. But the article was written in a way that Nick could read between the lines, which gave him a picture of what must have been going on behind the scenes while he'd been isolated from the world and passing his time jumping rope and riding an exercise bike to nowhere.

The feds had been able to gather enough evidence on O'Dell to put him away for a long, long time. While O'Dell had been sitting and stewing in jail awaiting trial, he'd had time to consider his options. When the federal prosecutor laid out all the evidence against him, O'Dell had flipped.

He'd cut himself a deal, and then he'd named names.

Nick's captain and a city councilman who'd had plans on running for mayor were among those arrested.

A few other local politicians and prominent businessmen were also named in the article as "persons of interest" in the on-going investigation. Nick would be willing to bet none of those businessmen had a net worth measured in the hundreds of millions. He would also be willing to bet other people had been involved. People whose net worth was much, much higher.

He'd always suspected that O'Dell wasn't keeping all the cash in the envelopes he collected from local businesses. Sure, O'Dell probably got a decent percentage, but it seemed that a bunch of other higher-ups all got their own cuts.

Some businesses in O'Dell's beat never paid protection money, and now Nick knew why. The men running those businesses had either been in on the scam or supported the right local politician. Businesses that tried to buck the local power brokers paid more or they didn't stay in business long.

The feds had cast a wide net. They'd busted a corrupt organization of cops, politicians, and influential businessmen. And Nick had started the whole ball rolling because he'd talked to the old hardcase who'd taught him how to box, and then he'd talked to the hardcase's friend.

Now he knew why he'd been cut loose so abruptly. The feds had kept their word, they'd set him up in a new life, but they'd never given him any details about how far the corruption reached.

After O'Dell's arrest, Nick had given the feds a long and detailed statement before a videographer. From the questions the feds had asked him about O'Dell, Nick knew O'Dell was up against some serious charges in addition to accessory to murder. He knew what kind of prison time O'Dell had been facing.

The article noted that O'Dell had pled guilty to a variety of felony charges. O'Dell wouldn't have pled guilty unless he got a deal for a reduced sentence, something less than life behind bars. When the feds had cut Nick loose, they'd assured him O'Dell would be in prison for a good long time.

Apparently not long enough.

Nick resisted the temptation to look for articles about what had happened to the other people who'd been arrested by the feds—he was especially curious about what had happened to his old captain, the one who'd blocked Nick's attempts to transfer to another precinct —but he really didn't want to go down that rabbit hole. His problem now was O'Dell, and he only had half the story.

He scrolled down the list of articles until he reached the last one that mentioned O'Dell's name. It was dated nine years ago and reported on O'Dell's release from prison.

O'Dell had only served six years.

What the hell? Six years for covering up the murder of a kid? Not to mention all the other charges the feds must have brought against him.

Nick sat back in his chair, dumbfounded. O'Dell must have made a hell of a deal with the feds. And why not? The feds didn't care about one single corrupt cop. They'd been focused on taking down O'Dell's whole network. They'd probably promised him the moon if he agreed to name names.

Nick rubbed his face while he considered the fact that O'Dell had been out of prison for nine years.

Nine years. And Nick had never known. Suddenly all his precautions to keep himself off the grid didn't seem so paranoid.

What had O'Dell been doing in all that time? He would have been on parole initially, so he would have had to keep his nose clean. No associating with his old network, if they'd even talk to him again. In fact, given that O'Dell had flipped, it was a wonder he'd not only survived prison, but that he hadn't been killed the minute he'd set foot in the outside world.

Nick did know one thing. Living off the grid to keep himself safe wasn't O'Dell's style.

He went back to searching O'Dell's name, only this time he concentrated on social media sites. He found a few Oscar O'Dells, like the deli owner in Elizabeth, New Jersey. That particular Oscar O'Dell had a busy Facebook page filled with pictures of all the community projects the man was involved with. But he got no hits on social media for the right Oscar O'Dell.

When Nick finally found a fairly recent link for the right Oscar O'Dell, the link was to an article about a gun show in Reno.

The three-year-old puff piece was part of a blog highlighting local events. The blogger had talked to O'Dell about a company called Blue Lake Protection Agency. The company provided private security for everything from organized hunting trips to concerts and events like the gun show, and could even supply highly skilled bodyguards to people who thought such things were necessary.

"Like in the movies?" the interviewer had asked.

O'Dell had replied that his guys were better than the guys in the movies. "In real life there's no do overs," he'd been quoted as saying. "You have to get it right on the first take."

Good quote for the article, the kind of quote journalists probably drooled over, but it made Nick's blood run cold.

If O'Dell had gotten it right the first time, Nick would be dead now. Pure, simple luck was the only reason he was still alive.

The last thing he wanted was to give O'Dell another shot at killing him.

He'd lived in Vegas long enough to learn just how fickle luck could be. The house always came out the winner. This time around, he'd have to make sure he was the house. That he held all the cards, not O'Dell.

The odds on that happening?

Somewhere between slim and none, but a man could hope.

20

The first time O'Dell had tried to kill Nick, the feds had caught it all on tape.

The feds hadn't taken Nick into protective custody right after he'd given them a preliminary statement. First they'd wanted him to wear a wire.

"We need corroborating evidence," they'd told him. "This thing could be big. This can't be just one corrupt cop, not if what you've told us is true. We need to make sure it is, you understand that, right?"

He'd understood, all right. All that time he'd spent watching detectives build cases against suspects, he understood exactly how the system worked.

Without corroborating evidence, it would be Nick's word against O'Dell's. The feds needed more than the word of one beat cop who was still wet behind the ears compared to O'Dell. And who, by the way, already had one excessive force beef in his jacket.

So Nick had agreed to wear a wire.

"Just do what you always do," the feds advised him. "Don't do anything to make him suspicious."

Only what Nick usually did on his beat with O'Dell turned out not to be enough.

O'Dell always took Nick with him when he collected his payments, but the man was smart. He didn't say anything about what was in the envelopes, even when it was obvious the envelopes were stuffed with cash. He just took the envelopes and stuffed them inside his pocket and gave Nick a self-indulgent smile that had no humor in it.

The closest O'Dell came to incriminating himself was when he'd clapped Nick on the shoulder after tucking an extra thick envelope into his pocket and said, "Is this a good life or what, Nicky?"

The feds said that wasn't enough.

They'd picked up Nick on his way home. In the backseat of a nondescript midsize sedan, they'd told Nick they needed something better. Something definitive.

"We're going to set up video surveillance," one of the feds said. He was the stereotypical federal agent straight out of central casting. Square jaw, unwavering direct gaze, serious tone to a voice that had no trace of an accent, odd enough in a place like New Jersey.

"We'll try to catch him on video that we can sync with audio from the wire," the other fed said. This one was older and looked like someone's middle-aged uncle. He might have been as stereotypical as his partner when he'd been younger, but time had taken some of the intensity from his gaze and rounded out the angle of his jaw.

He'd been sitting in the front passenger seat, and when he turned around to talk to Nick, he'd looked relaxed. Like this was all going to be easy-peasy, just another day on the job. Nothing to worry about here, kid.

"It would be great if he did something else with that drug dealer," the older fed said. "Think that'll happen anytime soon?"

The implication had been "can you make something like that happen?" Like the kindly older uncle asking his nephew for a favor.

Nick realized they were double-teaming him. Not the good cop, bad cop cliché of television dramas, but the real life version: intense cop, mellow cop.

He didn't have any influence on the things O'Dell did, and he told the feds that.

"That's all right," the older fed said. "Just give it your best shot."

Kindly older uncle was now disappointed with his nephew. But don't worry, uncle still loves you. The only thing missing was the understanding pat on the shoulder before he was sent away with a lollypop and the wire still taped to his chest.

So Nick did his best. The next day he tried to bring up the drug dealer in casual conversation, but it apparently hadn't been casual enough.

O'Dell was a lot of things, but stupid wasn't one of them.

Nick had never been a match for O'Dell when it came to manipulation. He'd tried his best, but O'Dell got suspicious. Nick could read it in the man's flat expression, but he told himself he was only imagining things because he was so nervous.

Right up until they took a domestic disturbance call. Then things became deadly real.

The call was on the edge of their patrol district, but O'Dell told Nick to radio in that they'd handle it.

"It'll be good experience for you, kid," O'Dell had said.

Nick didn't need the experience. He'd been on his fair share of domestic disturbance calls before he'd been partnered with O'Dell, and even more since then. The neighborhood was rough. Most of the neighborhoods they patrolled were.

They could hear screaming from a third-floor apartment as soon as they exited their shop. The building's elevator was broken, and by the time they'd climbed to the third floor, O'Dell had been wheezing.

Nick should have known something was up. O'Dell had a bunch of years on Nick, but the man was in pretty good shape.

As if he'd known what Nick was thinking, O'Dell had told Nick he thought he was catching a cold. "You do the honors," he said, pointing at the apartment door.

So Nick had knocked on the door and identified himself as a police officer. He stood off to one side of the door so he wouldn't present himself as a target. He'd unsnapped his holster, ready to draw his weapon even though he hoped it wouldn't be necessary.

The only thing he'd done wrong was not wait for O'Dell to cover the apartment door from the other side. The woman inside the apartment had gone from shouting in anger to shrieking in pain, and Nick didn't want to wait.

Without warning, three shots blasted through the center of the door right at the spot where the suspect inside expected Nick would be standing.

The bullets went through the wall on the other side of the hallway. Nick learned later that the apartment was rented by an elderly woman, who lived there with her caretaker. Two of the bullets hit the caretaker. She lost full use of her right arm, but she survived.

The caretaker's screams made Nick turn his head.

That was the only reason he saw O'Dell standing less than six feet away, a gun in his hand. Not his service weapon, but a small caliber handgun.

Pointed directly at Nick.

"Nobody likes a snitch," O'Dell said, and then he fired.

If Nick had frozen, O'Dell's shot would have killed him. All the years Nick had spent in the gym learning how to box the right way had given him fast reflexes. He'd thrown himself down and away a split second before O'Dell pulled the trigger.

O'Dell hadn't aimed center mass. Like all patrol officers, Nick wore a bulletproof vest. Hitting him in the vest would have temporarily incapacitated him, but it wouldn't have killed him. Instead, O'Dell had aimed at Nick's thigh, shooting for his femoral artery.

Nick's quick reflexes saved his life. The bullet only dug a channel along the outside of his thigh.

His leg erupted in pain as he hit the dirty, cracked linoleum. Women were screaming on both sides of the hallway, and a man was shouting obscenities. Nick's ears were ringing and he realized he was yelling himself.

He rolled, freeing up his service weapon. He fired two quick shots at O'Dell even as O'Dell fired again. This time O'Dell's shots hit the floor where Nick's head had been a moment before.

Nick's shots weren't any more accurate than O'Dell's, but he caught O'Dell high in the vest, and one of the shots might have nicked his shoulder. He didn't wait to find out. As soon as he got his feet under himself, he took off running down the hallway toward the stairwell at the other end.

He didn't know if the feds were listening to him live. Even if they were, how far away were they? He was in trouble and he needed help. His leg was screaming at him now. Unless he'd actually wounded O'Dell, Nick wouldn't be able to outrun him. Not going down three flights of stairs with a bum leg.

"Bastard shot me," Nick said, hoping the wire was picking up his voice. "If you don't get me out of here, he's going to kill me."

He hoped to hell the feds were paying attention. Hoped to hell that they were close enough to actually help.

They were.

When he hit the street, the feds snatched him up almost immediately. He was put in the back of a panel van while other members of the team took O'Dell into custody.

The feds took about a million photographs of Nick's leg before and after the wound was cleaned and stitched. As soon as he was released from the hospital emergency room, they'd taken him to a house in the suburbs.

That had been his first night in a government safe house. His old life was officially over. It was a good thing he'd never had a pet. He barely had time to call his parents from the hospital, tell them he'd been wounded in the line of duty but he'd be okay.

And now here he was, sitting in a library in Las Vegas, ready to go up against O'Dell armed with what? He didn't even own a gun, but the thought of running away and starting over again somewhere else made his stomach turn.

He spent a few minutes trying to find out anything he could about Blue Lake Protection Company, the security company O'Dell had apparently been working for three years ago when he'd been interviewed in connection with the gun show in Reno. Business records in Nevada were public and most of them were online, but nothing came up for either the company or O'Dell. If Blue Lake was doing business in Nevada, it hadn't registered its existence with any state agency.

Next Nick tried googling the company itself, but the words "blue" and "lake" were too common. He got about a zillion hits on various bodies of water throughout the world, but nothing about a security company.

He supposed that a whole lot of nothing he could find about the company itself said something about the business. What kind of business these days didn't have a web presence? Even the strip club where he worked (used to work now, no doubt) had a rudimentary web page. Websites were the new Yellow Pages. Customers expected to find information about a company on the web.

But maybe Blue Lake didn't have to advertise. Maybe it brought new business to its doors, wherever the hell those doors were located, strictly by word of mouth.

Which said a whole lot about the type of protection services the company offered and the type of clients it served.

The type of clients who wouldn't hire a legitimate security agency because the clients—and their businesses—weren't exactly legitimate themselves. O'Dell must have been at the gun show to make connections. To put a public face on a company that could only be found on the dark web.

Was that why O'Dell was in Vegas? Was he on a job? Or was he looking to drum up more business for his company?

Nick did a quick search on events happening in Vegas. He didn't see any gun shows listed, but that didn't mean anything. Any sufficiently big event could be a draw for a company like Blue Lake, and Vegas was the home of mega-conventions and enormous trade shows.

Something else Janine had said struck him.

Mobbed up. That's how she'd described the men who'd been looking for him at the club.

From anybody else, Nick would have shrugged off the remark. Lots of people west of the Mississippi thought everyone with a Jersey accent was part of the mob. Thank you very much, *Sopranos*. But from Janine, who had more skills and a much more varied—and apparently shady—background than Nick had ever given her credit for, he'd take her assessment at face value.

Was that what O'Dell was doing these days? Was he on the payroll for some local mobster? Or some east coast transplant?

That put a whole new spin on Nick's plans to confront the man. Nick wasn't stupid enough to think he could go up against the mob. Not now. Not on his own without law enforcement backing him up. He wasn't the star of some action movie, the lone hero who could dodge a barrage of bullets. He couldn't even successfully dodge one. He had the scar to prove it.

He was lost in thought when Janine sat down in the chair next to him.

"I've been going through some newspaper archives," she said. "The library system keeps an archive."

She handed him a printout of a newspaper article.

"The woman in that picture on Leon's wall?" she said. "The couple you were asking about? I thought she looked familiar. Stacy Peck."

Until that moment, Nick had been so preoccupied with Blue Lake Protection Company and Oscar O'Dell that he'd forgotten about Janine's odd reaction to the picture of Leon with Stacy and Gregory Peck.

Nick didn't bother to do more than scan the article. It had something to do with a local fundraiser. He paid more attention to the picture accompanying the article.

Janine pointed at the picture. "That's Stacy and her husband."

Stacy Peck and her husband, Gregory Not-the-Actor Peck, were featured along with a local radio personality. A few other people could be seen standing behind the couple, including a slick-looking younger man standing off to Stacy's right.

"And that," Janine said, moving her finger to the younger man, "is one of the guys who came into the club looking for you. The one who told me to mind my own business."

Nick sat forward in his chair. "Is he security, you think?" he said. "O'Dell apparently had some kind of gig with a security company at one time that didn't appear to be exactly aboveboard. If he's still doing that, he could have brought a couple of the security guys with him."

Janine was shaking her head. "Read the caption."

The picture had been taken two years ago according to the date next to the caption. The people in the photograph were identified as Stacy Pucinelli, Gregory Peck, and a local DJ. The guy standing to Stacy's right with the slicked-back haircut and the *don't fuck with me* attitude was identified as Gino Pucinelli.

Nick couldn't keep his surprise from showing. "That's her brother?"

Why would Stacy's brother come looking for Nick in a strip club?

"Cousin," Janine said. "I'd never met him before, wouldn't know him from Adam. But the family, I've heard of them. The Pucinellis own controlling interests in a lot of places around town." She shrugged, as if in response to an unasked question. "I hear stuff. People talk when they come to the club, you know how it is. They must not think we can hear them."

Nick understood that. The cliché was that drunks told their troubles to a bartender. That didn't happen in Chub's strip club. There the drunks told their troubles to the strippers, but they had to talk loud over the music. Nick overheard a lot, but he didn't remember anyone ever mentioning the Pucinellis.

"Gino's dad is the real deal, someone you don't want to cross," Janine said. "You know what I'm talking about when I say 'real deal,' right?"

Nick nodded. He'd grown up in Jersey. He'd been a cop in Jersey. He knew all about men who were the real deal.

"The way Gino threw his weight around when O'Dell came looking for you," Stacy said, "I'm guessing the kid thinks he's a real deal too."

O'Dell had brought Stacy's cousin Gino into the bar looking for him.

Nick thought it through.

None of this had anything to do with him initially. It couldn't have. No one, least of all him, could have predicted he'd be in that convenience store at the same time Peck was killed. O'Dell hadn't known Nick would be there. The robber couldn't have known Nick would be there either.

Hell, the man who'd hired the robber to kill Peck—and Nick was becoming more and more convinced that the robbery had just been cover for a hit on a man who was quite literally married to the mob—that unknown backer hadn't known Nick would be there or that Nick would interrupt the robbery.

The fact that Nick had appeared in an amateur video and that O'Dell happened to spot him was just one more layer of icing on the cake.

But the thing that would come back to bite Nick in the butt even more than O'Dell being hot on his heels after all these years?

The fact that O'Dell had brought Gino Pucinelli with him to the strip club when O'Dell came looking for Nick. Gino Pucinelli, who thought he was just as real a deal as his old man.

Nick rubbed the back of his hand against his mouth, which had gone as dry as the Nevada desert.

"Son of a bitch," he said. "I think I crossed the mob."

21

———————

Everything Nick had just found out pointed to the fact that somehow O'Dell had hooked up with the Pucinellis.

Not as a partner. Not as a made man either. A wannabe tough guy like Gino Pucinelli might hire someone like O'Dell as muscle, but no one would let O'Dell into the family. He wasn't important enough. Disgraced ex-cops were probably a dime a dozen in the Pucinellis' world.

Gino though? O'Dell would be just the kind of man a kid trying to prove how tough he was would hire. Having a guy like O'Dell at his beck and call probably made Gino feel important.

So when O'Dell had shown up at the club with Gino, it was because Gino was the one looking for Nick, not O'Dell. A kid who thought he was a real deal mob guy would never tag along on O'Dell's personal business. He might not even know that O'Dell had a past with Nick.

There was only reason why Gino would be looking for Nick—because Nick had gotten in the way of family business.

It didn't matter that the robber had ended up killing Peck anyway. He was probably supposed to kill everyone in the convenience store *except* Stacy, then get the hell out, leaving no one behind except a traumatized woman who might not be able to identify him. Or who wouldn't if her family told her not to.

But thanks to Nick, the robber hadn't gotten away clean. He'd been arrested. Now the Pucinellis had two loose ends to tie up: the robber, and Nick.

No good deed goes unpunished.

Had Gregory Peck, the nice older guy Nick met at the convenience store, known he was marrying into a mob family when he married Stacy? He was an investor, but that didn't mean he was smart. He might have thought he was marrying into money, that he was making a new type of connection for his business. Or maybe he really had fallen in love with the girl. It certainly looked to Nick like the man was smitten, as Nick's mom used to say.

But why would the Pucinellis want to kill someone in their own family?

The more Nick stared at the picture Janine had found while he tried to work out the logic behind why he was totally and completed fucked, the more he started to think it hadn't been the family who wanted Peck out of the way. Maybe it was just one Pucinelli.

Gino Pucinelli had a thing for his cousin Stacy.

Once Nick realized what he was looking at, the signs were totally obvious.

When Nick first saw Stacy at the convenience store, he'd thought she was maybe late teens or barely twenty. The photograph had been taken two years ago, which would have made her what, eighteen at the time? If that?

The photographer had snapped the photo while Peck had his arm around Stacy's waist. Gino had been standing close to Stacy and just a little behind her. Nick had initially thought he was a security guard because of the way Gino had been hovering over the girl. Now that Nick had given the photo a closer look, he could see the man's barely controlled jealousy. His hands were balled into fists, and he was shooting daggers at Peck behind Stacy's back.

In the photograph, Gino looked to be in his mid-twenties. Much more age appropriate for Stacy than a guy who was in his sixties. Peck had the look of a well-groomed, health-conscious older man. One of those guys who ran five miles a day without breaking a sweat, but still more than three times Stacy's age. Which said a lot about Stacy's taste in men. Daddy issues much?

Gino had probably been harboring a secret crush on his beautiful cousin for years. He could have been waiting for her to get out of school—high school at that—before he did anything about it. But then Peck had come along and swept her off her feet, so to speak.

Had this all started with a love triangle gone wrong?

Could it really be that simple?

From his background in law enforcement, as relatively brief as it was, Nick knew the basic reasons most people got themselves killed was over money, over power, or over love. Peck might have gotten himself killed over all three, but if Nick had to bet on one motive alone, it would be love. Or rather the flip side of love: jealousy.

"You're sure this is the guy you saw?" he asked Janine.

"Yeah," she said. "Gino Pucinelli. I told you." She peered at him. "You look like a guy who just figured out grass is green and the sky's blue and you should have known that all along."

Maybe he should have.

The library's computers weren't all that busy. A couple of other people were sitting further down the row. One was a college-age kid. He had three thick hardback books open on the table, with the keyboard balanced on one of them, and was taking notes on a legal pad. The other computer user was a middle-aged businessman in a suit and tie. He had a leather briefcase parked on the floor next to his chair.

The college-age kid had never looked up once from his books, but the businessman kept shooting surreptitious glances in Nick's direction.

Did he work for the Pucinellis? Or O'Dell?

The chances of that were astronomical, Nick knew that. He had better odds of winning a mega-jackpot, and he didn't gamble.

He was probably being ridiculously paranoid, but he didn't want to talk to Janine about any of this while they were in earshot of someone else.

"We need to get out of here," he said. "Go someplace quiet where we can talk."

She gave him a look that said she thought he was nuts. How much quieter could a place get than a library?

He gestured with his chin in the direction of the guy in the suit and tie. Janine glanced that way just in time to see the guy look back at his computer screen.

"Really?" she said to the guy in a voice loud enough to carry, but she picked up the printout of the article, folded it, and stuck it in the pocket of her jeans just the same.

Once they got outside, she gave Nick a sidelong glance. "Getting a little paranoid, are we?"

He shrugged. "Paranoid's how I stayed in one piece for so long." Especially since he was sure all of O'Dell's old gang didn't end up in prison.

She chuckled. "You ever consider that Mr. Businessman might have been looking at me?"

He hadn't, and the realization made him blush. Even dressed down, without her strip club makeup and wearing significantly more clothes, Janine was someone who could turn heads.

"Yeah, well," he said, "I guess there's that."

"You guess there's that," she repeated in a sing-song voice, but her grin let him know she was just teasing him.

Once they were alone in his car and he had the air conditioning going, he told her everything he'd found out about O'Dell, and then he started to lay out what he thought had happened given what she'd told him about Gino and the Pucinellis.

She took it all in without interrupting him until he started to tell her he thought the Pucinellis might be involved with the shooting at the convenience store.

"Wait a minute," she said. "What makes you think the robbery had anything to do with the Pucinellis? I mean, that's a pretty big leap. Just because the family's mobbed up doesn't mean they're involved in every bad thing that goes down in this town. I thought we were going on the assumption that it was just bad luck that O'Dell saw you on the same news report I did."

"That's what I thought at first," Nick said.

"Then I don't understand what that has to do with the shooting..."

She trailed off as her eyes narrowed.

"Why did you want to know who Stacy and her husband were when you saw their picture at Leon's?" she asked. "They have a lot of pictures on their wall, but you only asked about that one. I mean, I know why I was interested. I thought she looked like someone I used to know. When Leon said her first name was Stacy, I wanted to make sure, so that's why I looked in the newspaper archives. I mean, Pucinelli's not exactly a last name you want to look for online, you know?"

He didn't say anything. It wasn't really a question that needed answering.

"The only reason I printed that picture was because I recognized Gino from the club," she went on. "I used to know Stacy when she was just a kid, but you were interested in them before you even knew who they were. How come?"

The last couple of days' worth of newspapers must not be part of the library's newspaper archives. She didn't know that Gregory Peck was the victim. His name hadn't been mentioned in the television report.

"They were in the store," he said. "It was her husband..."

He didn't need to finish the sentence.

Her eyes got shiny bright, and she looked away from him, blinking rapidly.

"Damn," she said, that one word a low prayer.

She was quiet for a few moments. Nick let her have the time. Outside the Vegas day was hot and merciless. The air conditioning in his car was doing its best, but he could feel the heat baking off the windshield. It wasn't even full summer yet.

In another couple of weeks the city would be filled to overflowing thanks to the Memorial Day weekend. If he survived that long—it he was able to deal with O'Dell by then—bugging out of town with all the tourists after their long weekend was over might not be such a bad idea.

He could head north. Go find a job somewhere with a cooler climate. Take the kitten and start over someplace new, someplace where the Pucinellis couldn't find him.

"You said you crossed the mob," Janine finally said. "Because you broke up the robbery?"

He shrugged. "That's the only reason I can think of that would make Gino come looking for me at the club. He doesn't know me, and I've sure as hell never done a damn thing to him."

She leaned back in the passenger seat and stared out the windshield, her eyes squinted against the bright sunlight. Her eyes had that faraway look of someone trying to visualize a memory.

"He did act like he was the guy in charge," she said. "I only ever knew Stacy, and not all that well. She seemed pretty well adjusted for someone who was growing up in a family like the Pucinellis. If you're right, that means the Pucinellis wanted her husband dead and they wanted it to look like a random act of violence."

There was a lot of that going on these days, especially in a big city like Vegas that was undergoing a lot of growing pains.

"I wonder what he did, Stacy's husband," she said. "It had to be for a reason."

A few things, Nick thought but didn't say. Peck could have screwed up a deal for the family, or maybe he'd wanted in, to be treated like a full member of the family. Or maybe he'd been screwing around on her, although that seemed less likely.

If Nick had to bet, he'd put his money on Gino doing the hit on his own. Jealously made a hell of a motive for murder even in families that weren't mobbed up.

Janine heaved a sigh and then turned toward him. Her eyes were dry now, but a small frown line remained between her eyebrows. "So what's the next step?" she asked.

He honestly didn't know. He'd come to the library looking for a way to track down O'Dell so he could confront the man and be done with this business once and for all. He'd thought he had a better than even chance of winning a knock-down, drag-out fight against a guy who'd waved goodbye to his fifties and didn't have the police department to back him up.

But nobody in their right mind went up against the mob. That was a good way to get dead and have your rotting corpse dumped in the middle of the Nevada desert for the buzzards to feast on.

"I need to get out from under O'Dell," he said. "And I need to make things right—somehow—with the Pucinellis."

Or maybe just one Pucinelli. If he could figure out a way to talk to Gino's old man without getting himself killed, Nick might be able to talk his way out of that part of this mess.

If the old man would even listen to him.

If the old man didn't already know what Gino had done and was even now in the process of covering it up.

And most importantly, if the old man hadn't ordered the hit himself and sent Gino to take care of it.

If, if, if.

There was so much Nick didn't know, and all of it could get him killed.

Even with the air conditioning, sweat had started to break out on Janine's forehead. It plastered the wispy ends of her short auburn hair to her damp skin. She was watching him, waiting for him to go on. To come up with some kind of a plan. He just didn't have one.

Finally, she wiped the sweat away from her forehead. "I might have an idea, but we're going to have to stop by my apartment first."

That might not be safe, not if O'Dell and Gino had gone back to the club and pressured Chubs to give up her address.

Nick was about to tell her that when she interrupted him.

"I need a change of clothes," she said. "This t-shirt's getting rank, and I don't even want to think about my underwear. Neither of us can afford to buy the kind of clothes we'll need for what I have in mind. Not even second hand."

"It might not be safe," he said, because he felt he had to get that out there. She needed to understand the potential danger. "You sure there's not an alternative?"

"You're worried Chubs is going to give me up, aren't you?" She shook her head. "I'm smarter than you were. I didn't give him my real address. It's not like he reports my wages to the government. Even if he gave Gino the address the club has on file for me, all they're going to find is a construction site." She grinned. "Renovation's a bitch, baby. The apartment building that used to be there was an eyesore, and it's gone now."

Nick shook his head. "Who are you?" he asked. "Really?"

She gave him a short laugh that had no more humor in it than her determined grin. "I've been a lot of things. Still am, if I'm being honest. Why do you think I wear all those wigs?" She brushed at her short, sweat-soaked hair. "You're the only one who's seen the real me in a long time."

He kind of doubted that. He had a feeling that just because she wasn't wearing a wig or hiding her face behind a ton of makeup, he had yet to see the real person sitting in the car with him.

"So what's your idea, then?" he asked.

She gave him a sideways glance. "I told you I used to know Stacy when she was a kid. I used to be a different person back then, but I think it'll be enough."

"Enough for what?"

"For me to pay a condolence call on the widow," she said.

22

"This is a stupid idea," Nick said.

They were in Janine's apartment. She lived in a nice area of Vegas, one of the neighborhoods that had undergone modernization. Her apartment was one of a multitude of cookie-cutter units in a complex you needed a map and a good compass to navigate.

She could clearly afford better clothes than the oversized t-shirt and jeans she wore after she got off work from the club. She'd been in the bedroom for a good fifteen minutes, throwing clothes into an overnight bag and changing into something "more appropriate for paying her respects," she'd said through the half-open bedroom door.

"Stupid idea," Nick said again, louder this time.

"I heard you the first time," she said. "You want to take care of this business once and for all, but that's going to be hard to do if you can't find O'Dell. If you're right, if he's working for Gino, the best way to find him is to find Gino."

If Gino really did have a thing for his cousin, he'd probably be hanging around Stacy every second of every day. He'd want to be her protector. To provide a convenient shoulder to cry on. To eventually worm his way into her bed.

And if Gino was using O'Dell as his personal bodyguard, chances were that O'Dell would be hanging around Stacy too.

That wasn't good. Nick wanted to get O'Dell alone. He could beat O'Dell one on one. Running into O'Dell on what amounted to the man's home turf was about the stupidest thing Nick could think of.

And he'd be putting Stacy—and Janine—smack dab in the middle.

"So what, you're going to be bait?" he said.

Nick didn't want Janine risking her life for him. If Gino felt he could get away with murdering a rich investor who just happened to be married to his cousin, he wouldn't have any problem getting rid of some random woman from his cousin's past.

On the drive to Janine's apartment, Nick had come up with what he thought was a better plan. All he had to do was update the phone number on the witness statement he'd given the police. He could tell the cops he got a new cell, and give them the number of a burner phone he'd buy just for that purpose. O'Dell had to have a connection with the Vegas cops, or maybe the connection was someone who owed the Pucinellis a favor. Either way, updating his phone number on his witness statement would essentially send an engraved invitation to O'Dell to give him a call.

O'Dell would want to set up a meet. It would be an ambush, of course, but Nick thought—he hoped—he'd be able to get the jump on O'Dell instead and beat the crap out of him. O'Dell was a bully, and bullies were cowards at heart. Once Nick had O'Dell down for the count, Nick could use O'Dell to get in to see Gino's old man. The "real deal" of the Pucinelli family according to Stacy.

From that point on, Nick was a little vague about how to convince Pucinelli Senior that it would be in both their interests to part ways in one piece. But he had to deal with Pucinelli one way or the other, or he'd just be trading one badass who hated his guts for an even more powerful badass who'd consider wiping Nick off the face of the planet as a matter of honor.

Janine had nixed his plan. "You can't control that situation. O'Dell will have too much time to set it up to kill you and make sure it never comes back on him. He's got at least one cop out here on his side, remember? You'd never live long enough to get a meeting with Gino's dad. I don't want to see you dead."

He didn't either, but if that's the way things ended up? Problem solved. Leon would give the kitten a good home. They might rename her, but that would be all right. Connie was kind of a stupid name for a cat anyway.

And with Nick out of the way, Janine would be okay too. O'Dell was a dick, but he'd leave her alone, especially if Nick went to meet O'Dell alone. She wouldn't be a witness to whatever O'Dell did. He'd let her fade into the woodwork. She could reinvent herself again. Apparently she had a lot of experience at it.

"I'm not bait," Janine said as she opened the bedroom door, tugging a rolling carryon suitcase behind herself.

Nick's jaw fell open. He couldn't help it. She looked totally different. If he'd passed her on the street, he wouldn't have recognized her. Not in a million years.

The wig she wore now was shoulder length, a natural-looking dusty blonde shot through with lighter blonde highlights. Not at all the long, curly style of the wigs she wore at the club. This hairstyle was simple—relaxed curls with wispy bangs that framed her eyes. She wore just enough makeup to tone down her freckles and accentuate her eyes.

It was the business suit that threw him off the most. He had no idea what the fabric was, but the dark peach suit looked light and airy, as did the cream-colored blouse she wore beneath the jacket. The suit was cut to minimize, not accentuate, her ample chest, and the low heels she wore did the same for her muscular legs. The only accessories she wore were a simple watch on her left wrist and understated earrings.

All in all, she looked like a business professional more at home in a boardroom than a waitress who worked nights at a shady strip club.

"You're a damn chameleon," he said.

She smiled. Even her smile was different, with just the right touch of self-assured professionalism combined with pleasure at receiving an honest compliment.

"I've had an interesting life," she said.

No shit, he thought. He shook his head and grinned at her. "You going to tell me about that life someday?"

"If we get out of this mess in one piece, I will." She glanced at her watch like she'd been wearing one all her life. He'd never once seen her wear a watch even once before, and given what she wore—and what she didn't wear—at the club, he would have noticed. "Probably should leave," she said.

For the first time since he'd bought his beater car, he felt embarrassed by it. Janine looked like someone who deserved a nice new car, a sedan maybe, or something a touch sporty.

He put her carryon in the trunk. He didn't ask her what was in it. Probably a few changes of clothes or a few other wigs from her stash, just in case.

"You know where we're going?" he asked as he navigated his way back to the apartment complex's entrance. He had no idea where the Pecks, now just Stacy Peck, lived.

Instead of giving her the Pecks' address, Janine gave him directions to a pawn shop east of the Arts District.

"Don't get me wrong," she said. "We're not selling anything. A friend of mine runs the place, and he owes me a favor."

"What favor?" Nick asked.

She gave him that half professional, half friendly smile again. "You'll see."

Ace High Pawn took up all of a long, low, nearly windowless building bracketed on both sides by narrow parking lots. The sign out front proclaimed that Ace High Pawn was open 24 hours. It might be busy after sunset when gamblers looking to raise enough cash to stake a comeback would be lining up to pawn wedding rings and diamond earrings, but in the middle of the afternoon, the parking lot was nearly deserted.

Nick parked on the far side of the building in a space near the back, away from the busy street out front. When he got out of his car, he had to squint against the bright sunlight reflected off the building's whitewashed walls. He was rarely out and about so early in the afternoon, and he missed the quiet of the night and the anonymity of its shadows.

A blast of cold air hit him as they went in through the front door. Janine gave a nod to the heavyset black man seated on a stool just inside. The man wore a neon vest that made him look like a roadside flagger instead of a security guard, but Nick caught sight of the taser attached to his belt. The security guard's eyes, deep set within folds of thick flesh, took in Nick's wrinkled and sweat-stained clothes. In comparison to Janine, Nick probably looked like someone who should be panhandling out on the Strip.

"How you doing, Miss Janie," the security guard said to Janine.

Janie again? Nick was beginning to think that Janine was just a name she used at the club.

"Just fine, Bo," she said. "Jenkins around?"

Bo's eyes flicked over to Nick. "Your friend got business with the man?"

Before Nick could say anything, Janine rested a hand on Bo's forearm. "He's with me," she said. She was smiling, but her tone had taken on the chill of pure business.

"You vouch for him?" Bo asked.

"He's a friend," she said. "Good enough?"

Bo didn't relax, but he did send a smile in Nick's direction. The smile had no warmth to it at all.

"For now," Bo said. He gestured toward the back of the store with a tilt of his head. "He's in his lair."

Nick followed Janine past glass cases filled with trays and trays of jewelry, watches, and weathered coins he didn't recognize. The store's few customers were too busy browsing to pay much attention to Nick and Janine as they passed by.

He'd been in pawn shops in Jersey. Always as a patrol officer responding to a robbery or an attempted robbery, never as a customer. He hadn't owned much of anything valuable enough to pawn, and the idea of buying something that someone else had sold at the worst moment of their life—or worse, buying stolen property —didn't appeal to him.

Janine stopped in front of a solid metal door at the far end of the store. The door was painted the same off-white as the walls. A plain paper exit sign stuck on the door pointed to the store's official back exit on the other side of the store.

She rapped on the metal door three times in rapid succession, waited a beat, and then did it again.

The squeal of a desk chair with squeaky wheels came from the other side of the door. Then the distinct thunk of a deadbolt being thrown, and the door opened inward.

A man about Nick's height stood in the semi-gloom of the darkened room beyond. He had the long, wavy, shiny black hair of a stage musician and a neatly trimmed goatee. His eyes were dark and surrounded by thick lashes and topped by thicker eyebrows. He had the muscular neck of a gym rat who worked free weights like there was no tomorrow, and Nick could see the faint outline of a heavily muscled torso beneath a loose black t-shirt. The shirt bore the same Ace High Pawn logo that was on the store's sign out front.

He didn't smile at Janine, but he didn't seem hostile either. "Haven't seen you in a while," he said. "What's with the getup?"

"I have a need to be respectable," she said. "You have a minute?"

His eyes slid over to Nick. "For the two of you?"

"That's right," she said. "Nick, this is my friend Jenkins." She didn't look at Nick as she made the introduction.

"Friend now, is it?" Jenkins didn't offer Nick his hand. "He my replacement?"

"Hardly," she said. "We just came for your clothes. And your car. You don't have a problem with that, do you?"

23

Nick had never been inside a limousine before.

He'd seen them, of course. Limousine rental services did a brisk business in Vegas. Casinos sent limousines to the airport to fetch high rollers. Wedding parties rented limousines for bridal showers and bachelor parties. Indulgent parents with more money than sense rented limousines for their preteen's birthday party.

He definitely hadn't driven one before.

"I don't have the right kind of license for this," he said as he pulled out of the lot next to Ace High Pawn.

He'd left the partition down between the driver's seat and the luxury seating in back. Janine sat at the far end of the limousine in her sensible business suit, sipping sparkling water from a green bottle.

"Then don't do anything stupid that gets us pulled over," she said.

He shifted on the seat. His borrowed clothes—black suit, white shirt, black tie, and black leather shoes polished to a high gloss—didn't fit quite right. Jenkins had bulkier muscles than Nick. Even when Nick had been working out on the heavy bag six days a week, his shoulders couldn't hold a candle to Janine's old friend.

"Just who is that guy, anyway?" he asked. People didn't go around handing over limo keys to a casual acquaintance. "And why does he call you Janie?"

He could see her sigh in the rearview mirror. "Part of a different life," she said.

"I gathered that."

He waited for her to elaborate. When she didn't, he stared at her long enough in the rearview that she said, "Eyes on the road." She paused for a moment, then gave him a smile that quirked up one side of her mouth. "Driver."

Driver. Right. All part of Janine's plan to pay her respects to Gregory Peck's widow.

On the drive over to Ace High Pawn, Janine had told him that Jenkins would be able to figure out where the Pecks lived even if it wasn't listed in any public databases. Besides owning a pawn shop and a limousine, Jenkins was apparently very good with computers.

"One of the best," Janine had said.

Jenkins had tapped away at the computer in his office—his "lair," as the security guard had called it—while Janine watched over his shoulder. Nick had hung back by the door leading to the public area of the pawn shop.

Lair was an apt description of the back office at Ace High Pawn. The only illumination came from dual computer screens and a flatscreen television mounted to the outside wall. One of the computer screens displayed constant video feeds from security cameras placed throughout the pawn shop. The code or whatever Jenkins was typing scrolled across the other screen, dull off-white letters on a black background. The television was playing *Oceans Eleven*, not the one with George Clooney but the original movie starring the Rat Pack. The audio on the movie was turned down low, barely audible over music coming from what looked like a state-of-the-art sound system. Nick recognized the heavy bass beat of a classic rock song.

The pawn business must pay well.

Janine had made a small *hmph* sound when the Pecks' home

address showed up on Jenkins' computer along with a map of the area.

"What?" Jenkins had asked, glancing back at Janine.

"Nothing," she said.

Nick didn't believe her. It was pretty clear Jenkins didn't either, but he let the subject drop. He'd leaned back in his computer chair and stared at her as she explained why she wanted the limo. All the while his fingers beat out a rhythm on the padded black leather arms of his chair.

It took Nick a minute to realize Jenkins was tapping out a counterpoint to the beat of the old rock song playing on the sound system. If Jenkins wasn't a musician, he was a wannabe who'd never stopped looking the part.

The conversation had stalled when Janine said she needed to borrow his uniform to go along with the limo. Jenkins' fingers had stopped tapping on the chair and his eyes narrowed. The look he shot Nick was something Nick had seen often when he'd been a teenager and he'd managed to tag a more experienced boxer in the ring with a shot that made the older man stagger back.

Jenkins was sizing him up. Wondering if Janine had told him the truth when she'd said that Nick wasn't his replacement.

"We need to look convincing," she'd said. "That's all. I'm all set, but limo drivers don't wear t-shirts and jeans. Especially not if they've been living in them for two days." She gestured with her head toward Nick. "He's almost your size."

On the television, the Rat Pack was having a good old time pulling off the heist of the century. The sound system started up with another heavy bass beat as a different classic rock 'n roll song blared from the speakers. Nick saw more than heard Jenkins heave a sigh.

"Always knew someday you'd be back to take the clothes off my back," Jenkins said to Janine. "Thought the circumstances would be a little different."

"Dream on." Janine held out her hand, palm up. "Keys and clothes, if you please."

Jenkins unlocked a drawer in his desk and fished out a set of keys, then tossed them to Janine. She caught them easily. When Jenkins stayed sitting in his chair, she arched an eyebrow.

"Fine," Jenkins said with a sigh. "Tell Bo I said to give you the clothes." He gave Nick the once over. "Don't do anything in my suit to make me regret this."

The driver's suit came complete with a black cap, which was currently sitting on the passenger seat next to Nick. He didn't like hats. Not even when he was out in the hot Vegas sun.

"I told you about my other life," he said now as he glanced at her in the rearview. Well, he'd told her about part of his other life, not all of it. "You can at least tell me how Jenkins figures in yours."

She was looking out the side window. The limousine's tinted windows kept the sun off her face and the interior was air conditioned, but she still looked uncomfortable in her businesswoman outfit. Or maybe Nick was just projecting since he felt more than a little uncomfortable in his driver's uniform.

He'd slicked back his hair and taken the butterfly bandage off the cut on his forehead, which thankfully hadn't bled, but he'd drawn the line at shaving. The scruff on his face had grown out a little overnight. In a couple of days he'd have the beginnings of a decent beard, which might not be such a bad disguise. He'd been a cleanshaven cop back in Jersey, and O'Dell hadn't gotten that good a look at him last night.

"He's my ex," she finally said. "We're civil. Sometimes even friendly."

She'd been married to Jenkins. That surprised him, although maybe it shouldn't. Vegas was a city of easy marriages, and it was almost as easy to get a divorce when those marriages didn't work out.

"Kids?" he asked.

She snorted. "Oh, hell no. Jenkins was a kid himself when we got together. He had big dreams. Rock star dreams. I was just part of this image he had of who he wanted to be. Kids weren't in the plan."

"How'd he end up with a pawn shop?"

"Life." She shrugged and took another drink from the green bottle. "How about you?" she asked. "Ever been married?"

"Nope."

"Come close?"

He thought about Connie. That crush had been so long ago she didn't seem real anymore. More a dream of who he thought he'd spend his life with. Sometimes it felt like his entire life before O'Dell had been a dream.

"No," he said. "Not really."

She gave him a long, sober look. "I didn't think so. Lonely way to live. *Nick*."

He hadn't come right out and told her that he was living under a new identity, but admitting he'd been in witness protection certainly implied it. The way she said his name now made it clear that as long he was using a name that wasn't his, she wasn't about to explain why people like Leon and Jenkins called her Janie.

We all have a past, he thought. We all have secrets we don't tell anybody. He'd told her his, or most of them anyway. He hadn't told her about the kid the drug dealer had killed or that O'Dell had intimidated Nick into helping him cover it up. Even all these years later, he was still ashamed of the coward he'd been back then.

But that didn't mean she owed him a quid pro quo. She had already done more for him than he had any right to ask, and she wasn't finished yet. She had a right to keep her big, dark secrets to herself.

She caught his eye in the rearview mirror. "You ready for this?" she asked.

"Ready?" Not hardly, and he had the easy part. "I should be asking you that."

The plan they'd worked out had about a million moving parts, any one of which could go horribly, dreadfully wrong.

If Stacy agreed to see her, and Janine was pretty sure she would, Janine would go pay her condolences to the widow while Nick stayed with the limo. While she was inside, she'd be able to see if Gino was there and if O'Dell was with him.

"Don't worry," she'd said. "If he's there, he's not going to recognize me, and I won't start anything. I'll just leave, and then when he leaves, we can follow him. Find out where he lives, and you can go from there."

Although how Janine figured they could follow someone in a borrowed limo without being obvious about the tail, Nick didn't know. Tailing someone wasn't as easy as it looked on television and in the movies. Vegas might have a lot of limos on the road at any one time, but even so, O'Dell was bound to figure out he'd picked up a tail after only a few blocks.

He also wasn't real happy about the idea of Janine going into the house by herself, but they didn't really have a choice. If O'Dell was inside, he'd recognize Nick on sight. Hell, even Gino might recognize him if O'Dell had shown him Nick's picture. Any photograph O'Dell had of Nick would be an old one, but Nick hadn't changed all that much over the years. He was older and scruffier, sure, but he wasn't a chameleon like Janine. The woman riding in the back of Nick's limo looked nothing like the waitress Gino had talked to at the club or the woman O'Dell had probably only gotten a glance of from one story up while she ran away from Nick's apartment.

That was why Nick was posing as a driver. Limo drivers always stayed with the car. Add to that the fact that drivers were the kind of hired help most rich assholes ignored. Nick thought he stood a good chance of fading into the background.

Janine was also hoping that if Stacy's dad was around, he might remember her too. At least enough to be polite.

"Maybe I can feel him out about the shooting," she'd told Nick when she came up with this plan. "Men like talking to me, and I'm pretty good at reading them."

Nick didn't like that part of the plan at all, and he'd told her so. He was going to need to smooth things over with the Pucinellis. While Stacy's dad might be able to set up a meeting with Gino's old man, Nick didn't want Janine to put herself in the middle of that particular mess.

She'd ignored him. Then she'd told him again not to worry, that she'd been taking care of herself around men like the Pucinellis a long time before he came along.

That might be true, but all it did was make him worry more. He hoped she wasn't one of those people who got off on being in dangerous situations. He'd met a few people like that in Jersey. Witnesses who were a little too excited to be close to the action. Who enjoyed being part of the investigation, even in a small way.

He would have felt better if he had a gun, but that was one thing Janine hadn't asked Jenkins for. The pawn shop had plenty of guns, but Janine said the business was all strictly above board. No stolen property, no handguns with the serial numbers filed off. Any gun Jenkins gave them could be traced back to him, and that was out of the question.

If Nick had had access to the cash in his bank account, he could have bought a gun on the street. He knew the right neighborhoods and the right way to ask. If it came to that, he'd get the money one way or another and get a gun. He just hoped it wouldn't come to that.

At least the limo came equipped with a blackjack. He'd found it when he first settled into the driver's seat. The blackjack was tucked beneath the driver's seat within easy reach. It wasn't as good as a gun but it was better than nothing.

If things went south and he needed a weapon other than his fists, it would have to do.

24

The Pecks, now only Stacy Peck, lived in a sprawling Spanish-style home in the middle of a private golf course in southwest Vegas. The golf course was surrounded by an eight-foot tall concrete retaining wall the color of desert sand and decorated with silhouettes of native plants and wildlife.

Nick turned onto a private road and drove a quarter mile to the golf course's gated entrance. Off to one side of the wrought-iron gate was a closet-sized guardhouse manned by a stocky black man with a badge over the breast pocket of his uniform.

Nick rolled down the limo's window and smiled what he hoped was a professional smile at the guard.

The guard didn't smile back. He left the guardhouse a little reluctantly, Nick thought, a clipboard in his hands. The guardhouse was probably airconditioned. His uniform was midnight black. Not something anyone would want to wear out in the sun on a hot Las Vegas afternoon.

"Member name, sir?" the guard asked. His tone was professional, not deferential. He clearly wasn't impressed with the limo. He probably saw them all the time.

"Tell him Janie Trejo to see Stacy Peck," Janine said from the back.

Nick raised an eyebrow, but he relayed the information.

He expected the guard to go inside and make a call. To clear their visit with Stacy Peck, but he all he did was write something on the clipboard. His fingers were the size of sausages, and the pen he held looked like a twig. If the guard had been a boxer, he would have been a heavyweight. One punch from hands like that would have landed Nick on the canvas, out for the count.

The guard looked back at Nick. "You been here before?" he asked.

Nick shook his head. "First time."

"Only one house in this place," the guard said. "Keep going on this road past the clubhouse. You can't miss it."

The house or the clubhouse? Nick guessed he'd find out once he got there.

He nodded at the guard—just two working stiffs doing our jobs, that nod said—and rolled up the window. The guard went back inside the guardhouse, and a moment later the wrought iron gate trundled open. Nick put the limo in gear and drove through at a stately fifteen miles an hour.

"Janie Trejo?" he asked Janine.

"Jenkins' stage name," she said. "Johnny Trejo."

That begged further explanation, but Nick didn't ask. He'd asked before and she'd clammed up. Maybe if he waited her out, she'd volunteer a little more information on her own.

She seemed lost in thought, staring out the window. They drove past a foursome gathered around a golf cart just off to the side of the road. All of them were men, and they were all dressed in golf clothes Nick wouldn't be caught dead in. Plaid pants, white golf shoes, pastel golf shirts, and all with little hats tilted cockily on their gray-haired heads. Not a one of them was under sixty, and they were all white beneath their outdoorsy tans.

Private club. Very private club. Nick wondered if men whose skin was as dark as the security guard's would be welcome on this course. He tried to spot a darker face anywhere on the greens as he followed the private road around a bend. He didn't.

Janine sighed. "This place hasn't changed a bit," she said. "Stacy's still living in the house Jenkins played at for her fourteenth birthday party. I was his manager at the time, which meant I hung around while he sang his retro rock 'n roll heart out." She looked at Nick in the rearview mirror. "You've seen him," she said. "He looked even better five years ago. Tight leather pants, black muscle tank. Johnny Trejo. The bad boy of rock 'n roll, and I was his old lady."

She smiled at the memory. Clearly, her time with Jenkins hadn't been all that bad.

"Stacy had a bit of a crush on him," she said. "Not enough that I made her jealous, but enough that she figured talking to me was a way to find out more about him."

Now he knew why Janine thought Stacy might agree to see her. Provided Stacy even remembered the wife of her childhood musician crush. The way Stacy's life had gone, that wasn't a given.

"I'm willing to bet you didn't look like this back then," he said. The wife of a rock 'n roll singer, even if she was his manager, wouldn't have dressed like a conservative businesswoman.

She shrugged. "Have to look like I've gone on to bigger and better things. That's half the battle in this town. Dress for the part you want, clichéd but true. Make everyone think you're something you're not." She shook her head and huffed out a smile. "Look at me, telling you something you already know."

True. He'd just gone the other way. He'd chosen to live the way he did to make himself into someone no one wanted to get all that close to. The ruse had worked pretty well for fifteen years. So well, in fact, that sometimes he forgot he'd ever been anyone else.

Then a little black kitten came into his life and wound him around her fuzzy razorblade-tipped paws. He wondered how she was getting along with Leon's cats. With any luck, he'd find out when this business was all over.

The private road took a meandering route around the greens on its way to the clubhouse. Once Nick had to stop to let a golf cart cross the road in front of him. Signs along the road warned that golf carts had the right of way. The two white-haired gentlemen inside this particular cart didn't give the limo a second look.

For a private golf course, the clubhouse didn't look all that special from the outside, just a low building sided with the same desert-colored blocks as the fence that separated this oasis from the rest of Las Vegas. Nick was willing to bet that the inside of the clubhouse was upscaled to the max. Heavy furniture upholstered in dark leather, a bar stocked with expensive booze, maybe even gold-plated fixtures in the bathroom. The cars parked in the lot next to the clubhouse would have made a luxury car salesman drool with envy.

"Just how private is this club, anyway?" he asked Janine.

"Private enough that if you have to ask how much the memberships cost, you can't afford it," she said.

And your ancestry had to be of a certain type, no doubt. "You'd think Jenkins would have performed at the clubhouse," he said. Better acoustics. Maybe even a stage.

She chuckled. "Are you kidding? The walls would have collapsed at the horror of it all. Sinatra could have given a private little show there back in the day. He might have for all I know, but certainly not a musician named Johnny Trejo."

Which confirmed Nick's thoughts about the skin color of the club's exclusive membership.

"No, Stacy's daddy threw her a private party at the family's estate," Janine said.

"Estate?"

"Just wait," she said. "You'll see."

The private road kept going for a half mile past the clubhouse before it ended at a gated driveway bordered by so much greenery that it made the place look like a Mediterranean villa, not a private estate in the Nevada desert. The gates stood open with no guard in sight, so Nick drove up the long driveway to the house. Marble statues of half-naked Greek goddesses that would have been at home in Caesar's Palace stood on either side of the two-lane driveway.

More marble, this time a fountain, was the centerpiece of a court-yard that marked the end of the driveway. Cobblestones formed a border around the fountain, and the driveway circled around between the house and the fountain. A mosaic pattern had been etched into the concrete on this part of the driveway.

Two other limos were already parked near the steps leading up to the main house. Nick pulled up behind the last limo. He grabbed his hat from the passenger seat and put it on with the brim tipped low on his forehead before he got out to open the door for Janine.

No, Janie Trejo, he reminded himself. While they were here, she was Janie Trejo.

"If Gino's in there," he said, "be careful. You're a damn good chameleon, but he still might recognize you from the club."

"All I am in a place like that is a nice set of tits." She gave him a tight, professional smile. "The regulars might get to know me by my face, but a guy like Gino? No tits on display today, he won't make the connection."

Nick understood now why she'd chosen a business suit that minimized her chest and hid her cleavage. She wasn't just a damn good chameleon, she was a savvy chameleon.

"Good luck," he said. "And don't push the dad too hard, if he's there."

She gave him a look that would have put a lesser man in his place, but Nick wasn't a lesser man. He was a man who was getting used to being with her.

A man who was genuinely worried about sending her in alone.

She must have realized that because her expression softened. "I used to tell Jenkins to set the strings on fire," she said, "and he'd tell me 'it's the world, baby.' That he'd set the world on fire. That was our good luck wish."

"Then go set the world on fire," Nick said.

The wish hadn't been enough for Jenkins. He hadn't set the world on fire. Somewhere along the line, his dreams had beaten him down. He'd given up the rock 'n roll and opened a pawn shop. Now he tapped along to the beat of old rock 'n roll music with his fingers while he kept the books and watched the security cameras.

Whatever Janine's dreams had been back then, they must not

have panned out either. Working in a strip club for a guy named Chubs was nobody's idea of setting the world on fire.

Nick hoped the wish actually worked for her this time around.

25

On a cloudless day in Vegas, the afternoon sun was brutal. Nick could feel it cooking his skin through his borrowed clothes. The black limo uniform only served to amplify the heat. Whoever had decided that limo drivers should dress in black was one sadistic son-of-a-bitch.

He understood now why Janine had referred to Stacy's childhood home as an estate. He also understood why an investor or real estate developer—or both—like her husband would want to live in a place like this even if it was owned by the Pucinellis rather than live in a penthouse suite in downtown Vegas.

It was all about appearances, just like Janine had said. This place shouted old Vegas money, and a lot of it, at the top of its lungs.

The Pucinellis' house took up almost as much real estate as Nick's entire apartment building, and that didn't include the outbuildings. The land alone had to be worth a pretty penny considering the place was located in the middle of a golf course.

He wondered what had come first—the golf course or the estate. Or maybe they'd been built together, the house intended to be a place where the original owner of the course could live and look out over his creation. Lord of the links.

Did the Pucinellis have something to do with that? If not, they must have offered the previous owner a screaming deal to give up a place like this. Or else they'd made him an offer he couldn't refuse. That was always a possibility with a family used to getting its way.

The sprawling two-story residence wrapped around the courtyard's fountain in a gentle arc. Two more low buildings bracketed the driveway, one on each side. Narrow rollup doors marked one of the buildings as a garage. Arched windows in the other building gave Nick a view of an indoor pool.

The doors in the garage were all closed, but he'd bet the Hummer he'd seen at the convenience store was parked inside. No one appeared to be using the indoor pool.

Four wide, curved steps led up to an oversized set of double doors. Janine walked up those steps like she belonged in a place like this, her head held high, eyes hidden behind dark glasses she'd pulled from her bag.

The question of whether Stacy Peck would remember the woman she'd known as Janie Trejo was answered before Janine reached the top step. One of the heavy wooden doors swung open and Stacy flung herself into Janine's arms. Nick caught the moment's hesitation before Janine hugged Stacy back.

The guard at the gate must have called the house to let Stacy know she had visitors, but if that was the case, he'd waited until after the limo passed through the security gate. That seemed odd. Shouldn't the guard have gotten authority first before he even let them through? But maybe the Pecks did things differently.

A man dressed all in black stood just inside the front door. From his ramrod straight posture and the sheer bulk of him, Nick guessed he was private security. Probably a bodyguard, maybe even someone on O'Dell's crew. One thing was certain—the man wasn't O'Dell himself. Even if O'Dell had taken up bodybuilding to increase the size of the muscles he'd neglected when he'd been on the force, he'd never been as tall as this guy.

If Nick had to guess, the bodyguard was probably packing a holstered gun beneath his sportscoat and maybe a stun gun on his belt. He'd be the kind of man who'd call his employer "sir" even if he thought his employer was a dick, and his eyes wouldn't miss a thing.

If you booked an actor to play the part of a bodyguard for a mob boss, this was the guy you'd hire.

He was also a guy Nick didn't have a shot at knocking out with a single punch. Or a flurry of punches, if he even managed to get off more than one or two before the guy decked him. The blackjack beneath the driver's seat seemed more inadequate than ever.

Nick stood beside the limo, the brim from his cap casting a shadow on his face, and watched the women hugging like long-lost sisters. So far, so good, but this was just the preliminaries.

After a few moments, Stacy let go of Janine and led her into the house. The security guard closed the front door behind them.

This was the part Nick didn't like. He was stuck outside babysitting the limo while Janine was locked away inside where he couldn't see her, much less help her if something bad went down. But he was playing the part of the limo driver in this little scenario, and limo drivers didn't accompany their employers inside. Limo drivers stayed with their rides. Nick couldn't call attention to himself by acting out of character.

He was sweating inside his borrowed black suit. He could feel his hair wicking up the sweat on his scalp beneath his driver's cap. Jenkins probably wouldn't like sweat stains on his clothes, but Vegas was Vegas and there wasn't much Nick could do about the heat. He wasn't about to take the cap off. The cap was part of his disguise, and it did serve to keep the sun off his head. You took the good with the bad.

The courtyard fountain was going full blast, splashing water over a set of gradually increasing, ornately carved bowls. Like the water features on the Strip, it was supposed to make things feel cool, like all that splashing water was supposed to convince you it wasn't really all that hot outside. All it did now was make the courtyard humid.

The other two limo drivers were nowhere in sight. He supposed they were sitting inside their rides where the air was presumably cooler and dryer. He could do that too, but he was too wired to just sit and wait.

So he paced across the patterned concrete, past the other two limos parked in front of his. He couldn't see inside either one thanks to heavily tinted windows. Both limos had their engines running. He could do the same thing, but he didn't have a lot of cash to waste on gas. He didn't think Jenkins would be happy if the limo was running on fumes when they brought it back.

He felt more than useless out here. He could walk around the driveway, keep pacing back and forth on the patterned concrete, but that was it. He couldn't even strike up a conversation with the other limo drivers. The windows on the limos were rolled up tight against the heat, and he didn't feel like knocking on any of the doors.

And what would he say, anyway? *Hi. How 'ya doing? You seen a guy around here named Oscar O'Dell?*

No, he couldn't see himself doing something that monumentally stupid. And it would be stupid. The only reason he even considered it, just for a moment, was because he was worried about Janine.

She could have bailed on him this morning. Should have bailed on him. Taken some cash and clothes and left town. They'd been in her apartment for a decent amount of time, longer than he'd liked, and no one had shown up. No one had tailed them when they left. No one was watching her period. She wouldn't have a thing to worry about if she bugged out now. O'Dell would never find her.

So why hadn't she left, really? He was grateful she hadn't. He wouldn't have gotten anywhere near this place without her. But why was she staying with him?

And why had she decided to head straight into the lion's den? Didn't she have any idea how dangerous it was to try to play people like the Pucinellis? Nick had to do it to save his own skin. She didn't.

A trickle of sweat ran down the side of his face. The heat had turned his black suit into an oven. He decided the other drivers were a whole lot smarter than he was. Nerves or no nerves, he couldn't stand outside and pace.

He got back inside the limo and tossed his cap on the passenger seat. He started the engine so he could run the air conditioning. Screw the cost of gas.

While he waited for Stacy to come back, he tried to turn his mind off. Just switch it off. That's what the detectives back in the precinct used to say they did when they were on a stakeout. Switch their minds off, go into a kind of standby mode that wasn't quite meditation and definitely wasn't dozing on the job. You just had to stay alert enough to catch movement around you.

Far easier said than done. Nick had only begun to learn the technique when he'd told his story to the old hardcase at the gym and then again to the man the hardcase had introduced him to. He hadn't used the technique at all since he'd been in Vegas.

Practice makes perfect, and he was far from perfect. In spite of his best intentions, the heat and the waiting made Nick realize how incredibly tired he was. If he'd gotten four hours sleep the night before, that was a lot. He needed coffee. The back of the limo was well stocked with bottled water and booze, but no coffee.

One thing the limo did come equipped with was a cell phone. He thought about calling Leon to see how the kitten was doing and immediately dismissed the idea. Leon had given Nick their cell phone number and told him to call anytime to check up on his girl, but Nick couldn't do that. Not until this mess was over. He didn't want anyone to connect him with Leon in case things went south.

According to the clock on the limo's dash, Janine had been inside with Stacy for nearly an hour when the front doors finally opened. Nick half expected someone who belonged to one of the other two limos to walk down the steps, but instead he saw Janine and Stacy.

About damn time.

He got out of the limo and stood at attention near the rear door, cap pulled down low on his forehead again, the picture perfect image of a limo driver ready to open the door for his passenger.

Only it appeared he was going to have two passengers.

He tried not to act surprised. Both women were walking down the front steps. The bodyguard started to follow, but Stacy turned around and said something to him. The man started to shake his head, but Stacy interrupted him.

Her voice was loud enough that Nick clearly heard her tell him she was old enough to go wherever the hell she wanted by herself.

Nick worked hard to keep his expression neutral. Stacy might be a grieving widow and a young one at that, but she was no wallflower. He really had misjudged her the other night.

She walked down the few steps to the limo and got in the back without even glancing his way. Janine followed and Nick shut the door after them.

This should be interesting.

He slid into the driver's seat. The dividing panel between the front and back of the limo was still down, and the rearview mirror gave him a clear view of both women. They were sitting on the back seat next to each other, facing forward.

He didn't say anything. He guessed that's what a limo driver would do, just sit and wait quietly for instructions.

"I'm going with Stacy to make arrangements for her husband's funeral," Janine said.

She gave him the address of a well-known local mortuary. Nick had seen commercials for the place during the old movies he watched in the afternoons before heading off to work at the club. Tasteful commercials, of course, for a high-class place.

"Take the long way," Janine said.

Stacy hadn't expected that. She gave Janine a startled glance, but Janine was looking at Nick, so Stacy turned to look at him too.

He sucked in a steadying breath. This was where things could really go sideways, but he had no choice. Might as well get it over with.

He turned around in his seat so Stacy could get a good look at him. Considering everything that had happened to her since she'd first helped him out with the kitten, there was no guarantee that she would recognize him.

But she did.

Her eyes widened as she sucked in a startled breath. She looked back and forth between Nick and Janine, and he could see her trying to work it through. It didn't take her long.

She lost the wide-eyed look, but she was still looking at Janine when she reached into the bag she'd brought with her. It was larger than the shoulder bag Janine had grabbed from her apartment, and was probably from a big-name designer for all he knew. The bag was certainly bigger than the little clutch purse Stacy had been carrying in the convenience store.

Big enough to hold the handgun she pulled out and aimed at Nick.

She put her finger on the trigger, ready to fire. "I think now would be a very good time for somebody to tell me what's going on here," she said.

26

Nick's dad had been a big fan of the *Dirty Harry* movies starring Clint Eastwood.

Dirty Harry with his .357 Magnum and his *Make my day* attitude.

Sometimes Nick wondered if his dad secretly had the same kind of anger issues Nick had always wrestled with, only his dad had learned to control his anger far better than his son. Dirty Harry was a pretty angry character, when you thought about it. He just let his gun doing the talking.

One damn big gun. The whole reason to carry a .357 Magnum was intimidation.

A .22 pistol, like the one Stacy had pulled from her bag, had the same effect at close range. Intimidation, pure and simple.

When he'd been a cop, Nick had had guns pointed at him but usually from far enough away that he could fool himself into thinking the guy holding the gun might miss. There was no way Stacy could miss if she fired her .22 from the back seat of a parked limo.

"Put the gun down," Janine said from where she was sitting beside Stacy. "Nick's a friend of mine."

Her voice was calm and measured, the same kind of tone a

veteran cop would use when they were trying to talk a jumper off the ledge of a ten-story building. Not a single tremor. Nick gave Janine a lot of credit for that.

"He was at the convenience store," Stacy said. "How do I know he's not a part of it? That you're not a part of it? You showed up out of the blue and I thought you were my friend, but that's not really why, is it."

That last bit wasn't a question.

He'd underestimated Stacy, all right. She was a smart woman, not a plastic person out to nab a rich husband. Hell, she was probably worth more than ten Gregory Pecks put together.

"He tackled the asshole who shot Greg," Janine said. "Beat the crap out of him from what I understand. Would he have done that if he'd been part of it?"

At the mention of her husband's name, Stacy's gun hand trembled slightly. Not enough to miss Nick if she fired, but enough that a second shot might go wild. Not that she'd need a second shot at this range.

"Greg didn't get shot until after *he* got involved," Stacy said. Her eyes grew bright and shiny with unshed tears. "It could have been a cover. What's your name? Nick? You could have been sent there to take the guy out so he wouldn't talk to the cops. That's how these things work, right? Only you didn't finish the job."

She thought her husband had been murdered. That someone had set out to kill him deliberately. That was the "part of it" both women were talking about. Nick would have picked up on what they meant sooner if he hadn't had a gun pointed in his face.

"For all I know, you're the one who got him in the hospital," Stacy said. "Well, congratulations. Job well done."

What?

Nick shot Janine a glance. She nodded back, just the slightest movement of her head.

"The robber died in the hospital last night," Janine told him.

Nick hadn't hurt the guy bad enough to kill him. He'd never killed anybody with his fists. He'd messed up the guy's face, broken his nose, knocked out a couple of teeth. Maybe he'd broken a few ribs, but unless one of those ribs had punctured something inside, the guy shouldn't have needed more than a trip to the emergency room and some heavy-duty pain meds.

That meant Nick had been right. Someone wanted Peck dead and they'd found an amateur to do the job. But they'd expected the guy to get away clean. When he hadn't, when he'd been arrested instead, he became a loose end. Loose ends talked. Especially loose ends who had no particular loyalty and who thought trading information might get them out of a jam.

But taking the guy out in the hospital couldn't have been easy. Suspects who needed medical treatment were under guard at all times. Nick had pulled a few of those assignments. Whoever had done the job in the hospital was a professional.

"It wasn't me," Nick said. "Someone's tying up loose ends."

He was a loose end too. He'd proven back in Jersey that he had no problem talking to law enforcement about what he knew and what he suspected.

Whoever had killed the robber in the hospital would be after him now. Nick had a feeling that person was Oscar O'Dell.

And if killing Nick gave O'Dell an extra little personal thrill because of what had happened in Jersey? So much the better.

"Why should I believe you?" Stacy asked, and the hand holding the gun steadied.

"Because he was with me last night," Janine said.

Stacy gave Janine a quick sideways glance. "That's the truth?"

"Yes," Janine said.

Just that one word, but it seemed to do the trick. Stacy didn't lower her gun, but her finger moved away from the trigger. If Nick had been sitting in the back, he could have disarmed her now, but he wasn't.

"I'm still not sure I can trust you," Stacy said. "Give me one reason."

She'd aimed the question at Janine, but Nick answered her

instead. "Because they already came after me. If... a friend hadn't warned me, I'd be dead now too."

He'd almost screwed up and said Janine's name—Janine, not Janie—and that would have screwed everything up. He hoped Stacy hadn't noticed his momentary hesitation.

She must not have because she just closed her eyes and finally lowered the gun.

"Bastards," she said.

Nick felt like he could breathe again. She still held the gun, but it was resting in her lap now. The threat level had gone from defcon 5 down to about a 3. He could handle a 3.

"Stacy's pretty sure someone intended to kill her husband," Janine said, "but we didn't want to talk about it in the house. The police will be releasing her husband's body soon. She's got an appointment at the mortuary, so we're taking her there to give us time to have a private little talk."

She raised an eyebrow at Nick.

He got it. Either O'Dell or Gino had been in the house. He wanted to ask Janine if they'd recognized her, but he'd have to wait until later. Stacy knew Janine as Janie, the successful former manager of a musician she'd had a crush on what must seem now like a lifetime ago, not as a waitress at a strip club.

But it was more than that. Her raised eyebrow had been a sign that she wanted him to wait before he told Stacy who exactly had come to kill him. Before he shattered her world even more by telling her that her cousin Gino was involved somehow in this whole mess.

"I wasn't sure if you were just humoring me," Stacy said to Janine.

"No, I believe you," Janine said. "We both do. But if you thought I was humoring you, why did you agree to come with me?"

Stacy gave a sad little laugh. "I needed to get out of the house and away from my family. Gino—he's my cousin—he's hovering. He always hovers, but now it's like..." She paused, like she was looking for the right word. "Like he thinks he's the big man of the family and I'm some broken thing that needs looking after." She shook her head. "A widow at twenty. I can't even legally drink or gamble in this fucking city, but I can bury my husband just fine. Anybody want to tell me how that's supposed to be okay?"

She glared at Nick, daring him to answer. To give her some ridiculous platitude, but she'd probably heard enough platitudes in the last couple of days to last her a lifetime. So Nick kept his mouth shut.

"I'm not broken," she said.

"No, you're not," he said softly. As if anyone else's opinion mattered.

From what he could tell, she was one tough woman. Maybe she had to be like that if she wanted to have any shot at running her own life. Growing up female in a family like the Pucinellis must have taught her to push back against the overload of male ego that surrounded her.

If her family thought she was still a little girl who needed protecting from the big, bad world, they were delusional.

She seemed to be waiting for him to say something else. He wanted to ask her about Gino, but Janine was right. Now wasn't the time to broach that subject.

So he decided to ask about something else.

"Did your mom really foster rescue kittens?" he said.

Stacy blinked at the sudden change in subject, and even Janine looked startled.

"The kitten," he said to Janine. "My kitten. Stacy's the one who gave me the idea of feeding her baby food."

"That's right, you had a kitten," Stacy said. "Do you still have her? Is she all right? I mean, she didn't get hurt, did she?"

"She's fine," he said. "A regular little fluffball of energy."

He decided to leave out the part where he'd left the kitten with Janine's friend. He didn't want to mention Leon to anyone, not even Stacy.

"We did foster rescues," Stacy said. "Mom always liked cats, and we certainly had the room." She shrugged. "Made the place feel more like a home, she said. I just knew I got to play with a lot of kittens when I was little." Her eyes took on a faraway look. "I gave them all names even though we only got to keep a few after they started to grow up."

"He named the kitten Connie," Janine said.

"Connie?" Stacy scrunched up her nose, and for just a second, she looked like a typical twenty-year-old, not a twenty-going-on-forty widow. "I always named the kittens something like Fluffy or Snowball."

"I think he named her after an old girlfriend," Janine said.

Nick couldn't remember if he'd told her that, but maybe it was obvious. Janine did say she was good at reading men.

"I can always rename her," he said.

Stacy looked affronted. "Don't you dare," she said. "Not if you're going to keep her. You are, aren't you?"

Nick hoped he'd still be around after this was all over, that he could go back to Leon's and reclaim his kitten, but all he did was nod like it was a done deal.

"Mom used to tell me that cats—even kittens—will let you know their names once they've picked you as their person."

He wanted to ask if her mom still thought that, but he'd caught the past tense. Her mom wasn't around anymore. Whether she was dead or just gone, it didn't really matter. Stacy didn't have a mom, and now she didn't have a husband.

Movement at the front door of the house caught his attention. A man was standing in the open doorway, but it wasn't the bodyguard and it certainly wasn't O'Dell. This man was shorter, his dark hair slicked back from a low forehead, the cut of his suit not something you could buy off the rack.

Nick had seen the man's picture before. This was Gino Pucinelli, and he was standing in the doorway with his armed crossed, staring at their limo.

"I think we'd better head on out," Nick said, "or we're going to have company."

Stacy glanced out the window. "You're right." She slipped the gun back inside her bag. "He was supposed to take me to the funeral home. He's upset I told him no, but I just couldn't..." She waved a hand in front of her face like she was swatting away an annoying fly.

Nick started the limo. He spared a glance out the side window.

Gino had taken two steps down the short set of concrete stairs, but he stopped when Nick put the limo in gear and pulled around the other two limos still waiting for their passengers. Nick half expected Gino to get in one of the other limos and follow them, but he stayed on the steps.

Stacy relaxed back against her seat. She caught Nick's gaze in the rearview mirror. "That's my cousin, by the way," she said. "Gino. The pushy one."

They'd reached the end of the driveway. Nick drove past the open gates onto the private road that led out of the golf course.

"I know," he said.

A frown built between Stacy's eyebrows. "You know my cousin? But you never said..."

Janine had gone as still as one of the marble statues in the Pucinellis' driveway. "Maybe now's not a good time," she said to Nick.

There would never be a good time. They had Stacy on their side —at least momentarily. Who knew how long that would last? It was now or never.

"A good time for what?" Stacy said.

She glanced between the two of them before her gaze settled back on Nick. She wasn't relaxed now. She might even be thinking that putting her gun away had been a bad idea.

"Maybe I should ask how you know my cousin," she said.

Nick didn't hesitate. He didn't want her to think he was just making up some story.

"I saw him the other night," he said. "He's one of the guys tying up loose ends, and I'm one of them."

27
_____

The white-haired twosome who'd driven their golf cart across the private road in front of the limo on the way to Stacy's house had been replaced by a silver-haired foursome in two separate carts.

Nick slowed the limo to a crawl as the carts trundled across the road. Only one of the four, a white guy who had to be nearly eighty, turned his head to look at the limo.

The sun must have been at just the right angle, because the old guy could clearly see Nick through the tinted windshield. He gave Nick a jaunty salute with two gnarled fingers against the brim of his bright yellow gimme hat. Nick was still wearing his driver's cap. He gave a slight nod of his head and returned the same salute to the old guy.

Comrades in arms, that salute said, which made Nick wonder if the old guy was a guest, not a member. If he was somebody who called a slightly less rarified neighborhood home, he might only set foot on the golf course when his buddies needed a fourth. He might be someone who appreciated the hired help because he'd been one himself.

Cynical thinking, Nick knew that. But all the time he'd spent working at the strip club and jobs like that had made him a cynical observer of the unspoken class system that existed in big cities everywhere.

Back when he'd been a cop, there'd been good guys and bad guys. But out here, it was the haves and the have-nots. Tourists and locals. The old, white, straight farts who'd vote a dead conservative into office before they'd vote for anybody who didn't look and think like them.

Good guys and bad guys still existed, but until the other night, Nick hadn't given that distinction all that much thought. He wasn't a cop anymore. He didn't have to divide the world between criminals and law-abiding citizens.

Until two days ago, he would have said the only thing that really mattered in a city like Vegas were the haves and the tourists. The haves, like Stacy Peck and her husband, and the tourists, like the family Nick had seen the night before gassing up their car, made Vegas run. They gambled away their savings or sank their fortunes into can't-miss deals with the hope of striking it rich, all the while never really understanding that casinos weren't built because the owners lost money and most investors never recouped their investments much less made a profit.

Without the haves and the tourists, all the glitz and glitter of Vegas would dry up and blow away. No more destination casino resorts, no more mega-hotels, no more floor shows or trade shows or even cheesy strip club shows where the locals could go to blow off steam. Even the locals would eventually move on to the next city where they could earn just enough money to barely scrape by.

Stacy Peck had been a have since birth. Haves had money, and money equaled power. But she'd gotten a rude awakening the other night. Maybe for the first time in her life, she was on the receiving end of proof positive that no matter how rich she was, no matter how important her husband was, bad guys could still get to her.

And now Nick had told her that her cousin was one of those bad guys.

At least she hadn't pulled the gun from her purse again and shot him. Instead, she'd been sitting in the back of the limo next to Janine, staring out the window and not saying a word.

The limo was almost to the guard shack when she finally spoke.

"I'm supposed to take your word for this?" Nick could feel her eyes boring into the back of his neck. "I'm supposed to believe that Gino had Greg killed? I don't know you. I just met you. And I'm realizing I don't know you either," she said to Janine. "Not anymore."

"All I can tell you is what happened to me after I stopped the robbery," Nick said. "After somebody with a cell phone shot a video of me handing my statement to the cops and it ended up on the news."

The local news probably only included the video in their broadcast because he'd been holding the kitten. That made for a nice human interest angle to the story. He wasn't just some stranger who stopped a robbery. He was also a man taking care of a little kitten.

If he'd put down his real address on his witness statement, some news station might have sent out a reporter for a follow-up interview —provided he agreed to hold the kitten while he talked to them. People loved baby animals. Well, most people. The dickhead who'd dumped the kitten in the trash behind the club hadn't loved baby animals. Nick doubted they even knew what love—real love—felt like.

He stopped the limo when he reached the guard shack. The gate stood partially open, and this time the guard stayed inside with the air conditioning. He nodded at Nick through the bars of the gate, letting him know that he could drive right on through as soon as the gate opened all the way.

"If you want out," Janine said to Stacy, "now's the time. We'll understand. But I really hope you'll hear us out."

The gates finished rolling open, but Nick didn't drive through immediately. He wanted to wait a minute longer for Stacy to make up her mind.

That apparently alerted the guard. He came out of the shack and bent down on the passenger side of the limo.

Nick rolled the window down so the guard could look into the back of the limo. "Everything all right in here, Ms. Peck?" he asked.

"Fine, Winston," she said. "I have a meeting to go to, and I couldn't remember if I brought everything I needed, but it turns out that I did." She flashed him a quick smile that had no warmth behind it. "I didn't mean to worry you."

"That's all right." The guard—Winston—hesitated a moment, then he said, "I sure am sorry about your husband. I've been wanting to tell you that. He was always real nice to me. The wife and I, we want you to know if there's anything you need, you just let me know."

"That's very nice of you," Stacy said, and now her voice held the kind of warmth her smile hadn't. "But you should get back inside now, out of the heat. I'll be fine."

"Yes, ma'am."

He straightened up and backed away, but he didn't go back inside the guard shack. Nick could see him in the sideview mirror still watching the limo as Nick pulled away. Stacy had said the right things and without a moment's hesitation, but she hadn't been all that convincing. Nick just hoped that Winston wouldn't decide to go in the shack and call the police, just in case.

After Nick had rolled up the passenger side window and turned onto the short drive that led away from the gated entrance to the golf course, Stacy said, "While we're on the way to the mortuary, I want you to tell me why you think my cousin's involved. You've got that long to convince me."

So Nick did. As he negotiated afternoon Vegas traffic, he told Stacy about how he'd spotted the robbery going down in the convenience store's security mirror, which let him get the drop on the robber. He told her about how Janine came to his apartment the night before to warn him that guys came to his work looking for him.

"We work together," Janine said. "I'm the one who saw your cousin."

Janine didn't mention where they worked, so Nick didn't either. Instead, he told Stacy that Janine had been at his apartment when

Gino and the two men he'd been with had shown up, and how they had to flee out a second story window.

"We've been on the move ever since," he said.

What he didn't mention was Oscar O'Dell or how O'Dell tied into Nick's past. He would, but not just yet.

He also didn't say anything about the kitten. Stacy noticed.

"Where's the kitten?" she asked. "You don't have her with you. You said you've been on the move, but I don't see her. I don't want to hear that you abandoned her."

"She's with a friend," Janine said. "They're good with cats. She'll be safe until Nick can go back and get her."

"That's the plan?" Stacy asked Nick. "To keep her?"

He nodded. "That's the plan."

If he survived.

"Good," Stacy said. "I was wrong about you, made assumptions I shouldn't have, but it sounds like I at least got that one thing right."

Nick could relate. He'd made assumptions about what kind of woman Stacy was, and most of them had turned out to be dead wrong.

She went back to staring out the window, probably thinking through what he'd told her.

Janine had given Nick directions to the mortuary, but she'd also told him to take the long way. Instead of sticking to the main road, he drove down wide side streets that took them through cookie-cutter neighborhoods made up of large two-story homes with three-car garages and price tags, he guessed, that would be in the seven-figure range.

If Stacy realized he was taking them on a grand tour, she hadn't said anything. She might not be in a rush to meet with someone for the purpose of making her husband's final arrangements.

Nick wondered who would make the final arrangements for his own parents. He had no brothers or sisters. His mom was almost a decade younger than his dad, and it stood to reason that of the two of them, his dad would pass away before she did.

The idea of his mom having to make final arrangements for her husband without Nick there to help her was almost unbearable. Nick might have lost his old life, become a ghost living a new life with a new name, but that had been his choice. His parents had lost their only child through no fault of their own. Doing the right thing had come with a heavy price, and not only for himself.

Stacy kept looking out the window, not saying anything, until Janine finally broke the silence.

"Can I ask you something?" she said to Stacy.

Her voice was soft as cotton, as gentle as someone talking to a skittish animal. Still, Stacy jerked at the sound of Janine's voice, like she was waking up from an unexpected nap only to find that the dream she'd been having was far more pleasant than reality. She made a huffing sound that wasn't quite a laugh.

"Sure," she said. "Only you have to answer something for me first."

Janine shrugged one shoulder. "If I can, okay."

"You've both been on the move, that's what you said. You might as well have said you're on the run because you think you're a loose end. It doesn't take a genius to know you don't want anyone taking care of that loose end." This last part Stacy directed at Nick, meeting his gaze in the rearview mirror. "You could have run right on out of town. It's a big desert out there. You could have lost yourselves in Los Angeles or down in San Diego or maybe crossed over into Mexico, but you're still here. You claim Gino's involved, but instead of getting the hell *away* from him, you concoct this flimsy excuse to come see me."

Now she was looking at Janine.

"We met for what, a few hours back when I was a kid with a crush on your rocker boyfriend? It's not like we were great friends, but here you come, years later, ready to console me."

Nick had to give Janine credit. She didn't squirm or look away from the anger radiating from every pore of Stacy's body.

And Stacy wasn't just angry. She was furious.

"I'll admit, it felt good," Stacy said. "At least at first. Like someone really cared about me for *me*." She held up a hand to stop any protest Janine might have been ready to make. "And please don't tell me that you do. I'm not that naïve. We're not friends. We're not going to *be* friends. You got me out of the house, and I thank you for that."

There was a *but* coming. Nick could feel it.

"Greg told me I trusted people too easily, and maybe I do," she said. "Or I did. I relied on him too much because I thought he'd be there to look out for me. Not for always, but for long enough. But he's gone now and the only one who's going to look out for me is me, so I have to ask you both—and you damn well better tell me the truth."

She turned her angry eyes on Nick and then back on Janine.

"What, exactly, do you two want from me?"

28

____

That was the question, wasn't it.

What did they want from Stacy Peck?

Or a better question: what did they want from her *now*?

Nick stopped the limo at a traffic light. Heat waves were rising off the pavement, creating little miniature illusions of water where none existed. The afternoon had turned into a real scorcher, even by Vegas standards. No pedestrians were out and about in this neighborhood. They were all inside their air-conditioned houses or their air-conditioned cars.

When the light turned green, Nick didn't hit the gas immediately. Cross-traffic had been moving in a desultory flow, as if the cars themselves didn't want to be out on the hot pavement. But this was Vegas. Running red lights to beat the clock was almost a city-wide pastime.

As if to prove a point, a cherry-red Porsche zoomed through the light. Nick caught a glimpse of the driver, a business type with a cell phone plastered to his ear.

Would they be in this mess as deep as they were if he'd had a cell phone? Janine could have called him from the club to warn him instead of showing up at his door. With a warning like that, he could have taken off long before O'Dell and Gino kicked in his front door, and Janine wouldn't be part of this shitshow. They wouldn't even have known that she'd called him.

That was a whole lot of speculation for no good reason. He didn't have time for regrets.

What he had to do now was come up with a way to answer Stacy's question when he couldn't even answer it for himself.

Initially, the only thing Nick had wanted from Stacy was to find out if she had any connection with Oscar O'Dell, even if it was just through her cousin. If Gino had hired O'Dell, and if Gino was hanging around Stacy now that her husband had been killed, Nick had thought it was a good bet O'Dell would be in the house too. When he eventually left the house, they could tail him long enough to get him alone. Then Nick could have his final showdown with the man and be done with him, once and for all.

Of course that plan had gone out the window when Janine had offered to give Stacy a ride to the mortuary. She had her heart in the right place, and getting Stacy alone so the three of them could talk had been a good idea.

Only that talk hadn't gone well. Instead of enlisting her help, they'd pissed her off.

Nick had forgotten one of the cardinal rules he'd learned as a cop: people in emotional distress aren't predictable. Domestic dispute calls had been the worst for that very reason. People who had deep emotional ties to each other fought dirty. Fought until they rubbed those emotions raw. Then they turned against the people who tried to help.

So what did they want from her now?

"We're trying to find a guy named Oscar O'Dell," he said. "That's the first thing."

A frown line built between her brows. "The first thing? What else do you want?"

"That depends on you," Nick said. "You know anybody named O'Dell?"

She sighed. "He's Gino's head of security. Or that's what Gino calls him. He's just a glorified bodyguard. An old glorified bodyguard."

Interesting observation coming from a woman who'd married a man old enough to be her grandfather.

"For how long?"

"I'm don't know exactly," she said. "He's been hanging around with Gino for months. I thought he was just one of Gino's guys, you know? A Jersey guy, Greg called him. Somebody to make Gino look cool, he said. Make Gino feel important."

"Was he at the house with Gino today?" Nick had a feeling he already knew the answer, but he wanted to hear it anyway.

"For the last couple of days Gino hasn't gone anywhere without him, so yeah, he was there." Her eyes narrowed. "Why do you want to know all this stuff about O'Dell?"

Nick debated how much to tell her. He certainly wasn't going to lay out his entire backstory. Stacy wasn't an ally. He couldn't tell her he'd been in the witness protection program because of O'Dell. He couldn't trust that she'd keep that information to herself.

"We have a history," he said. "Let's leave it at that."

"He's a creep," Stacy said. "I hope you're not going to tell me you're old friends."

Janine had been sitting quietly next to Stacy, letting Nick direct the conversation. "They're not friends," she said now. "And you're right, he is a creep."

Stacy raised an eyebrow at that.

"He was with Gino," Janine said. "When he came to where we work yesterday looking for Nick, O'Dell was with him."

Stacy leaned back against her seat. "Yesterday was a blur," she said. "I don't remember much except that I couldn't sleep. I finally took a pill that knocked me out. I think Gino was at the house, but he could have left. I don't know."

She wasn't recounting her day for them. She was doing it to figure out if they were telling the truth about her cousin.

"I didn't wake up until this morning," she said. "I was alone. Greg was always taking business trips, and I was alone a lot. I actually had to remind myself that he was gone."

She turned her face toward the window, and a moment later Nick heard her sniffle.

Stacy had been a widow for less than forty-eight hours. She'd been in shock yesterday, but today she was coping. Hell, she was more than coping.

Nick suddenly felt like a creep himself for barging in on her grief. He could have found another way to locate O'Dell. He should have told Janine no when she came up with this idea, but maybe a part of him had been in shock himself. He'd created a carefully constructed life that left next to no paper trails, just like the feds had taught him, but he'd never really believed that O'Dell would find him.

While the last two days—less than two days, really—hadn't exactly been a blur, he'd lost all sense of time. He'd thought more time had passed. The fact that it hadn't raised one more question.

If the cops were releasing Peck's body to the mortuary soon, did that mean they'd already finished the autopsy? Even back in Jersey the coroner's office wasn't that fast. Nick had no experience with the coroner's office in Vegas, but this seemed awfully fast to him.

Something must have bumped this case to the top of the line. Which also didn't make sense. From the cops' perspective, this case was cut and dried, over and done with. They had the robber and they had his weapon. The robber was dead and only one civilian had been killed. The outcome could have been much, much worse, but the crime and its resolution was a done deal. There was no need to rush the autopsy just to confirm that Peck had been killed with the robber's gun.

Did the Pucinellis have that much influence in this city? Did they have the juice to bump the autopsy to the head of the line? If they did, that meant they controlled not only local politicians but key law enforcement personnel as well.

Now that was a sobering thought. Especially if it wasn't just Gino but the family itself that had set Peck up.

And even if it had just been Gino, did Nick want to be the one to tell old man Pucinelli that his son was a screw up? The old man might fix things with his son, but he also might decide to get rid of the one witness not only to his son's stupidity, but whose testimony might land his son in jail.

That meant Nick was right back where he started, only now with a much more powerful enemy. Crap.

And he'd been stupid enough to let Stacy know that Gino was involved. He couldn't retract that now.

Double crap.

He'd have to lose himself after he settled things with O'Dell. Forget about making nice with the Pucinellis. Tell Janine to reinvent herself—again—somewhere far away from Vegas and forget she'd ever known him.

Stacy seemed to give herself a mental shake. "You said that was the first thing, what I knew about O'Dell. So what else?"

Nick wasn't about to ask her to set up a meeting with her family, not now. Instead, he decided to ask her something that had been bothering him ever since this whole thing started.

"I know why I was at that store," he said. "I found a kitten—" or maybe she'd found him "—and she needed something to eat. Why were you there?"

"Because we were stupid," she said bluntly, and he could see anger bubbling once again just below the surface. "We'd been at this party, a launch for one of his projects, and we got lost going home."

The party, she explained, had been at a private club, not in one of the Strip hotels. They'd both had too much to drink, and Greg had turned down the wrong street. One wrong turn led to the next, but they were drunk just enough not to care.

"We joked that as long as we could see the Strat's tower, we could find our way back home. We'd never been in that neighborhood before. Greg said that forging through unknown territory was thirsty work, so when we saw the store, he stopped to buy a bottle. Then he said we should buy snacks in case we were stranded for days."

She sniffed again, a sad little mournful sound, but her eyes were dry.

"He said it was our own little adventure," she said. "It was a game to him. All the things he did, the developments he was involved with, even bringing investors into a project—all of it was a game. If life wasn't fun, what was the point?"

Now her eyes were shiny bright with unshed tears. Nick only caught a glimpse of her expression in the rearview mirror, but she reminded him of women he'd had to give bad news to back in Jersey. The ones who'd tried to maintain a tough-girl front even though their eyes betrayed just how much they were hurting inside.

When she didn't say anything else, he asked, "No one knew you'd be there?"

"We didn't even know that place existed before we stopped there."

He thought about that. If someone had sent the robber to kill Peck, the robber had to have been following them. But how would he have even known Peck would stop?

Unless the shooting really was supposed to be a road rage incident. Road rage wasn't all that uncommon in Vegas.

But shooting Peck in his car would have been dicey. Stacy could have been hit by accident. Nick didn't think a possessive prick like Gino would have risked something like that.

Stacy turned her face toward the window. "I don't want to talk about this anymore. In fact, I don't want to talk about anything. I have to get ready to do something that's going to be the hardest thing I've ever done, and I'd appreciate if you would both just leave me alone now."

Making arrangements wouldn't be the hardest thing. The funeral would be. Peck hadn't been shot in the face, so there was a good chance the funeral would be open casket. Nick had never been to the funeral of someone he loved. He couldn't imagine the pain.

So yes, he would leave her alone. He already had more than enough to think about.

If Gino had set the whole thing up, he would have given the robber very specific instructions. Hit Stacy and you die.

Nick could almost see the hitter's thought process when he saw the couple stop at the convenience store. Shoot at a moving target where you had a good chance of hitting the wrong person, or shoot a man at gunpoint on solid ground? The choice was a no-brainer.

Until the guy was actually inside the convenience store. Standing under bright fluorescents, play-acting at being a tweaked-out robber, all the while waiting for Peck to come close enough to shoot and not miss.

He must have realized his mistake almost immediately. He hadn't been wearing a mask. A mask hadn't been part of the instructions he'd received from Gino. It wasn't like he needed a mask for a road rage shooting, but for a convenience store robbery?

That's when he must have realized that he was a dead man whether or not he did his job right. His face would be out there for all the world to see, especially if the store had video surveillance, and in this day and age, what store didn't?

He was going to have to kill everyone in the store, even Stacy, then run like hell and hope Gino never found him.

That must have been when Nick stepped in and all hell broke loose. The guy had shot wildly, but he'd managed to do at least one thing right. He hadn't shot Stacy. But it didn't save his life.

Nick had always thought that the robber was an amateur. He was even more sure of it now. A pro would have gotten the job done the right way. He would have stepped into the store, shot the clerk without hesitation, then turned the gun on Peck. If he'd seen Nick, Nick would have been the next target. Then he'd clean out the register and split. All while wearing a mask, probably one of those clear things meant to mess with facial recognition software.

If the Pucinellis were anything like the old-school mob guys in Jersey, they would have hired a pro to take out Peck. But somebody like Gino? Somebody who, in Stacy's words, was trying to act like a big man? He couldn't use any of the family's hitters. Guys who'd get the job done and do it right would report back to the boss about what the kid planned to do.

No, Gino would have had no choice but to hire an amateur.

Had O'Dell helped him find the guy? Nick didn't think so. Gino wouldn't have wanted to involve O'Dell with the hit. It would have given O'Dell something to hold over Gino's head.

But when the plan went south and the robber got caught? Gino didn't really have a choice. If he went to his old man to confess what he'd done and beg for the old man's help, he would have lost face within the family. He'd forever be a screwup. The only option was to ask his head of security, a corrupt ex-cop, to take out someone who was about to turn against Gino and the family.

Nick could just imagine what O'Dell must have thought. Gino had handed him a golden ticket. He had leverage now, and a way into the inner circle of the family. Gino would never be able to get rid of O'Dell. Even if Gino grew a pair at some point in time, if he became the real deal and headed up the family and inherited all that power, he still wouldn't be able to take O'Dell out. He'd never know if O'Dell had confided in someone else. Someone who'd go to the cops if O'Dell died a sudden, violent death.

So either O'Dell had managed to kill the robber himself or he'd sent in a trusted associate to get the job done.

Someone who could blend in well enough to get by the cops guarding the suspect they had in police custody and not make the death arouse suspicion.

Nick had never earned his detective's shield, but it was time to put all that studying he'd done to work. If he could find evidence that O'Dell had been involved with the robber's death—any evidence at all—he might be able to rid himself of O'Dell once and for all. He wouldn't need to talk to old man Pucinelli about his son. He wouldn't even have to turn the evidence over to law enforcement. All he'd have to do was convince O'Dell that Nick had a golden ticket of his own.

A get out of jail free card.

A leave me the fuck alone pass for the rest of his natural life.

Then he could pick up his kitten from Leon, gas up his car, and get the hell out of Vegas once and for all.

29

Desert Sun Hospital was a sprawling complex of salmon- and sand-colored buildings with green-tinted windows located on a major thoroughfare four blocks east of The Strip. The complex took up an entire city block, a small city within itself.

Nick had driven past the hospital only a few times in all the years he'd been living in Vegas, but he'd never been inside. The main entrance was down a long driveway, nearly as long as the driveway on the Pucinellis' estate, lined with palm trees, stunted desert shrubs, and pulverized rock. The emergency entrance was around back, nestled in between buildings housing medical offices.

They'd left Stacy at the mortuary. Janine had offered to go in with her, but Stacy had declined. She'd also declined—firmly—their offer to wait and drive her back to the estate. Gino, she'd said, would be happy to come get her when she ready to leave.

The fact that she preferred that Gino pick her up told Nick all he needed to know about how Stacy Peck felt about him. Nick hoped he wouldn't need any further help from her because he wasn't likely to get it.

They'd returned the limo to Jenkins along with the driver's

uniform, no worse for the wear if you didn't count the sweat stains, and retrieved Nick's old car. Before they'd left the pawn shop, Jenkins had thrown a clean t-shirt in Nick's direction.

"Your clothes stink," Jenkins had said. "This shirt's marginally better."

The graphic on the front of the shirt featured a stylized depiction of a band Nick didn't know. It made him feel old, but he put it on anyway. Better than the flannel shirt he'd worn at the club, and far better than the plain black tee he'd worn underneath it.

He drove around the hospital three times, trying to think of a way to get what he wanted.

"You sure this is the right hospital?" Janine asked.

"I'm sure," he said.

He flexed his right hand on the steering wheel. The first two knuckles on his right hand were still swollen and sore to the touch. Maybe he had broken something after all. The paramedics who's tried to talk him into getting an x-ray had come from Desert Sun, and that's where they'd wanted to take him.

Maybe he should have let them.

Maybe he should let someone look at it now. At least it would get him in the door.

"I have an idea," he said. "Drop me off at the emergency entrance, park the car, and then come meet me inside."

She raised an eyebrow.

He held up his right hand. "I think I need x-rays."

"I thought you said..." Then she smiled. "I get it. You just want to get inside. What then?"

He gave a slight shake of his head. "I'm just making this up as I go along."

The emergency rooms Nick had been to in Jersey were loud, raucous, and always seemed to be overflowing with angry people who'd been waiting too long to have their emergencies attended to. The few times he'd accompanied a suspect to the hospital, Nick's uniform hadn't afforded him any leeway. Quite the opposite. The sight of a cop in the emergency room immediately raised the noise level, as if Nick could do anything about the long wait times.

Desert Sun's emergency room was only slightly less crowded, but the noise level was tolerable due in large part to the fact that most of the people waiting for their turn to see a doctor were glued to their cell phones. Nick was going to be the odd man out because he didn't have one. Then again, he didn't plan to stay in the waiting room for long.

He checked in at the front desk where a weary intake clerk handed him a clipboard and told him to fill out the three forms clipped there, front and back. Nick held up his hand, making sure she could see his swollen and scabbed knuckles.

The intake clerk sighed. "Do the best you can," she said.

He found a seat toward the back of the room and went to work on the forms. He could grip the pen better than he'd implied, but now he pretended that his hand was too painful to let him write well. When he got to the line where he was supposed to sign his name, he scribbled something that looked like he'd given the pen to his kitten to play with.

He was just finishing up the last form when Janine walked in. She'd not only parked his car, she'd changed her wig *and* her clothes. Now she was wearing a short mousy brown wig in a style that could only be called *I got caught in a hurricane*. She'd also ditched the businesswoman suit for faded jeans and a scoop-neck woman's tee in dusty rose.

He wondered how the hell she'd managed to change so quickly, and out in the open at that. It wasn't like his car came equipped with drapes or even heavily tinted windows.

Then he remembered his initial impression of her. That she was someone who might have worked in one of the showrooms around town. Quick changes were probably just one of the many skills she'd honed along the way.

She sat down next to him and grinned. Thanks to her newly dressed-down outfit and wig, she looked like someone you'd find in a big city hospital waiting room in the middle of the afternoon. Pretty and shapely, but not drop-dead gorgeous.

She also looked like someone who'd be with a guy with a full mustache and a scruffy beard who was wearing a t-shirt for a band he didn't know and who'd obviously punched something a little too hard in the not-too-distant past.

"You're pretty fucking amazing," he said. "That's what you had in your roller bag?"

"You don't want to know all that I have in there." Her grin took on a mischievous glint. "And no, I didn't flash anyone out in the parking lot."

"I didn't ask," he said.

"You didn't have to."

Nick got up with an exaggerated groan and took his completed forms back to the intake clerk. As he handed the clipboard over, he caught a glimpse of the sign-in sheet. At least a dozen people were ahead of him.

The clerk saw him looking. "It's gonna be a while," she said. "We've got a pile-up on the 15, and they're gonna take priority."

Nick could hear the wail of distant sirens getting closer. Ambulance crews had a separate entrance to the emergency room, one that bypassed the public waiting room. He'd seen it when Janine had dropped him off.

"That's all right," he said. "But I'm going to need a restroom. Can you point me in the right direction?"

He'd scoped out the waiting room while he'd been filling out the forms, but he hadn't seen a sign for a restroom. Looking for a restroom would give him an excuse to prowl the hallways. He hoped.

"Out the double doors to your right, down the hall past records. You can't miss it." The clerk narrowed her eyes at him. "You're not gonna pass out in there, are you? Take something you shouldn't?"

He assured her he wouldn't. He wasn't quite sure she believed him.

His stomach chose that moment to rumble. There was a soda

machine and another vending machine with snacks in the waiting room, but his complaining stomach gave him a better idea.

"How about a cafeteria?" he asked. "If it's gonna be a while..."

He trailed off, letting her fill in the blanks. He hadn't eaten anything since the bad breakfast sandwich from the gas station mini-mart that morning. Hospital cafeteria food might actually be in his budget.

"Yeah. Follow the directions on the reader board in the hall." The clerk held up one finger—a warning, not a sign to wait. "You miss me calling your name, you go back to the bottom of the list."

He gave her a wan smile. "Got it," he said.

When he got back to his seat, instead of sitting down, he gestured with his head toward the emergency room exit that led into the hospital. "Let's go grab a bite to eat," he said to Janine.

She got up without a word. Once they were outside the waiting room, she asked, "We're not really going to eat hospital food, are we?"

She'd clearly overheard his conversation with the clerk even at the back of the waiting room. That wouldn't have happened back in Jersey. Or maybe it would have now. Cell phones apparently made even hospital emergency rooms tolerable.

"Not immediately," he said.

She huffed out a breath. "You sure know how to show a girl a good time."

He grinned at her. "You haven't seen anything yet," he said.

30

Hospitals were a warren of long hallways separated by central nursing stations and double doors marked *No Admittance* that could only be unlocked with keycards. Desert Sun was no exception.

Nick and Janine walked past closed doors marked *Private* and *Imaging*, past the hospital pharmacy and a gift shop. They found signs pointing them to the cafeteria, but they didn't follow them. They retraced their steps when they came to locked doors at the end of hallways, made a few wrong turns, and found themselves headed back toward the emergency room.

"What, exactly, are we looking for?" Janine asked.

Nick had only given her a general explanation, that he wanted something that would tie O'Dell to the robber's death.

"The jackpot would be video of who went in and out of the guy's room right before he died," Nick said, "but I don't think we can get that. At minimum, it would be nice to find something that tells us why he died."

"And we're supposed to get that how?"

That indeed was the question.

Nick had hoped that the records room the intake clerk had

mentioned, the one right before the restrooms, would be the logical place to start. No such luck.

Unlike all the locked rooms they'd passed, the records room was the most open office they'd seen so far. It was located at the corner of two hallways near the emergency room entrance. Large pass-through openings overlooked both hallways and were equipped with sliding glass panels. Both panels were currently open, and two clerks sat inside the room typing away at computer terminals. Not a paper record or chart was in sight.

Nick guessed this wasn't the hospital's main record room, only a records area for the emergency room. That could have worked if the room contained paper charts. The robber/hitman had been brought to the hospital via ambulance, which meant he would have been taken to the emergency room for triage and from there been admitted to the hospital.

But without paper records, even if he could get access to a terminal, Nick wasn't a hacker. Maybe they should have convinced Jenkins to tag along.

That's why he'd been looking for a more general records area. One that actually had paper records. He couldn't believe that even in this day and age, the hospital would rely solely on digital records. Computers crashed. Computers got hacked. Paper records might burn up, but computers crashed all the time. He couldn't remember the last time he'd heard of a hospital catching on fire

But everywhere they'd looked, they hadn't found another area marked *Records*.

This idea was turning out to be a bust. He didn't have the authority of a badge to get someone to let him take a look at records he shouldn't have access to without a court order. He should have stuck with his first idea—get a burner phone and then get O'Dell to call him to arrange a meet up.

Janine squeezed his arm. "I have an idea," she said.

Two firemen stood by one of the record room's sliding windows chatting with the clerk inside. Muscles strained at the sleeves of their t-shirts, and Nick would bet they had well-defined six-packs beneath those shirts. He hadn't seen men so toned since he'd left the boxing gym far behind. They'd even make Jenkins look like a ninety-pound weakling.

Janine went up to one of the firemen. "Jerry?" she asked with a smile, touching him on the arm.

The fireman glanced at her, a puzzled look on his face,

"Oh my God," Janine said, covering her mouth with one hand. "I'm so sorry! I thought you were my friend Jerry. I haven't seen him in a while, and he was trying out to be a firefighter, and I thought..." She shook her head, an actual flush blushing her cheeks a delicate pink. "You look a lot like him."

The fireman smiled back at her. "Lucky Jerry," he said. "Don't worry about it."

"Stuff like that happens to him all the time," the other fireman said, sending a playful elbow toward his friend's ribs.

"Why are you guys here?" Janine asked. "Is there a fire?"

Nick had to hand it to her. She had the wide-eyed look of an innocent, and her freckles only added to her girl-next-door charm. Both men were responding to her, being friendly in return. Whatever she was trying to do, it looked like it was working. Nick just didn't know what she hoped to accomplish.

"No fire," the one she first approached said. "We responded to the accident on the 15. We brought in one of the victims."

"You're paramedics?" Janine asked. "I mean, you look like firemen."

"We are," the other one said. "We get called in too."

"Wow," Janine said. "I had no idea."

Nick heard a soft snicker in the hallway behind him. An orderly had wheeled a sixtyish woman in a wheelchair into the hallway next to Nick. The woman was wearing a hospital gown over faded jeans and had a tote bag on her lap and earbuds hanging around her neck. The orderly was a skinny guy in his mid-twenties with oversized black-framed glasses and the complexion of someone who'd had serious acne when all those puberty hormones hit.

The orderly was watching Janine. Nick caught his eye.

"She's laying it on a little thick, isn't she?" the orderly said.

"She usually does," Nick said with a grin.

"You're with her?" The orderly sounded incredulous.

Before Nick could answer, the woman in the wheelchair snickered again. A small smile was playing at the corners of her mouth.

"Not everyone's overly possessive these days," the woman said to the orderly. "This gentleman's clearly enlightened."

Nick didn't know about that. He might be many things, but he'd never thought of himself as enlightened.

The orderly cleared his throat. "They warned me about you, Ms. Nightingale," he said to the patient. "You're a troublemaker."

She shot Nick an innocent look. "Do I look like a troublemaker to you?"

He chuckled in spite of himself. "No, ma'am."

"See?" She craned her neck to look back at the orderly, but the movement made her wince. "Concussion," she said to Nick. "Not that anyone will *tell* me that. Just tests and more tests, and then when they need my bed they decide to park me out here."

"We're not parking you," the orderly said. "Exactly."

The woman shot the orderly a look that wasn't exactly annoyed. More fatalistic, Nick thought.

"You're going to leave me out here while someone somewhere decides what hospital will take my insurance," she said. "They don't," she added to Nick. "So here I will sit and wait. At least there's eye candy."

The orderly raised an eyebrow and shared a look with Nick.

"I saw that," the woman said. "I'm old. I'm not dead… yet."

Nick had to stifle a chuckle. He was beginning to like this woman.

"But I am hungry." She looked up at the orderly. "If you can stop ogling this man's girlfriend for a few minutes, do you think you can find me a sandwich?"

"She's not my—" Nick said, but that was all he got out before the orderly talked over him.

"That's not—" the orderly began.

"Part of your job." The woman sighed. "Well, do you think you can find someone whose job it is to find me something to eat? It's going to be hours before the paperwork is finished, and don't tell me otherwise."

Apparently deciding retreat was his only option, the orderly said, "I'll see what I can do," before he disappeared through a set of double doors down the hall. The sign over the doors read *Trauma Center – No Admittance.*

"I won't see him again," the woman said. "This place is going to be hopping for hours. I heard all about the wreck. My bed was next to the nurses' call station. I heard the first ambulance reporting in." She started to shake her head, then thought better of it. "Very bad. Head trauma. They really will be needing my bed when the next ambulances get here." She gave Nick a sober glance. "I got very lucky, you know. When you get to be my age, a fall can be much worse."

He wondered how lucky she really was since she wasn't being released, just transferred to a different hospital.

"So why are you here?" she asked.

He held up his right hand. "Doing something stupid," he said, which wasn't that far from the truth.

"Looks painful. At least you're mobile. This thing," she said, tugging at the wheels of her chair, which didn't budge, "is a two-person operation. I guess they don't want me wheeling myself around the hospital."

Nick gave the wheelchair a closer look. He'd never seen one like it. Instead of dual handles on either side of the backrest that someone could grip to push the chair, two long handles ran horizontally across the top of the backrest, one thinner than the other. He guessed the two handles had to be squeezed together to get the wheelchair to roll.

"And to think I was being good today." She patted the tote bag on her lap. "Just my knitting and a book, no snacks."

Janine was still busy flirting with the two firemen. She'd shifted positions so that she was standing between the two men.

She was also standing where she'd be able to see one of the computer screens in the records room. Smart woman. If she glanced at the screen at just the right moment, she might be able to figure out a way to get into the computer system.

How did she know how to do that? What exactly had she been in her prior life? Besides Jenkins' ex. Maybe she'd learned how to do this by watching over his shoulder, like she'd done earlier that day.

In the meantime, she didn't need him. He might even be a deterrent to further firemen flirting. His stomach rumbled again, and he realized he was seriously hungry.

"I'll tell you what," Nick said to the woman in the wheelchair. "I was heading toward the cafeteria. How about I get you a sandwich?"

Her face fell. "I don't have any cash on me," she said. "Just a debit card." She clutched the tote bag with a hand that looked surprisingly young. "I wasn't exactly prepared for a hospital visit today. Thank goodness I have a couple of movies downloaded to my cell phone. And my paperback."

"Don't worry about the money," Nick said. "My treat." How much was a sandwich from a hospital cafeteria going to cost anyway?

"That's very sweet, but I can't take your money." She was silent for a moment, then her eyes took on a mischievous glint. "You could always take me for a ride."

Nick blinked. "Aren't you supposed to wait here?"

"They're not going to miss me," she said. "They parked me out here to get me out of the way. As long as I've got this on—" she plucked at the hospital gown "—and this—" she held up her left hand to show the hospital band on her wrist "—I'm invisible out here."

He thought it should be the opposite. Wouldn't staff keep an eye on her since she wasn't in a room, just out in an open hallway?

She must have read the doubt on his face. "Here, watch what happens."

Two women were walking down the hall toward them from the emergency entrance. Both wore nurses' smocks and white pants and shoes. They weren't talking to each other, and while they both gave the firemen a friendly smile, they totally ignored Nick and the woman—Ms. Nightingale—in the wheelchair. The nurses didn't even glance their way.

I'll be damned, Nick thought.

"This isn't my first rodeo," Ms. Nightingale said. "So, how about that sandwich?"

A mob guy and an ex-cop with a deadly grudge were chasing him —and he was trying to turn the tables on them—and the only friend he had in the world was chatting up two good-looking firemen while spying on the computer terminals in the records room. And here he was, cooling his heels in a hospital hallway.

So sure, why not take a sandwich break? It wasn't like he had anything important to do.

He grinned down at Ms. Nightingale. "Let's go," he said.

31

Over egg salad sandwiches in a cafeteria that looked like it had been built thirty years before the rest of the hospital, Nick discovered that his side trip to get something to eat hadn't been a total waste of time after all.

Ms. Nightingale, who told him to call her Eleanor (*not Florence?* he'd joked), had retired two years earlier after putting in twenty-three years in the administrative offices of a mid-size hospital in a mid-size city in Washington State.

"I've seen nurses and aides and orderlies walk past patients like that more times than I can count," she said. "Too many patients, not enough time. And not enough staff these days. The ones who are here can't afford to be distracted from the patients they're actively treating. I've just never experienced being invisible from a patient's standpoint."

She'd treated herself to a vacation in Vegas, she told him, and was staying at one of the hotel/casinos on The Strip. She'd passed out in a buffet line and smacked her head on the tile floor.

"Had a pretty good bump," she said, touching the back of her head gingerly. "When you're my age, things like that can be serious. So they had an ambulance bring me to the nearest hospital." She shrugged. "Luckily mine isn't. Now they're trying to figure out why I fainted. Rule out any underlying conditions so they don't turn me loose on the gaming floor only to have me faint again."

She took a bite out of her sandwich. She'd refused to let him pay for hers, and she'd offered to buy his as well. He'd refused in return. He might be low on cash, but she was looking at an unexpected hospital stay, and that wouldn't be cheap.

"Only they can't do that here or my insurance won't pay for it," she said. "That's when administration takes over. They'll be working to find a hospital that takes mine. That's what I used to do. Coordinate coverages. I know how long it takes."

Which was why she'd known she had time enough for a side trip to the cafeteria before anyone wondered where she went.

She gave him a look over the top of the half of the sandwich she was holding.

"And no, I'm not old enough for Medicare. If I was, it wouldn't be a problem. I could stay here. Or at least I could if they had room."

Nick chuckled. It had been so long since he'd had insurance—since he'd been on the force—that he'd forgotten the red tape most people lived with.

The cafeteria was furnished in steel and Formica. The walls were dull metal that had never seen a paintbrush. Tables were bolted to the floor and topped with chipped Formica. The serving plates looked like the ones Nick had eaten off of in his middle-school cafeteria. And the smell... except for the overall medicinal odor that permeated hospitals everywhere, the basic smells in the cafeteria were the same from that long-ago middle-school cafeteria. A combination of greasy French bread pizza, thick spaghetti (no meatballs), and fried chicken.

Only here the smell of coffee overlaid everything. Eleanor was nursing the single cup she'd allowed herself.

"Now that I've told you my story," she said, "are you going to tell me what wall you punched to land yourself in here?" She gestured at his right hand with her sandwich. "It doesn't seem to be bothering you all that much."

He took a bite of his own sandwich, more as a stalling tactic than anything else while he tried to decide what to tell her. Contrary to the reputation of most hospital food, the sandwich was actually pretty tasty. Or else he was just incredibly hungry.

"I used to be a boxer," he said. "I don't think anything's broken, but I thought I should make sure."

Eleanor lifted one eyebrow. "Were you any good?"

"I thought I was pretty tough. Let's leave it at that."

She put what was left of her sandwich on her plate and took a sip of coffee. The coffee must have been bitter because she made a face. "So who did you punch?" she asked without looking at him.

A guy who deserved it, he thought but didn't say.

"A guy in a bar," he said instead. "He... uh... let's just say he was incredibly rude to my friend."

"The one chatting up the firemen?"

"That's the one."

She gave him a mischievous look. "Did you win?"

Yeah, he'd won. And lost at the same time.

"I hit him too hard," Nick said. "I heard he ended up here. I wanted to drop in and apologize while I'm here since I have a wait in front of me, but I don't know the guy's name." He shrugged. "Kind of a stupid idea, I guess."

"Kindness is never stupid." She leaned back in the wheelchair and sighed. "People are so busy these days, a lot of them don't take the time to be kind. Or thoughtful."

The windows on one side of the cafeteria looked out on a central courtyard. Tall palm trees like the ones out front provided scant shade while the rest of the landscaping, which was predominately hardy desert plants and crushed rock, filled in the open area in an attempt to make the spot look appealing. Cement walkways crossed the landscaping, and a few weather-worn benches next to the palm trees might be shady spots to sit at the right time of day.

A young couple was sitting on one of the benches. The man had an arm around the woman's shoulders, and she was resting her head against him. The picture they made might have looked romantic except for the strain evident on their faces. Nick wondered if they had a child in the hospital or maybe an elderly relative whose prognosis wasn't good.

No one in their right mind hung around hospitals unless they had a good reason. He'd thought he had a good reason, but right now he felt like the only good thing to come of it was the sandwich he was eating and some unexpected company.

He must have looked dejected because Eleanor reached across the table and patted his left hand, the one whose knuckles weren't as swollen.

The touch surprised him, and he almost pulled his hand away. How long had it been since another person had actually touched him in a comforting way? He couldn't remember.

"Let me guess," Eleanor said. "No one would give you this guy's name."

"Nope," he said, which wasn't exactly true since he hadn't asked.

"Confidentiality," she said. "Hospitals take that very seriously." Her eyes narrowed. "Tell me, are you comfortable with the occasional small lie?"

He'd been lying about who he was for more years than he cared to remember, and that wasn't exactly a little lie.

"Depends on what the lie is," he said, hedging his bet.

"The kind you tell over the phone," she said. "The kind where you pretend to be someone you're not in order to get the kind of information you need." She paused, and one corner of her mouth quirked up in an almost-grin. "Like the name of someone you're looking for."

Like the name...

Nick hadn't even thought of trying to bluff his way over the phone, and he should have. The detectives he'd shadowed back in Jersey used to do that sometimes. Call a witness or a lead and pretend to be someone they weren't just to get a bit of information. But they'd had years to hone the skill of being bullshit artists. He'd adopted a new persona so thoroughly that he'd made it his new life. It wasn't bullshit to him. The lie had become who he was now.

But even if he called the hospital and pretended to be someone else, he had no idea what to say, and he told her so.

She patted his hand again. "Don't worry," she said. "I'm going to give you a crash course on exactly who to ask for and what to say."

And for the next ten minutes, she did.

32

Nick bought a second egg salad sandwich for Janine before he wheeled Eleanor Nightingale back to her parking spot in the hallway outside the trauma center. She'd wrapped the second half of her sandwich in a napkin and stowed it in her tote bag.

"For later," she said, "since I'm sure I have a few more hours to wait."

He wished her the best, and on impulse, placed a gentle kiss on the top of her head. "That didn't hurt, did it?" he asked, remembering only after the fact exactly why she was in the hospital.

She gave him a wistful grin. "Only that it made me wish I was a couple of decades younger."

He felt his cheeks warm up at the compliment, but he didn't say anything. He bet she'd been a flirt herself when she'd been younger.

He found Janine sitting on a bench just outside the emergency room entrance. He handed her the sandwich in lieu of hello.

"Thought you got lost in there." She unwrapped the sandwich. "Egg salad?"

"Seemed safer than the tuna." He squinted at the bright sunshine. The sun was noticeably lower in the west, but the desert sky still looked flat and washed out by the day's heat. "You see any pay phones around here anywhere?"

"Pay phones?" she asked around a mouthful of sandwich. "What are you, seventy? Or maybe you've been holding out on me and you're Superman in disguise."

He raised an eyebrow but didn't say anything.

"No," she said. "No pay phones. You might want to join the 21st century and get a cell."

"Paper trail," he said. He wasn't even happy about the bank account, especially since he couldn't access any of that money at the moment.

"Burner phone," she shot back. "I'm sure you've heard of them, what with your prior profession."

Of course he'd heard of burner phones. He'd just never seen the need before, and he kind of doubted the hospital gift shop stocked burner phones next to the candy and bags of potato chips and *Get Well Soon!* balloons.

She reached into the back pocket of her jeans and pulled out a plain black cell phone. "Like this one." She thumbed it on and handed it over. "Should I even ask who you're calling?"

He didn't answer. Instead he entered the number Eleanor Nightingale had looked up on her own cell phone. He'd memorized the number instead of writing it down.

For the next five minutes he worked his way through various layers of hospital administration while he pretended to be someone he wasn't. An officious-sounding someone. He put what he hoped was the right amount of authority into his voice.

Janine just sat and watched him, her expression unreadable, while she polished off the rest of her sandwich.

By the time the call ended, he had a name.

"Winston Jackson," he said.

"Who?"

"The guy who robbed a convenience store and shot Stacy Peck's husband." He handed the phone back to her.

She shoved the phone back in her pocket. "I'm impressed. I didn't know you had it in you. I thought I was the only chameleon in our little gang of two."

"I had a crash course," he said.

"The woman you wheeled down the hall?"

She'd seen him leave with Eleanor. That figured. Janine didn't miss much.

"So what did you learn from the firemen?" he asked.

"That it's a shame I'm not really available." She gave him a wicked grin. "Another time, another place, I would have tried harder."

"And what did you learn about the records computers?"

"You saw that," Her grin got wider. "I thought you might have. You're no slouch yourself."

He didn't say anything, just raised one eyebrow while he waited for her to answer the question.

"Okay," she said. "I'm pretty sure I caught a password."

He shook his head. She was better at this covert stuff than he was. "I'd ask you how, but I'm not sure I want to know."

"Trade secrets." She stood up and brushed a few crumbs from the bread off her shirt, then threw the sandwich wrapper in the trash can next to the bench where she'd been sitting. "Now I'm guessing we're going in search of an abandoned workstation?"

He stared at the trash can. It must have been emptied recently because there was hardly anything in it. With the Vegas heat, the hospital probably had to empty the trash often to keep deadly germs from breeding out of control.

"My thoughts exactly," he said as a new idea began to form. "We just need to pick up a few things first."

It wasn't until much later, when it was far too late, that he realized he'd met another man that day named Winston. And he realized that two men with such an unusual name was just one damn coincidence too many.

PATIENTS SITTING in hallways weren't the only people the hospital staff ignored.

They also ignored janitors.

At first Nick had thought they could borrow white doctor's coats or orderly scrubs, but when he'd stared at the trashcan outside the emergency entrance, he got a better idea.

So they went looking for a maintenance room instead.

The first one they found that was unlocked was little more than an oversized closet chock full of cleaning supplies, a rolling bucket with a long-handled mop, and an industrial sink. Best of all, three olive green overalls hung off a hook fixed to one of the shelving units. No name tags, but maybe the overalls would be good enough.

Nick fit into the overalls just fine, but the cut didn't exactly fit Janine well. The legs were too long, the waist too large, and the chest just barely big enough to zip closed, especially since they had decided to wear the overalls over their own clothes, just in case they had to ditch the disguises in a hurry.

He filled the bucket with hot soapy water from the sink and ran the mop through the wringer a few times just to give it a well-used look. Then he handed a spray bottle to Janine along a pack of wipes and a roll of black trash bags.

"You look like you've done this before," she said. "I'm surprised Chubs didn't have you swabbing out the john at the club."

"I've done a lot of disgusting things since I left Jersey behind," he said. "Cleaning up puke in a strip club restroom isn't one of them. But yeah, I've done janitorial before."

Not that he intended to do any actual mopping now. The bucket and the mop were just camouflage. And, he hoped, the cleaning supplies would gain them entry to areas where the general public wasn't allowed. Although the one thing he hadn't found that they could really use was a passkey.

"Isn't it a little early in the day for maintenance?" Janine asked as they left the maintenance room behind. "Won't we stand out?"

"Not if we look like we belong." He glanced at Janine. "From what I've seen, you have a lot of practice at that."

While he'd been in the cafeteria with Eleanor Nightingale, a janitor had come in pushing an oversized trash bin. He'd changed the trash bag out of the can near the entrance to the cafeteria. No one had given him a second glance.

He would have felt better if Janine was pushing one of those over-sized trash bins, but there hadn't been one in the maintenance room they'd raided. The trash bags would have to do.

They'd decided they'd keep up with the ruse until they found an unattended room with a computer terminal. That turned out to be harder than even he'd thought. The unattended rooms they passed were all locked, and without a passkey, they couldn't get inside. The rooms that were open had at least one staff person inside.

But he'd been right about one thing. No one paid any attention to them other than to scoot out of the way when Janine reached for a trash can under a desk or around a dividing wall. The doctors and nurses and orderlies they passed in the hallway ignored them just like the nurses had ignored Eleanor in her wheelchair.

Until one person didn't.

Another janitor dressed in the same type of coveralls that Nick and Janine had borrowed peered at them as they passed by him in a long hallway full of mostly locked doors.

"What you doing?" the man asked.

He was a short and stocky Hispanic in his forties. He had one of the oversized trash bins that was now mostly full of black plastic trash bags. The laminated I.D. tag clipped to the breast pocket of his overalls identified him as Ernesto.

"You not supposed to be in this wing," Ernesto said. "This my wing. And where your nametags?"

Shit. Nick froze up for a moment, not sure what to say. The trick to getting away with something like this was to act like you belonged, but Nick had never felt less like he belonged.

Janine stepped into the silence. "We just started today," she told Ernesto. "They didn't give us nametags, just told us to get busy, that we'd get our badges later."

Ernesto shook his head. "They cut corners then get mad when we don't follow the rules. They tell you to work this wing?"

"Admin offices," Janine said. "We're supposed to clean the admin offices. Claims. Insurance. Patient records, but we haven't seen any of those rooms."

Ernesto checked a cheap watch on his wrist. "You're early. Not time yet. You sure that's where they send you?"

"That's what we heard," Nick said. "I didn't want to ask a second time." He managed a sheepish grin. "Didn't want to look stupid on my first day, you know?"

Ernesto looked back and forth between them. Nick's heart was beating fast in his chest. If Ernesto didn't believe them and called security, they were screwed.

Finally, the other janitor heaved a long-suffering sigh. "Admin offices in B wing. You take elevator to basement, follow signs to B wing. Admin offices on second floor."

He grabbed Janine's half-full trash bag and put it in his bin as he muttered something in Spanish, then he kept pushing the bin down the hall.

"Guess we're going to the basement," Janine said. She sounded far cooler than he felt. He'd been sure that Ernesto was going to rat them out, but Janine had convinced him otherwise.

He'd wanted to be a detective, but he'd never had a desire to go undercover. That required skills he didn't think he had. Which was kind of ironic when he thought about it now. His entire life for the last fifteen years had relied on the same skills that made for a good undercover cop.

Too bad he'd never be a cop again. He might actually be good at it now.

He blew out a puff of air to get rid of the rest of his nerves. At least they had some idea of where they needed to go.

B wing. They just had to follow the signs.

As maps went, it wasn't exactly a big red X that marked the spot, but it was better than nothing.

The way things had been going lately, Nick would take it.

33

Nick thought they'd finally struck pay dirt in the third office in B wing that they pretended to clean. Or actually did clean.

He was getting pretty good at mopping floors, but he wasn't sure he was doing any good. The water in his bucket was filthy. If he'd been a real janitor, he would have found another maintenance room and changed the water. But if he'd been a real janitor, he wouldn't be in this mess to begin with.

The office had no sign identifying the department, just a suite number on the door: 237.

He'd expected the door to be locked. Half the doors in the hallway were locked, the others had staff persons busy on computer terminals or on the phone. Janine emptied trash cans while he mopped the portions of the floors that weren't carpeted. Unlike the cafeteria and the hallway, most of the administrative offices were carpeted. No blood or bodily fluids to clean up in here.

The door to Room 237 was not only unlocked, the overhead fluorescents had been turned off. The only light came from the screensaver on a computer monitor in a corner cubicle.

The multicolor swirling pattern lit the office just enough for Nick to see there was no one inside.

"Someone screwed up," Janine said, her voice barely audible.

Nick wheeled his bucket inside and she followed, closing the door behind them. "Lucky for us," he said.

It took his eyes a few moments to adjust to the dim light.

The office had been divided into four cubicles, but only one was equipped with a computer. The other three looked like they'd been turned into storage areas for office supplies. The drawers at the one remaining workstation were locked.

Janine sat down at the workstation and pressed the spacebar on the computer, and the screen came to life with a login window.

"Wish me luck," she said. "I'm no Jenkins."

She entered a login name that looked like gibberish to him and typed in a password. The computer responded by telling her the password was incorrect.

"Crap," she said.

She tried again, and again the computer told her the password was wrong. She typed in a different series of letters for a login name, and this time the computer told her the login name wasn't recognized.

She leaned back in the computer chair and blew out a frustrated puff of air. "We should have brought him along," she said. "I really thought I had it."

"Try again," he said. "This time close your eyes and let your fingers remember."

"My fingers?"

"It's a technique I saw used once."

"When you were a cop?" she asked.

"Not exactly."

He wasn't about to tell her it was something he'd seen on a television show he'd watched one afternoon. He didn't know if it was bullshit or not, but they weren't getting anywhere with what she was trying.

She stared at him for a minute, then she licked her lips and turned back to the computer. "Right," she said, but she put her fingers on the keyboard and closed her eyes.

After a moment, her fingers moved on the keys. She typed in a login name—more gibberish—and a password. Her movements were sure and steady.

This time instead of denying them access, the login window disappeared. After a moment, the computer displayed a home screen.

"Holy crap," she said as she opened her eyes. "That really worked."

"I'll be damned," he said, peering over her shoulder.

Their victory was short lived. Although Janine clicked on various icons on the screen, most of them opened programs that also required user names and passwords. She tried the same key combinations that logged into the workstation, but that didn't work.

There was a telephone in the cubicle next to the computer. The extension number was written on a label next to the handset: 20237.

Second floor, room 237.

"Try 20237 for a user name," he said.

She typed in 20237, and a new window popped up asking for a password.

She picked up the keyboard and looked underneath. "Sometimes people hide passwords in the most obvious places," she said, but there was nothing pasted to the bottom of the keyboard.

The most obvious places.

The cubicle held nothing of a personal nature. It was possible that this workstation was shared among several staff members since there were no framed family photographs, no plants (real or fake), no flowers (real or fake), and the only pens were generic black and blue stick pens in a mug advertising a local casino's restaurant.

"The mug," Nick said. "Check that."

Janine took out all the pens and looked inside, then she turned the mug over.

A hot pink sticky note was attached to the bottom with the word **LogIn!** written in block letters, but nothing else.

"We already know the login," Janine said. "We need the password."

Nick snorted. "I think that's the password."

"You've got to be kidding me." But she typed it in, complete with the asterisks and exclamation mark.

It worked.

"You are one lucky son-of-a-bitch," she said.

The icon she'd selected opened a program that in turn opened a window on the screen. The window contained at least two dozen dialog boxes, most of which were labeled with alphabet soup abbreviations. Nick was scanning each option in the window when Janine pointed to one box near the bottom.

"Patient name," she said. "I have no clue what anything else means, but we have a name."

She typed *Winston Jackson* in the box. A moment later another window appeared, this one with a series of Y/N selections for the types of records available.

Janine clicked Y on all of them and was about to hit enter when the lights went on overhead.

Their luck had just run out.

"You two better have a damn good reason why you're in here."

A big black woman stood in the doorway, hands on her hips. She wasn't wearing hospital whites or a nurse's uniform. She was dressed in civilian clothes, in her case a navy blue pantsuit that would have done Hillary proud if Hillary had been nearly six feet tall and built like a NFL linebacker.

Nick straightened up and shifted sideways so that his body blocked the woman's view of the computer screen. He hoped that Janine would use the time to exit out of the program and close the window.

The woman took two steps into the room. She wore a name badge clipped to her suit jacket and a set of keys hung from a lanyard around her neck. Unlike the janitor, her badge included a photograph of her with a much more pleasant look on her face. The name printed beneath her picture was too small for Nick to read.

"I said, what are you doing in here?" the woman demanded again. "Or do I call security?"

"No, you don't have to do that," Nick said. He held out his left hand, palm out in what he hoped was a calming gesture. He didn't want her to see the scabs and swelling on his right hand. "We didn't mean—"

"We were just trying to find a map of the hospital," Janine said, standing up behind him. "It's our first day, and nobody told us how to get where we needed to go."

Janine was giving the woman her most innocent, most honest, mostly embarrassed grin. It made her look about twenty-five.

It had no effect on the woman in the pantsuit.

"You couldn't find someone to ask?" the woman said.

"The door was open," Nick said. "When no one was here and the computer was on..." He let the sentence trail off with a shrug. "I'm sorry if we did something wrong."

The woman glared at them. "The computer was on? And the door was unlocked?"

Janine nodded. "I am sorry if we overstepped. I just thought—"

"Well, you thought wrong," the woman said.

She walked past them, her attention on the computer screen. Which, Nick was happy to see, now displayed the computer's home screen.

"Son of a..." The woman clicked on the icon for the same program Janine had opened. The login window appeared, which was the first thing that seemed to make the woman happy.

Nick tried not to breathe a sigh of relief.

"You two don't have name badges," the woman said, turning her attention back to them.

She was close enough now that Nick could read her name. Patrice Washington. He doubted she went by Pat. She didn't seem the type.

"They didn't give us—" he started, but she interrupted him.

"Everyone needs a badge," she said. "You march yourselves back down to H.R. and tell them I said that no matter how short staffed they are, no employee runs around my hospital without a badge. And if they have a problem with that, they can call me and I'll be happy to explain it to them."

When they didn't immediately march out of the office, her eyes narrowed.

"You *do* remember the way back to H.R.?" she said.

"Yes, ma'am," Janine said. She sidled her way past Nick on her way out the door.

"And take that smelly thing with you," Patrice Washington said, wrinkling her nose at Nick's bucket of filthy water. "This is a hospital, not a rest stop. You want to spread germs all over this place? Or do you think you might want to mop with *clean* water instead?"

"Yes, ma'am," Nick said.

He grabbed the mop handle and scooted the bucket out of the office as quickly as he could without risking a spill. She'd probably make him clean it up on his hands and knees if any of that water sloshed on the office's carpeting.

When he'd escaped the office and Patrice Washington and the office door was closed safely behind him, he shared a look with Janine, and then they both burst out in quiet laughter.

They really didn't have all that much to laugh about. They hadn't found out anything about Winston Jackson other than his name, and they'd just lost their best shot at accessing his records. But the situation was so absurd, and they'd escaped on the flimsiest of excuses, Nick couldn't help but laugh.

"I think whoever left that door unlocked is going to be in a world of hurt," Janine finally said.

Nick felt a little bad about that. Washington was probably going to ream that poor employee for not logging out of the computer as well, even though they had.

The thought made Nick sober up fast. He didn't want anyone else to get hurt because of him. It was bad enough that Janine was involved up to her rather shapely eyebrows just because she'd wanted to help him.

He gestured with his head down the way they'd come. "We better head out in case she comes back out."

"Where to?" Janine asked, walking alongside him with her cleaning supplies.

"Basement," he said. "We need to ditch this stuff."

He'd rather find another unattended computer, but he didn't want to risk it. Besides, if Patrice Washington was any example of how supervisors ran their departments—and she had to be a supervisor of something, even though her badge hadn't said—the odds of finding another unattended computer Janine could log into were somewhere between slim and none.

He mentioned as much to Janine as they rode the elevator down to the basement. They had the elevator to themselves, and Janine had already started to unzip her coveralls.

"We don't need to find another computer in the hospital," she said. "All we needed was the login and the password, which we now have."

"And that does us any good how? I don't think the library computer's going to help us this time."

The elevator arrived in the basement and the doors opened with a ding. The basement level of the hospital served as the physicians' parking garage. Two young doctors, barely out of medical school from the looks of them, got on the elevator without waiting for Nick and Janine to get off first. The two of them were talking about a case and didn't give Nick or Janine a second glance, even though Janine's coveralls were unzipped halfway to her waist.

They would have paid plenty of attention to Janine at the club, but here? Here she was as invisible as he was. Or as Eleanor Nightingale had been sitting in her wheelchair in the hallway outside of the Trauma Center.

Once the elevator doors had closed and whisked the two young doctors away, they found a shadowy corner of the basement where they could leave the janitorial stuff behind.

Janine leaned in toward Nick. "We don't need the library computer," she said as she finished stripping off her coveralls, revealing the jeans and t-shirt she wore underneath.

He unzipped his own coveralls. All the good humor he'd felt not that long ago was gone. They'd come so close only to come away with nothing.

"What we needed was the computer we found upstairs."

He stepped out of the coveralls and flung them at the wall, right by where he'd left the mop and bucket. Childish, yes, but better than punching the concrete wall out of frustration.

"We already have what we need," she said again. "We have a secret weapon."

She folded up her own coveralls and placed them on the concrete floor of the garage, then she grinned at him.

"We have a Jenkins."

35

Jenkins. Aka Johnny Trejo. Janine's ex.

Former musician, current pawn shop owner, and a man with mad computer skills.

"If there's a back door into the hospital's computer system," Janine said from the back seat of Nick's car, "he'll find it. We already have a login and password. That's more than what he usually has to work with."

After they'd left the hospital, they'd made a quick stop at a convenience store to buy two burner phones, one for Nick and one for Janine. Sooner or later Nick was going to want O'Dell to contact him, and the only way O'Dell could do that was if Nick had a phone.

He wasn't sure why Janine wanted a second burner phone. When he'd grabbed one from the spindle, she'd grabbed a second one and put it on the counter next to his. Maybe he'd used up too many minutes on the one she already had when he'd bluffed his way into getting Winston Jackson's name.

He'd paid for both phones. After she'd paid for the motel room the night before, not to mention everything else she'd done for him, if she wanted a phone, he'd buy it. It was the least he could do, even though the cost had burned through a good chunk of the cash left in his wallet.

"He'll do that for us?" Nick asked her now. "Jenkins?"

Jenkins had already loaned them his limousine and his driver's uniform. There was a limit to how many favors a man would do for a total stranger like Nick.

"He'll do it for me," Janine said. "If I ask. Nicely."

He thought she was banking far too much on her past association with Jenkins. The man still had feelings for her, that much was clear. But hacking into the hospital's computers to take a look at confidential patient records was a whole different level of favor, one that could land Jenkins in serious trouble if he got caught.

After they'd bought the burner phones, Janine had retrieved her carryon bag from the trunk. Now she was busy changing clothes—and wigs—yet again. Nick did his best to keep his eyes on the traffic, but it was a losing battle. It was late enough in the afternoon that the crush of Vegas traffic had them almost at a standstill, and that was on surface streets. Driving didn't demand his full attention.

"He'll still be there?" Nick asked.

"He's there all the time," she said. "He doesn't trust anyone else to price the stuff people pawn. He thinks his employees are too generous."

In other words, he was afraid his employees were ripping him off. Which made Jenkins a cautious man.

Nick had a bad feeling about this. He wanted something—some kind of evidence—to hold over O'Dell's head. Proof that the convenience store robber, Winston Jackson, had been killed by O'Dell or one of his security guys would do it, but the chance of getting that kind of information from the hospital's computer system seemed slim. If there had been any evidence pointing at foul play in the hospital, the hospital would have called the cops just to cover their own ass, and the cops would have been all over those records. Even if O'Dell had friends among the cops out here, they couldn't make all evidence of something like that go away.

But what if they could?

He'd underestimated how deep O'Dell's network of crooked cops had been back in Jersey. And back then, O'Dell hadn't been connected with as powerful a crime family as the Pucinellis. At least he didn't think so. He didn't want to make the same kind of mistake again.

Janine had slipped off her rose-colored t-shirt. Nick had seen her often enough at the club wearing next to nothing that the sight of her without her shirt on shouldn't have done anything to him. Still, the late afternoon sunlight lent a glow to her skin, offset nicely by the lacy cream-colored bra she was wearing. He couldn't help but think of how soft and smooth her skin might feel if he touched her.

She never let any of the customers at the club touch her, not even a pat on her back or on her bare ass. More than once he'd seen her deftly move out of the way of questing hands without making it seem like a brushoff.

Would she let him touch her like that? There had to be something going on here beyond mere friendship.

When she lifted up her arms to slip her new shirt on, he saw something besides just smooth, soft skin.

She had a purpling bruise on the underside of her upper right arm, just about the size and shape of a thumb. A big, powerful thumb. The last time he'd seen her without a shirt on had been at the club. He'd had a half-decent view of her bare arms when she'd leaned over the bar to look at the kitten, and he could swear the bruise hadn't been there then. He hadn't seen her without a shirt on since then.

The bruise looked new and angry.

He was about to say something when she caught him staring at her in the rearview mirror.

"Eyes on the road, mister," she said with a warning grin as she pulled on the new shirt, this one a silky, stretchy, black long-sleeved V-neck that looked like it was tailor made to fit all her curves.

He smiled back, but he went back to watching the barely moving traffic.

After a few minutes of silence, he said, "Can I ask you something?"

"Sure," she said, but the way she stretched out that one word spoke volumes. It told him he could ask but she might not answer, depending on the question.

He shifted in his seat. Stop-and-go traffic always made him antsy.

"Why are you doing this?"

"Changing clothes?"

He glanced back just in time to see her put on a new wig. The straight black hair on this one hung down past her shoulders and looked just as silky smooth as her shirt.

"I like to change the way I look," she said as she ran her fingers through the hair.

"Not that," he said. "I mean everything. Helping me. You should have left this morning. Left when we went by your apartment. Told me to take a hike."

She didn't answer for long enough that he thought she wasn't going to.

"You need me," she said finally.

That was it? "You think I need you."

He wasn't quite insulted. He'd been on his own for a long time, and he'd gotten along just fine. Hell, he was only in this mess because he'd opened himself up enough to rescue a helpless kitten. Maybe he shouldn't have done that, but there was no way he could have walked away and left her in that dumpster. He wasn't built that way.

"That's not what I meant." She sighed, then shook her head. "Men have wanted me all my life. Ever since I started to get tits. Some even before..." Her voice caught at that, and she stopped to clear her throat. "Jenkins wanted me. He thought I made him look good, and I was okay with that, at least while I still thought there was more to our relationship than looks and great sex."

Jenkins still wanted her, but Janine was smart enough to know that. In fact, she was relying on that. Playing to it. Making herself look sexy before they went to see him.

He wondered about the great sex part. Maybe she still wanted that too, just not enough to stay with the man.

Something inside Nick twinged at the thought. He tried to tell himself it was none of his business who she slept with, but the twinge wouldn't go away.

"The guys at the club, they want me," she said. "It's why I don't dance. Why I don't go in the back room with any of them. They all *want* the person they think I am. Whoever they think I am. I'm their fantasy woman."

That's probably how she got the bruise. Some men who wanted things didn't think that no was a real answer. For the club's primary clientele, the women who worked there were just things that existed for their amusement. Things didn't get to say no.

"You have no idea what it's like to be useful to someone as the person I really am when everyone else wants that fantasy woman," she said.

He didn't know how to respond to that. He hadn't expected that kind of raw, naked emotion.

The traffic started to move. Whatever bottleneck had slowed traffic down must have worked itself out.

"The radio in this thing work?" Janine asked, clearly changing the subject.

The whole time they'd been in his car, he'd had the radio switched off and she hadn't seemed to mind. The speakers weren't in much better shape than the car, but the radio did work. If she wanted music, he'd give her music.

"You have a preference?" he asked.

She gave him the frequency of a local FM station. It turned out to be an oldies station. The same kind of rock music Jenkins had been listening to in his cave of an office rattled the speakers in Nick's car.

She was getting in character, he realized. Rocker chick. She wasn't so sure Jenkins was going to help them after all, and she was getting ready to not play fair.

"You don't have to do this," he said.

"Yeah, I do," she said. "And here's the hard part. You can't be there."

What?

He opened his mouth to voice his objection, but she shut him down.

"No argument," she said. "He'll only do this for me, and only if I ask nice."

She was putting on makeup that made her eyes look deep and dark and bedroom husky. His imagination provided him with a vivid image of how exactly she was going to ask nice.

"If you're there," she said, "he won't do a thing. Trust me."

He thought about telling her again that she didn't have to do this, but again, it wasn't his business what she did or didn't do with Jenkins. For all he knew, she could be dropping by to be "nice" to her ex on a regular basis.

He certainly had no right to that twinge of jealousy he felt at the thought of her with Jenkins.

No right at all.

36

When Nick dropped Janine off at Ace High Pawn, she told him to cool his heels for at least an hour.

"It might not be an easy hack," she said. "Even with a password."

Only she didn't look him in the eye when she said it.

The hack might take time, but what would really take time was Janine doing whatever she planned to do to get Jenkins to agree to the hack in the first place. Nick wondered if the man would know he was being used. Hell, for all Nick knew, Jenkins might be the kind of man who got off on it. Some men did.

With an hour to kill and nowhere in particular to go, Nick drove to a second-rate casino a couple of miles away from the pawn shop. Eastern Shores billed itself as a resort casino, but from what Nick could tell, the only resort-type things about it were the fake potted palm trees scattered around the edge of the gaming floor and the little paper umbrellas in the drinks the cocktail waitresses carried on their trays.

He found a vacant barstool at a bar in the back of the casino near the sportsbook. He had just about enough cash in his wallet to pay for an overpriced gin and tonic.

He could always get some cash out of the trunk of his car where he'd stashed it beneath the spare tire. He considered that cash his emergency fund, and if this wasn't a damn emergency, he didn't know what was. It just wouldn't be smart to retrieve the money in the middle of a casino parking lot, especially not this casino parking lot.

He could think of a half dozen ways to part with his cash that would be less painful than getting mugged, including throwing the cash off the roof. He could defend himself with his fists well enough, but muggers who'd attack a man usually struck hard and fast and more often than not were armed with guns or knives. Or both. He'd only managed to get the drop on Winston Jackson because the man hadn't seen him. Nick had had the element of surprise. He wouldn't have that against a determined mugger.

Thinking about the robbery made him think about O'Dell. And Gino Pucinelli.

And how hard Nick had been working to keep himself off their radar until he had something on them.

But really, what could he possibly get? His best bet had been with Stacy Peck, but he'd blown it. Instead of getting her to confide in him, to elaborate on why she thought her husband had been murdered, she'd clammed up.

He couldn't blame her. Whatever her suspicions might be, she couldn't go to the police. Anyone whose last name was Pucinelli put family first, and Stacy had been a Pucinelli long before she'd been a Peck.

He took a sip of his drink. He didn't much like gin and tonic—he preferred a quality bourbon—but he'd ordered it so he wouldn't drink it too fast.

Stacy was between a rock and a hard place. Peck had been her husband, so he was family too. If the hit had been authorized by Gino's dad, Stacy was going to have to learn to live with it. But if Gino had taken it on himself and she found out?

The lights over the bar glinted off the surface of Nick's gin and tonic. For all that it billed itself as a resort, Eastern Shores was a dark casino. It was one of the reasons Nick had chosen it. It reminded him of the bar at the strip club—without the bump 'n grind music. And the mostly naked women. The cocktail waitresses here wore skimpy outfits with a Middle Eastern theme that didn't leave much to the imagination, but they still wore far more clothes than Janine did while she was working.

It would be easy enough for Stacy to take care of things herself if she confirmed to her own satisfaction that Gino was behind her husband's death. Nick had already planted that seed. Time would tell if it bore fruit. If it did, Gino had better watch his drinks whenever he was around his cousin. Women liked using poison.

He took another sip of the gin and tonic. He'd planned to get O'Dell's attention by updating his witness statement with a burner phone's number so that O'Dell's cop buddy would pass it on. He had the burner now so that Janine could call him when she wanted him to pick her up. He could still update his witness statement, but there might be a faster way. And with Janine putting her ass on the line for him, faster looked a hell of a lot better.

There was an ATM machine off to one side of the sportsbook. While Nick had been nursing his drink, he'd been watching people use the ATM to get a few hundred bucks before they headed back to the gaming tables or to the windows to place a bet.

Nick could do the same thing. Use the ATM to take money out of his account.

By now O'Dell had to know about Nick's bank account. Nick had around five grand in the account, give or take a few pennies. O'Dell was a greedy son-of-a-bitch. He wouldn't walk away from that kind of money, so he'd assume Nick wouldn't either. And it was a safe bet that O'Dell not only employed hackers, but that the hackers O'Dell kept on his payroll had a higher skill set than Jenkins.

Nick relinquished his barstool and wandered over to the an ATM. He set his drink on the top of the machine and proceeded to take out the maximum amount his bank allowed. It wasn't all that much, nowhere near his balance, but at least he had more cash on him now.

He'd hate to walk away from what was left in his account. He'd worked hard for that money. He'd lived in crappy apartment after crappy apartment. Poured watered-down drinks in a strip club and done day labor in the hot desert sun for that money. But if he had to —if he couldn't get himself clear of whatever he'd stepped into with the Pucinellis—he would.

He found an empty seat in the sports book and sat down to wait for Janine's call. The bank of television monitors were showing horse races and baseball games and soccer games. Nick could have cared less about anything on the screens. Give him an old movie any day of the week.

He'd never followed sports, not even boxing. His interest in boxing hadn't extended beyond his own skill set. Boxing had taught him how to fight by the rules. Had taught him how to control his temper. But boxing had never become his passion. Being the best police officer he could be had been his passion until being the best had no longer been possible.

Vegas had a pro football team now. A few of the men in the sportsbook were wearing team jerseys, but they were little guys for the most part. Not nearly big enough to be part of the team. If Nick was an undercover cop, he'd probably be wearing one of those jerseys himself just to blend in with the crowd.

Half his drink was gone and he still had a half hour before he could reasonably expect a call from Janine. He tried not to think about what she might be doing with Jenkins. If she'd had to do something special to convince him, surely that part was over by now. Maybe it hadn't been a hardship for her. She might have even enjoyed it. He didn't know, and he sure as hell wasn't about to ask her.

In a few hours the strip club would be doing bang-up business. Tonight was one of the nights when the customer who always wanted a glass of milk and a separate shot of Amaretto came in. If Chubs was stuck manning the bar himself, he'd look at the guy like he was nuts. Nick could almost hear Chubs giving the man grief.

Would Chubs have replaced Nick already? It wouldn't be that

hard, not in a city like Vegas. A guy like Chubs would know people who could get him people. The city, and especially businesses like the one Chubs managed, ran on connections.

Like O'Dell and Gino Pucinelli. Connections. Or better yet, a match made in hell.

Nick's burner phone rang. The generic sound startled him, and he almost spilled what was left of his drink.

He fished the phone out of his pocket. The display listed the caller's phone number. It was Janine's. They hadn't programmed each other's numbers into their phones, but Nick had memorized hers.

Had she finished early? Had Jenkins?

He stood up as he answered the phone. He left his drink behind as he started walking toward the exit closest to where he'd parked his car.

"Nick?" he heard Janine say.

"Yeah," he said, feeling foolish for talking on a cell in the middle of a casino. Not that anyone could overhear him. Like all casinos, Eastern Shores was non-stop noise. "Are you ready?"

Instead of answering, she said, "Where are you?"

There was something wrong with her voice, and not just because it had been bounced off a cell tower somewhere and came to him through a cheap cell phone.

Then she said, "Did you get ahold of Connie?"

His blood went cold when she mentioned the kitten's name. That stupid name. She was using it as a kind of code. An S.O.S. That's all it could be.

She was in trouble.

He broke into a run.

"Hang on," he said into the phone. "I'm coming."

He didn't disconnect the call. He wanted to hang onto that lifeline between them, like a string attached to two tin cans. That old trick had been generations out of date when he'd been a kid, but it had still amazed him.

So he heard the scuffle on the other end. He heard the sharp crack of a slap, and he heard Janine cry out. He heard the phone hit the floor. Heard it being picked up. Heard heavy breathing as a new voice came over that thin electronic string.

"Hello, asshole," said Oscar O'Dell. "Can't wait to see you."

And the call went dead.

37

Nick didn't have to wonder how O'Dell had found them. He'd found them because Nick had been stupid.

Not because he'd made a withdrawal from his bank account. It had to do with the license plate on the limo he'd driven to the estate where Stacy lived.

He'd known O'Dell had at least one buddy on the Vegas police force. That's how O'Dell had figured out Nick had a connection with the strip club in the first place. O'Dell's buddy on the force had looked up Nick's witness statement.

But it had never occurred to Nick that he shouldn't drive up to Stacy's house in a car that could be traced back to someone who knew him. And it should have. Running a license plate was practically Cop 101. He'd done it often enough in Jersey—run a license plate to see if a car he'd pulled over had been reported stolen.

O'Dell had been at the estate because Gino had been there. O'Dell had probably been watching Nick through a window the whole time. He couldn't make a move on Nick then because there'd be too many witnesses, including Stacy. Then Stacy had inadvertently saved them from becoming victims in a staged road rage shooting when she accepted Janine's offer to take her to the mortuary.

None of that mattered to O'Dell. He had the limo's license number. He could afford to bide his time.

And he had. They'd taken such a meandering route to the mortuary that O'Dell would have had more than enough time to beat them to the pawn shop when they dropped off the limo. But maybe Gino had kept him busy and O'Dell couldn't get away to take care of a little personal business. Or maybe O'Dell's buddy had been out to lunch and it took longer to run the plates. Whatever the reason, O'Dell hadn't shown up to brace Jenkins until later.

Then they'd made it easier still when Janine went back to the pawn shop to entice Jenkins to hack into the hospital's records.

O'Dell must have thought he'd died and went to heaven. He had Janine. That's all he needed.

Why chase after Nick when Janine could get Nick to come to him, right?

Stupid.

Nick should have known better.

The pawn shop was a trap. He knew it, but he couldn't do anything about it. He had to play this hand out and wait for an opportunity to turn the tables on O'Dell.

If he got the opportunity.

Ace High Pawn looked deserted. The *Open* sign was still lit up, but there were only a couple of cars in the parking lot when Nick pulled in.

He got out of his car and breathed in deep. The day was finally starting to cool off just a bit. There was still a lot of traffic on the street in front of the pawn shop, but the cars had their lights on now, almost like they were competing with all the neon over on the Strip.

All those cars, all those people, and not a one of them had any idea about the confrontation about to go down inside Ace High Pawn. Probably just as well. What was the old slogan? Vegas—what happens here, stays here? Something like that. Too bad what happened in Jersey couldn't have stayed there too.

There were no customers inside the shop. The black guard who'd been sitting just inside the front door that afternoon, the man Janine had called Bo, was gone. A wiry guy with slicked-back dark hair and a flashy suit had taken his place. He had a little earpiece in one ear attached to a curly wire that disappeared beneath the collar of his shirt in the back.

The cut of the guy's suit jacket didn't quite hide the bulge of a holstered gun clipped to his belt.

"Hey, asshole," the guy said when Nick stepped inside. "You been causing my man a bit of trouble, I hear."

Nick didn't say anything.

The guy didn't like that. He had mean little eyes that got meaner, like Nick had insulted him by not responding.

"Didn't your mom tell you it's polite to say hello when you come in a room, asshole?" the guy said.

Asshole must be this guy's favorite word. He'd probably picked it up from O'Dell.

Nick still didn't say anything.

"If the boss didn't say otherwise, I'd beat the crap out of you myself," the guy said.

Nick gave the man an icy stare. "You'd try."

The wiry man held Nick's gaze for a long moment. Whatever he saw there must have made him reconsider whether it was wise to piss off the guy his boss had been looking for because he broke eye contact and shifted his stance so that his hand was a little closer to his gun.

"They're waiting for you back there," he said with a little jerk of his head toward the back room. "But I gotta frisk you first."

That was fine. Nick wasn't armed.

He'd considered buying a gun on the way to the pawn shop. He had enough cash on him now to get a street piece, but he figured it wouldn't do him any good. Not unless he decided to come in shooting, which he didn't want to do. He wasn't John Wick. He wasn't even John Wayne. The only person he want to wipe the floor with was O'Dell.

The man's pat-down was rough and thorough. He grunted when he was done, whether in satisfaction because he'd grabbed Nick's crotch through his jeans just hard enough to hurt, or because he was surprised Nick wasn't packing. Probably in his world guns made all the difference.

The man pressed the earpiece. "He's here," he said to whoever was on the other end of this particular electronic string and tin can. "And he's clean."

His eyes lost their focus as he listened to the other end of the conversation. He kept one hand up by his ear. Given where his gun was clipped to his belt, the hand by his ear was his gun hand. He was still standing as close to Nick as he'd been when frisking him. All in all, not that smart.

At this distance, Nick could knock the guy out with a solid punch to the bridge of his nose before the guy had time to react. Hell, he could ram the palm of his hand up the guy's nose at just the right angle to jam bone into the guy's brain.

He'd seen that done in a movie once when he'd been young. He'd asked the old hardcase at the gym whether something like that would work in real life or if it was just movie magic.

The hardcase hadn't answered, but the look he'd given Nick told him he'd better not ever try it.

Nick considered doing just that, but he didn't know how many of O'Dell's crew were with him in the back room, and whether any of them had a gun on Janine. And he really didn't want to kill this guy unless he absolutely had to. He had a feeling that if could manage to take out O'Dell, the rest of his crew would scurry into the desert like cockroaches.

The guy took his hand away from his ear a moment later, and the opportunity was gone. "Go on back," he said. "But remember I'm out here in case you think about doing anything cute."

Nick ignored him. He turned his back on the guy and headed toward the room in the back that served as Jenkins' private little cave. Only it wasn't so private anymore.

He'd only taken two steps when the guy who'd frisked him shoved him in the back, hard.

Nick hadn't seen it coming, and he stumbled forward three steps before he caught his balance.

That had been stupid. The pawn shop had round security mirrors mounted on the ceiling just like the one in the convenience store. He could have seen the guy coming if he'd been paying attention. He should have kept one eye on the guy, but instead he'd just turned his back, his attention focused on what was ahead.

On Janine.

He hadn't even been with her a week, and he'd already lost the edge that had kept him alive these last fifteen years. He couldn't afford to do that again.

He didn't turn around and deck the guy. Didn't even acknowledge what had happened. He just straightened up and kept on walking.

"Pussy," he heard the guy behind him mutter, followed by a derisive chuckle. "You're not such great shakes, asshole. The boss is gonna eat you for lunch, then puke you up and make your girlfriend clean up the mess."

A red tinge began to creep in around the edges of Nick's vision. An old rage he hadn't felt in years started to ball up his hands into fists. Tensed up the muscles in his arms until the tendons in his wrists stood out like bands of steel. But he made himself keep right on walking, his pace as steady and deliberate as his breathing, until by the time he reached the solid metal door that opened into the room at the back of the shop, his hands had relaxed and the red tinge had faded.

Maybe he did want to kill this guy after all. But it wouldn't be right now. He had other things to take care of first, and if he survived that, maybe then he'd pay this guy a return visit.

He thought about knocking on the closed door, but hell, they knew he was coming.

He took a deep breath, then he opened the door and stepped inside.

38

The house Nick had lived in when he'd been a kid hadn't been much. Just a Jersey row house with two bedrooms and a bath on the second floor, and a closet-sized toilet and sink on the ground floor along with a narrow kitchen and dining room that looked out on a postage-stamp backyard. The house had a basement that was always cold and dank, and an attic on the third floor where his mom had her sewing machine set up among boxes of old clothes and old books and older photos of relatives he didn't know.

The best room in the house, according to his mom, was the living room. It was small like all the rooms in their house, with barely had enough room for his father's easy chair, a television set, a three-person couch, and a small coffee table. But it had a great view of the street and the little front porch where his mom would sit and knit on summer evenings after she'd finished the dinner dishes and his dad fell asleep in his easy chair.

His parents didn't have a lot of money, something he hadn't realized until he was older and his dad had that frank talk with him after Nick had beat the living snot out of the kid he'd sent to the hospital. When he was younger, he just thought that was the way everyone lived, with secondhand clothes from the Goodwill and leftovers for dinner a couple of times a week.

Nick's dad sold tires for a living and his mom worked at a neighborhood bakery part time while Nick was in school. Most nights when his dad came home from work, he'd park himself in his easy chair with a beer and watch whatever was on television while his mom made dinner and Nick went out to play.

All his friends lived in row houses, each house indistinguishable from the other on the outside except for the bicycles chained to iron handrails on the concrete steps leading up to front doors and the holiday decorations in the windows come Christmas. New toys and new comics were cause for celebration and more than a little envy. They played ball in the street and listened to music on a boombox one of the older kids had gotten for his birthday.

Typical lower-middle-class suburban life for a typical lower-middle-class suburban family in Jersey in the last decade of the last century. And a far better life than Nick had been living the last fifteen years.

Back then on winter nights when his mom said it was too cold—or too snowy or too wet—to play with his friends outside, he'd go up to the attic and read. He'd dig dusty books out of dusty boxes and let them take him to exotic faraway places. Like California. Or Hawaii. Or the moon.

Some of the books he read featured villains intent on taking over the world, and some of them had evil lairs where they planned their evil plans. Nick used to imagine the attic was his own lair, only his wouldn't be evil. His lair would be where he plotted how to take down the villains, like Batman did in the comics some of his friends let him read.

The back room at Ace High Pawn was Jenkins' lair. The room had given Nick that impression the first time he'd realized Jenkins was totally at home sitting in his office chair with its squeaky wheels surrounded by music and movies and computers. But now O'Dell was sitting in Jenkins' chair like it was his own personal throne, and the room felt more like the evil lair of a comic book villain.

Only the blood on the floor was very real.

The classic rock 'n roll music had been turned off, and the room was eerily silent. The flatscreen television had been smashed, probably with Jenkins' face. He stood off to one side of the room next to another one of O'Dell's lackies, who was holding a gun on him. Dried blood from a broken nose was caked in Jenkins' goatee and more blood was still seeping from his forehead where the skin had split over an impressive purpling knot.

Jenkins' eyes weren't totally in focus and he didn't look all that steady on his feet. To his credit, the lacky didn't look much better. One of his eyes had swollen nearly shut, and he was holding himself stiffly, like something inside hurt. Score one for Jenkins, the gym rat.

Nick took all this in a single glance before he focused on Janine.

She had a blossoming bruise on one cheek. Not from a punch, but from a hard, open-handed slap. Probably from O'Dell. Back when they'd been cops, Nick had seen his old partner slap around more than one prostitute just because he could. O'Dell didn't have a problem with hitting women. It had infuriated Nick at the time, but he'd been too green and too scared of the good old boys system O'Dell was part of to do anything about it.

Some of Janine's makeup had run down her cheeks. She must have cried, probably from the shock of being slapped, but she was dry-eyed now. Her wig was still in place, and although one sleeve of her shirt was ripped, she didn't look like she'd been hurt anywhere else.

Jenkins had probably been the object lesson. See what we can do to him? Behave, or we'll do worse to you.

She'd behaved. She'd called Nick. She'd tried to warn him off, but O'Dell had never been stupid. Greedy and vicious, but not stupid. She'd deviated from the script he'd told her to say, so he'd hit her.

He'd hurt her.

That red tinge was threatening Nick's vision again. He clenched his fists, then he made himself relax. The lacky next to Jenkins wasn't the only bad guy in the room with a gun.

O'Dell was holding a gun in his lap.

The only person missing was Gino Pucinelli.

"Where's your boss?" Nick asked. "He let you off the leash?"

O'Dell laughed. The sound had no humor in it.

"That little shit?" he said. "You've got it all wrong, *partner*. Again." He shifted in the chair, leaning back. The move actually puffed out his chest. He would have looked ridiculous if he hadn't had the gun. "I run him. He doesn't know it, but I run him."

"How about his daddy?" Nick asked. "You run him too?"

O'Dell's cheeks reddened, but he didn't say anything.

"Or are you just biding your time until junior's in charge?" Nick said. "Get in good with the kid, make him think he needs you, make him think he can always count on you, no matter what dirty piece of work he tells you to do. That the plan?"

O'Dell's hand holding the gun twitched. He didn't have his finger on the trigger. If he had, he might have shot his lacky, the way the muzzle was pointed.

"Just come whenever he calls," Nick said. "Like a good little lap dog."

Nick caught the lacky shooting O'Dell a look that clearly said *why are you putting up with this shit?* But O'Dell didn't do anything. He just sat there, getting red in the face because everything Nick said was true, and they both knew it.

"Like killing Peck," Nick said. "Your *boss* have you set that one up? A nice little robbery to take out the one thing standing between him and his cousin?"

Nick hadn't planned on goading O'Dell. He hadn't planned on anything. But as soon as he realized how easy it was to get under O'Dell's skin about taking orders from a kid, a mobster wannabe, Nick couldn't stop himself. If he could get O'Dell made enough to rush him, to try to beat him to a pulp to show how tough he really was, that's when Nick might have a chance to turn this whole situation around.

But that last barb didn't hit home like Nick thought it would.

O'Dell laughed.

This laugh was fueled by ugly humor.

"You think I did that?" O'Dell said. "You think I'd do something that fucking stupid? Stage a convenience store robbery?" He leaned forward in the chair, the hand not holding the gun on one knee to prop himself up. "Let me tell you something, *partner*. The kid might have a hardon for his pretty cousin, but he can't do jack about it. His old man said no, and what the old man says goes."

The lacky holding the gun on Jenkins relaxed. He smiled an ugly smile of his own. "You said he was stupid, boss."

At that moment, Nick felt stupid. He'd gone too far. He'd been so sure O'Dell was involved in Peck's murder, he'd overplayed his hand.

"All we did was take out the loose end," O'Dell said. "After you fucked it up. As a favor for the family. In and out, death by natural causes."

A favor for the family.

That part sunk in. The loose end O'Dell was talking about was the robber. The man who'd been hired to kill Peck. O'Dell, or maybe one of his guys, had killed Winston Jackson in the hospital like Nick thought, but they hadn't done it for Gino. They'd done it as a favor *for the family*.

Holy shit.

The head of the Pucinelli crime family had put out a hit on Peck? He'd hired Winston Jackson to take the fall, or maybe one of his trusted lieutenants had handled the pesky details, like hiring a disposable gun hand. But the driving force behind the hit had been the real deal man himself. Not Gino.

And Nick had fucked *that* up?

The surprise must have shown clear as day on Nick's face because O'Dell laughed harder this time.

"I bet you're thinking the old man had Peck killed," O'Dell said. "Some development deal gone south, right? Well, the old man's not that fucking stupid either. If he wants you dead, not even the buzzards'll find you. Big-ass desert out there, partner. It hides a lot of dirty deeds."

If it wasn't Gino and it wasn't his old man, that only left one person.

Gino's uncle. The old man's brother.

Stacy's father.

"That's always been your problem," O'Dell was saying. "A failure of imagination. You don't consider all the possible moves. All the possible players. All the potential strategies." He jabbed a finger at Nick. "You never played chess, and it shows. Think you've finally got it all figured out now?"

"It was her father," Nick said. "He arranged the whole thing."

"Bingo!"

A father would only kill his daughter's husband for one reason.

"Peck was screwing around on her," Nick said.

He wouldn't have thought it was possible. Not with the way the two of them had been acting toward each other when Nick had met them that night. Peck had looked like a man in love. Hell, he'd even tried to shield his wife once the shooting started.

"Who knows?" O'Dell said. "Maybe her old man didn't like a guy older than him fucking his little girl."

O'Dell reached out and grabbed Janine by the wrist and yanked her close.

"Like this guy over here didn't like you fucking his ex," O'Dell said. "Not that I can blame you. She's a nice little piece. Great tits."

Janine spat in O'Dell's face.

He might have slapped her again, but he would have had to either let her or the gun go. Instead he just wiped the spit from his face with the back of his gun hand.

"What we have here is what us cops—"

"*Ex* cops," Nick said.

"Us *cops*," O'Dell said, "call a domestic dispute. People kill each other over stuff like this all the time. Right, *Nicky*? Or should I call you Davis?"

Davis Grant. The name Nick had been born with.

Back when he'd been assigned to work with O'Dell, Nick had been Officer Davis Grant, the man with the backwards name.

He'd been Officer Grant when O'Dell had tried to kill him in that hallway in Jersey.

This time Nick didn't have to stretch his imagination to know what O'Dell had in mind. He'd used Nick's real name to remind him of how he was supposed to die all those years ago, the victim of a domestic dispute gone bad.

O'Dell was setting the stage for another domestic dispute. He knew Nick had a history of using his fists, so O'Dell's lacky had beaten Jenkins stupid and O'Dell had slapped Janine in the face so she'd have a bruise. Jenkins still had a thing for his ex, something his security guard probably knew. Jenkins had done a big favor for her and her new squeeze earlier in the day. But when she came back, intending to seduce him into doing another favor for her new guy, Jenkins snapped. He'd slapped her around and made her call Nick, who ran to her rescue. Hell, probably a half dozen or more security cameras at Eastern Shores caught him running from the casino when she called.

Nick was willing to bet that the guns O'Dell and his lackies had were street pieces. Or maybe the gun the guy was holding on Jenkins was Jenkins' own personal gun. The plan was to make it look like Nick and Jenkins shot each other, with Janine catching a stray bullet. The lacky who'd patted Nick down would pretend to be a customer who'd just happened to be in the shop when all the shooting went down. He'd be the one to call the cops.

The recording from the security cameras out front would show the pat down, but O'Dell would probably delete the recording before he left. With no evidence to the contrary, his guy out front would be the only witness, and he'd swear the only people he saw go into the back room were Nick, Jenkins, and Janine.

Except...

What had happened to Bo? The black security guard who'd been sitting on a stool by the front door earlier in the day? The one who'd called Janine "Janie" and who'd only let Nick in the back room because she'd vouched for him.

"What about the other guy?" Nick asked. "The big black guy at the door? You already kill him?"

"Didn't have to," O'Dell said. "We got your buddy here to give him the rest of the day off. With pay."

Jenkins made a wheezing sound and spit up more blood.

Janine tried to go to him, but O'Dell held her wrist tight. She struggled, but O'Dell didn't let go. She drew one arm back, ready to hit him. All O'Dell did was twitch the gun in her direction.

The wheezing noise got louder. Incredibly, Jenkins was smiling. His mouth was covered in blood, and his face looked like something out of a horror movie, but his eyes were in focus now and he was smiling. Nick realized the wheezing was actually laughter.

"Stupid son-of-a-bitch," Jenkins said. "Can't wait to see what comes next."

The lacky jabbed the gun in Jenkins' ribs. "Soon enough, buddy boy."

Jenkins turned his head in the guy's direction. "Exactly."

The word was barely out of his mouth when a flat muffled pop came from the other side of the metal door. It was a sound Nick hadn't heard in years, but once you heard something like that, you never forgot it.

The sound of suppressed gunfire.

39

The way O'Dell had been sitting in Jenkins' chair, he had his back to the computer screen that displayed the feeds from the security cameras out front. Nick had been facing O'Dell all along. He had a clear view of the computer screen from where he stood.

Right before the gunshot, he'd caught movement in the camera aimed at the front door. He saw the flash of muzzle fire as a new figure out front shot the man who'd patted Nick down. The man fell backwards, and the shooter fired a second shot into the man's head.

Quick.

Professional.

The security feed abruptly cut out. Nick hadn't gotten enough of a look to tell if the shooter was a man or a woman. But the new player wasn't a cop. No street patrol uniform, no SWAT uniform, no visible bulletproof vest.

"What the hell?" O'Dell turned toward the computer.

He let go of Janine's wrist as he turned. His gun hand relaxed, the muzzle now pointing at the floor.

This was the only chance Nick was going to get, and he didn't hesitate. Just like he'd been trained.

"You want your body to know what it's supposed to do," the old hardcase at the gym had told him when Nick had complained once —and only once—about all the mindless repetition on the speed bag and the heavy bag. "But it's got to know what to do without you thinking about it. The only way for that to happen is to do it so many times it becomes as natural as breathing or walking down the street."

Nick hadn't worked out on a heavy bag or a speed bag in years, but his body still remembered what all that training had pounded into his reflexes.

His first punch landed hard enough to knock O'Dell out of the chair and send him sprawling on the concrete floor.

Nick's knuckles exploded in pain. He ignored the pain, made the pain his friend, and moved in to hit O'Dell again.

But O'Dell was no slouch. He hadn't gotten soft over the years, and he rolled to his feet, still holding the gun.

Nick had momentum on his side. Before O'Dell could bring the gun up, Nick hit him again. And again. And again. First a blow that knocked his gun hand away and a second chop down on his wrist that numbed the nerves and sent the gun flying. Then Nick landed a flurry of blows to O'Dell's ribs followed by an uppercut to his jaw.

O'Dell fought back. He fought dirty, and Nick matched him blow for blow, block and punch, block and punch.

As good a shape as O'Dell was in, as hard as he hit with his elbows and kicked with his feet, he was no match for Nick.

Nick had years of pent-up anger and resentment and long-buried fury fueling each and every blow. Why the hell couldn't this man just leave him *alone?* Why couldn't he see that as much as he blamed Nick for ruining his life, he'd ruined his own life and Nick's along with it. All Nick had ever wanted to do was be a good cop. H wanted to live his life in peace. Even if that life was hollow and empty now, it was his life, dammit.

All he could think about was taking his fury out on the man in front of him. He didn't think about O'Dell's man in the room with the other gun. Didn't think about the shooter out front. His vision was suffused with red. He'd become a punishing machine, his only purpose to rain down judgment on O'Dell.

Bones broke beneath his blows. Blood flew from O'Dell's mouth and nose. Nick knew that O'Dell had landed punches of his own, but he hadn't felt them. His hands had gone numb. O'Dell's bloody face seemed to morph into the face of the kid he'd beaten senseless all those years ago. The hands pulling at his back, trying to pull him off O'Dell, felt like the hands that had finally pulled him off the school-yard bully before Nick killed him. He didn't hear anything, not even his own shouted obscenities. He only heard the blood pounding in his veins.

Until he heard his mom's voice. Saw her disappointed face as she cleaned the blood off his clothes and put ice on his knuckles.

"You're a better boy than this," she'd told him. "A smarter boy. I will always love you, but a good man doesn't use his fists on the weak."

He'd tried to tell her that the bully wasn't weak, he'd been strong, so Nick had to be stronger. Only when he got older, when boxing had helped him tame his temper, did he understand she hadn't been talking about physical strength.

The memory of his mom's voice, of her words and the look of disappointment on her face, made him stop now. O'Dell was the weaker man. Nick didn't have to keep hitting him drive home that point.

Nick's last punch had sent O'Dell to the floor. This time he stayed there, hands raised in surrender.

But he wasn't surrendering to Nick.

Sometime during the fight, Janine had picked up the gun O'Dell had dropped. She was pointing it straight at O'Dell. Jenkins had managed to get the other gun away from O'Dell's lacky and was holding it on the man.

The lacky was taking shallow breaths, one arm held awkwardly against his side like his ribs were broken. That was new. Jenkins must have still had some fight in him even after the beating he'd taken. Nick was impressed.

As the pounding of his heart slowed and the red began to fade from his vision, Nick got a better look at Janine. Her lips were pulled back from her teeth in a snarl, and her eyes were blazing with anger. She looked like she was two seconds away from pulling the trigger and taking care of the O'Dell problem for good.

"You hit me," she said to O'Dell. "You fucking *hit* me. Nobody hits me. Nobody *touches* me unless I let them."

She held the gun in a two-handed grip like she knew how to use it. Her hands didn't tremble, and she stood far enough away from O'Dell that he couldn't knock the gun from her hands before she could pull the trigger.

O'Dell was smart enough not to say anything. Blood was running down his face and his nose was broken, but he made no move to wipe the blood away.

Nobody said anything.

For a moment Nick was afraid she was going to follow through and shoot O'Dell, but he could tell she must be fighting her own battle for control of her anger. She didn't lower the gun, but her expression changed, becoming less ferocious. She was still a force to be reckoned with, but she was no longer on a hair trigger.

Nick's whole body was trembling now with the aftereffects of the fight. Blood dripped onto the concrete floor from his abused knuckles, and the cut on his forehead had reopened. More blood was running down the side of his face.

He stared at O'Dell. Nick had beaten the man bloody and the good guys held all the guns in this little tableau, but the fight wasn't over. Not yet.

They were at a stalemate.

Nick had done what he wanted to do—he'd beaten O'Dell in as close to a fair fight as a battle between the two of them was ever going to get—but that didn't mean O'Dell wouldn't be back someday. Even if he promised to leave Nick alone—to leave all of them alone just so he could get out of this situation in one piece—promises didn't mean much of anything to a man like him. His ego wouldn't let him back down and just go away for good. He wasn't made like that.

Nick was going to have to kill him.

He supposed he'd known that all along, he just hadn't been willing to face it. It had always been either him or O'Dell in the ground. That was the only way something like this could end.

Did he have it in himself to kill a man in cold blood? Looking at O'Dell now, thinking about what the man had planned to do not only to Nick but also to Janine and Jenkins, Nick was afraid he might.

He'd forgotten about the shooter in the front of the store until three sharp raps on the metal door disturbed the heavy silence in the room.

Jenkins limped over to the door, never taking his gun off O'Dell's man. Jenkins waited until three more sharp raps sounded on the metal before he unlocked the door.

"The calvary has arrived," he said, backing away as a stocky man stepped through the open doorway.

The man held his own gun at the ready, but he dropped it to his side as soon as he saw that Jenkins was holding a gun of his own.

"Doesn't look like you need me," he said to Jenkins.

Jenkins started to shrug but winced with pain at the movement. He glanced at Janine. "You can put the gun down now, Janie," he said to her. "He's with me. Or I'm with him, however you want to look at it."

It still took Janine a long moment before she lowered the gun.

The shooter looked like the kind of man that O'Dell could only dream of being. He wasn't overpoweringly tall, only a couple inches taller than Nick, but he had the solid self-assurance of a man who knew he controlled whatever situation he found himself in. That kind of self-assurance didn't come from swaggering ego, and didn't come from a network of powerful buddies who'd have your back when things were going good and who'd throw you to the sharks when things went belly up. It came from the knowledge that you were the biggest badass in any room you found yourself in.

This was the kind of man you didn't want to meet in a dark alley. You didn't even want to meet him in a well-lit ballroom.

This was a man who'd eat Navy SEALS for lunch. His eyes were cold and as dark as his hair and the suit he wore over a bulletproof vest. Nick could see the bulk of the vest beneath the man's silk shirt and tie.

Those cold eyes fastened on O'Dell. "This the guy Bo told me about?" he asked Jenkins.

"That's the one."

Nick blinked as more pieces fell into place.

Telling Bo to take the night off had sent a message, but the real message came in telling him to take the night off *with pay*. Jenkins didn't even let his employees set the prices for items pawned in the store, so telling someone to take the night off with pay would be unprecedented.

Why?

Because Jenkins wasn't the real owner of this particular business.

Nick should have figured that out sooner. He'd assumed Jenkins owned the shop, but Janine had said he *ran* the shop. And besides, where would a wannabe rocker who worked birthday parties instead of casino showrooms come up with the kind of cash necessary to start a business like Ace High Pawn? He'd needed a backer.

Someone else was involved behind the scenes. Someone Jenkins didn't dare cross.

Someone who had the connections to hire a guy like this unnamed badass. Someone who would want to protect an asset like the pawn shop, a legitimate business that probably ran a tidy profit.

Bo might not even work for Jenkins. To the general public, he'd look like a simple security guard, but Nick was willing to bet Bo's real job was to keep an eye on the business to protect his real boss's asset. He'd seen O'Dell and his two guys come in the store and had recognized them for what they were—trouble. When Jenkins had told him to take off for the night with pay, Bo had gone directly to the guy he really worked for.

Nick had a good idea who that might be.

Mobsters and Las Vegas went hand in hand. Hell, the city even had a museum down by Fremont Street devoted to the mob's history in Vegas. It was a nice place for tourists, and it helped cement the idea that those bad old days were long past and the Vegas of today was a safe family destination.

Jenkins didn't necessarily have ties to the Pucinellis. Then again, he'd found the address for Stacy pretty quickly, and that probably wouldn't be easy for the average Joe Blow hacker. Stacy's dad was probably only a minor player in the family business—even though he'd killed Stacy's husband, if O'Dell was to be believed—but even a minor player wouldn't want random strangers to roll up to the estate just to say hello. No, the family would bury that piece of property beneath so many dummy corporations and partnerships that even the county assessor wouldn't know the real owner.

If anybody other than Janine had asked for the address, Nick would be willing to bet that Jenkins would have turned them down. But Jenkins still had a thing for her, so he'd handed over an address he probably knew by heart. It wasn't like Janine was going to go in guns blazing and wipe out that branch of the family. He must have counted on that decision never coming back to bite him in the ass. He might be losing a few brownie points with his boss over fucking that up.

O'Dell wiped blood off his face with the back of one hand. His skin had gone pallid. Even guys like O'Dell recognized when an unbeatable force entered their lives. An unbeatable force with a gun pointed in his direction.

That didn't mean he wouldn't try to weasel his way out of a situation far beyond his control.

"I've got no beef with you," he told the badass in the black suit. "What's say we just go our own ways and call it good?"

The badass' neutral expression didn't change. "I've got no 'beef' with anyone," he said. "I'm just a messenger. The boss sent me to deliver this message to you."

And he shot O'Dell once, right between the eyes.

The sound was unexpectedly loud in the small room. Janine dropped her gun to the floor as she covered her mouth with both hands, her eyes wide and round with shock. Jenkins just twitched as

O'Dell fell backwards on the concrete floor. Blood began to pool beneath his head as his vacant eyes stared upward.

O'Dell's man started to whimper, "Oh Jesus, oh Jesus," over and over again. He tried to back away, totally ignoring the fact that Jenkins was still holding a gun on him.

The badass turned his gun on the man. "The boss has a message for you too."

The scent of urine competed with the acrid smell of gunpowder and the sharp coppery odor of blood as the man's bladder let go. He was still whimpering to a deity he probably didn't believe in as a dark stain soiled the front of his pants.

"You get to live," the badass said. "You never fuck with anybody in this room again. You never talk about what happened here. In fact, you get the fuck out of town. If you don't follow these rules?"

The badass gave a slight nod towards O'Dell's body. He didn't have to be any more explicit. O'Dell's man was jerking his head up and down so fast his brains must have been rattling inside his skull.

"Now leave," the badass said.

The man scrambled out of the room, nearly tripping over his own feet on his way out the door.

Jenkins heaved a sigh and lowered the gun he was still holding. Some color was coming back to Janine's face, but her complexion was still pallid, a shocking contrast to her shiny black wig.

It was over.

Or not quite.

The badass gestured with his head toward Nick. "This the other one?" he asked Jenkins.

Jenkins closed his eyes for a long moment, his mouth a thin, tight line. "Yeah," he said.

The badass turned his attention—and his gun—on Nick, and Janine screamed. She took a step forward, but Jenkins held her back.

"Don't," he told her. "You're not part of this now."

Nick didn't look at the badass or at Janine. Instead he shot Jenkins a look that said he didn't blame the man for anything that was about to happen. Jenkins knew where his bread was buttered, and Nick couldn't fault him for that. Hell, he didn't even know Nick. Nick had come into his life asking for a favor. The bill for that favor was about to come due.

Nick knew he had no chance of punching his way out of this one. Fists wouldn't work against someone who clearly held the upper hand. He'd learned that in the boxing ring when the old hardcase, a man who had a good forty years on Nick, had put Nick down on the canvas more than once.

The badass was simply better than Nick could ever hope to be. He could try to fight, but the result was a foregone conclusion. And Nick simply didn't have the juice left to put up any kind of a fight. He'd thrown everything he had into beating the living shit out of O'Dell.

So he just stood there and waited for the badass to pull the trigger. Nick felt bad about Janine. He felt bad about the kitten. But both of them would go on with their lives without him. The kitten would have a loving home with Leon, and as for Janine? They'd never really had a thing anyway. She'd be fine. She'd always landed on her feet before and she would again.

The badass said, "I have a message for you too."

Nick closed his eyes and waited to die.

40

Nick's mom had been a nurturer. She'd always been there with a plate of homemade cookies at least once a week as an after-school treat. Nobody could bake cookies like his mom.

When he got into fights at school, she'd wash the blood off his hands and then bandage up the worst of the damage. She might look disappointed at the cuts and bruises, but she never made him feel like he wasn't loved and cared for. She'd give him milk to go with the cookies, and sometimes she'd give him aspirin and tell him to go lie down on his bed for a while.

"You'll feel better tomorrow," she'd tell him and she'd kiss him on the top of his head. "Give your body a chance to heal, and you'll feel better."

He'd always felt worse the next day. His hands would be stiff and sore, and his muscles would ache, but he never let her see how much he hurt. He wanted her to think that the milk and cookies, the aspirin and a soft bed, had cured all his aches and pains.

He could use milk and cookies and about a million aspirin now. He hurt in so many places that he couldn't appreciate the luxurious leather seats in the Escalade.

The badass who'd killed O'Dell sat beside him in the back seat of the big SUV. A second man, this one only slightly less intimidating than the badass in black, was driving. Nick didn't ask where they were going. Where didn't matter. The only thing that mattered was who they were taking him to see. Nick had a good idea who that might be.

They'd left Jenkins and Janine behind with the mess at Ace High Pawn. Jenkins hadn't seemed overly concerned once he realized the badass wasn't going to kill Nick. At least not kill him right away.

That told Nick that Jenkins' silent partner would be sending a cleanup crew. When the pawn shop reopened for business tomorrow morning, the place would be spotless and there'd probably be a new flatscreen television installed on the wall in the back room to replace the one O'Dell had smashed with Jenkins' face.

As for O'Dell and the dead man who'd patted Nick down, it was a big desert. Their bodies would never be found.

Nick was surprised he wasn't dead too. He should have been dead. He'd interrupted the hit at the convenience store and caused problems when he'd kept the robber from making a clean getaway. But the message the badass had been told to deliver to Nick wasn't a bullet.

"The boss wants to see you," the badass had said. "I have a car waiting."

That was as close to an engraved invitation as he was going to get. Nick had gone with the badass without complaint.

Early evening had turned into night while he'd been inside the windowless back room at Ace High Pawn. They were driving north through the heart of the Strip. There were quicker ways to get wherever they were headed, but the badass seemed content to let the driver take his time. Postponing the inevitable might seem cruel, but Nick didn't mind. It gave him more time to take a good long look at the world.

The explosion of neon that was the Strip always looked better after the sun went down. Nick had worked nights for so long that he'd taken for granted the beauty of all that neon, all that glitz and electronic glamour. He'd become jaded. For him the Strip had become the land of drunks and grifters and gamblers always looking for the one big win that was always the next hand or the next spin of the roulette wheel or the next jackpot away. He'd avoided going anywhere near it.

Now?

Now as he looked out the tinted windows of a luxury car that probably cost more than he'd made in the last five years, he felt some of what first-time tourists must feel at their first glimpse of Las Vegas at night.

Vegas was an exercise in excess, but it was an exciting exercise. It made the heart beat faster with possibilities. Life had made him a cynic. Not dying made him feel wonder.

Free spirits lived in Vegas. They performed weird street art down on Fremont Street, some of them almost as naked as the day they were born. Or they lived in a trailer with their cats and planted rainbow pinwheels in clay pots on a sunbaked front porch and worked in a museum devoted to the history of erotica.

Conventional folks lived here too. They rooted for the city's new pro football team and ran by the thousands in charity events. They shopped for groceries in chain stores and health food megastores and big box stores. They drank coffee in the morning and tucked their kids into bed at night, and never once would most of them ever encounter the type of organized crime that still lurked in the shadows of their city.

Nick snorted. Not dying had also made him philosophical.

The badass shot him a look. Nick didn't say anything, and the badass turned to face forward again.

Once they left the Strip proper, traffic moved faster. It didn't take long until they reached their destination: a new condominium building close to the Fremont Street Experience and an older casino with a railroad motif.

The driver stopped the SUV in a loading zone in front of the building. The badass got out and came around Nick's side to open the door for him. Nick got out, moving stiffly. He was definitely going to need some aspirin, or maybe something stronger. If he lived long enough.

The SUV pulled away, leaving him alone with the badass.

He could have run. The badass had tucked his gun in the shoulder holster he wore under his suit coat. His coat had been tailored well, and it hid the hard bulk of the gun. No one out on the street would have suspected the man was armed, and Nick might actually be able to lose himself in the crowd before the badass could draw the gun from beneath his suit.

The crowd at this end of the Fremont Street Experience had grown thick. Music was pounding from the outdoor speakers, which meant that the overhead show was about to begin. The odds were good that Nick could disappear into the crowd.

The fact that the badass didn't have a warning hand on Nick's shoulder told Nick that the badass didn't think he'd run.

And really, why would he? He didn't have his car. He'd left it at the pawn shop along with almost everything else he still owned. The only thing he had that was his besides the bloody clothes on his back was the roll of cash in his pocket, and that wouldn't last long.

O'Dell was dead, and the simple fact was that Nick was tired of looking over his shoulder. If he ran now, he'd be trading one enemy for an even more powerful one. He was tired of hiding on the wrong side of whatever town he happened to be in. He was tired period, and he hurt, and he could use a drink.

A dying man should be able to have one last drink, if for no other reason than to remember what a quality shot of bourbon tasted like. He regretted now that he'd ordered a gin and tonic at the casino. A man's last drink should be one he actually liked.

Whoever they were going to see, Nick hoped they'd offer him a drink—one last drink—before they killed him.

41

Nick had never been in a penthouse suite before. The view from this one was spectacular.

Floor to ceiling windows gave him a view of the Strip to the south and the Fremont Street Experience to the east. A huge art deco mural had been painted on the side of another nearby high rise. Glass doors opened onto a private balcony with its own firepit surrounded by overstuffed patio furniture, and sitting out there must have made the mural look close enough to touch.

The interior of the condo was light and airy, filled with comfortable furniture and bookshelves stuffed to overflowing with novels from bestselling authors. More hardback books were stacked on occasional tables strewn around the living area. A huge, long-haired tabby cat lounged in the top tier of a cat tree next to one of the windows. It regarded Nick with sleepy green eyes.

Not what most people would think of as the home for the head of the most powerful crime family in Vegas.

Victor Pucinelli wasn't what most people would think of as a mob boss either. He was dressed in faded jeans and a short-sleeve button-up shirt in a dusty pastel green, open at the collar. His graying hair was long and tied back at the nape of his neck with a strip of leather.

His face was lined and weather beaten, as if he'd spent a lot of time in the sun, and he wore tennis shoes instead of polished dress shoes like the badass wore.

The badass looked the part he played. Victor Pucinelli looked like he'd be at home spending his days on a golf course teeing off with a few of his old buddies. Like the golfers Nick had seen that afternoon when he was leaving the Pucinellis' estate with Stacy and Janine in the back seat of Jenkins' limo.

The only thing hard about Victor Pucinelli were his eyes. His dark eyes were as flat and emotionless as a rattlesnake's. Or a shark's.

He took in Nick's bloody hands and the dried blood on his face. The blood on his clothes.

"Our guest might like to clean up first," Pucinelli told the badass. His gaze shifted back to Nick. "Before we chat."

The badass took Nick to a bathroom that was nearly as big as his apartment. An oversized tub was raised two steps off the tile floor. It had a wide lip around the edge—for candles, he supposed—and more floor to ceiling windows would give anyone soaking in the tub a breathtaking view of the Strip. The sink had gold fixtures and the towels were monogrammed. Candles of varying heights were set around a fresh flower arrangement on the bathroom counter. Their fragrance only added to the unreality of the moment.

Nick gazed at himself in the mirror. He looked awful, but he was still alive. He didn't believe Victor would have him killed in a place like this. No, this was Pucinelli's home. Something else was going on here.

He splashed water on his face and washed his hands, careful to get all the blood off so he wouldn't leave any on the towels. He couldn't do anything about the blood on his clothes.

That's when he noticed a bathrobe on a free-standing towel rack off to the side of the counter. The bathrobe was new, made of the kind of thick white terrycloth he imagined you might find in a luxury hotel. One they'd charge you an arm and a leg for if you were audacious enough to pack the bathrobe in your luggage before you checked out.

"Hey," he called to the badass standing outside the bathroom door. "Is this for me?"

The badass looked through the half-open bathroom door to where Nick was pointing at the robe. "That's what it's there for," he said. "Up to you whether you wear it."

Nick didn't take long to decide. Victor Pucinelli had offered the robe in hospitality. Nick didn't want to piss the man off by not accepting it.

He stripped off the t-shirt Jenkins had given him and shrugged into the robe, belted it at his waist. The soft white terrycloth covered most of the purpling bruises on his chest where O'Dell had hit him. The older bruises from where the robber had landed a few blows had already started to turn a sickly green. A new bruise was blossoming on his left cheek from another one of O'Dell's punches. At least the cut on his forehead had stopped bleeding.

He gave himself one more look in the mirror. Except for the jeans he'd decided to keep on, he looked like a boxer heading into the ring when he hadn't healed up from the last bout. The sight, combined with the utter opulence of the bathroom, made Nick wonder if the badass hadn't killed him after all, and this was some fucked up version of an afterlife.

Victor Pucinelli gave Nick a hard look when the badass led him back to the living area, then he walked over to a side table where an ice bucket, two glasses, and a crystal decanter sat on a serving tray.

"Straight or on the rocks?" Pucinelli asked.

Crime bosses didn't pour their own drinks, and they especially didn't pour drinks for anyone else. They sat in leather chairs behind heavy mahogany desks and smoked expensive cigars. They had toadies who did mundane things like pour drinks and light cigars and shoot upstart wannabes who annoyed the boss.

"Straight," Nick said, further convinced this was all a dream.

Pucinelli poured two fingers of bourbon into cut crystal glasses and handed one to Nick. It was the good stuff. Nick could tell by the smell.

"Have a seat," Pucinelli said, pointing with his glass toward a small conversation area near a south-facing window.

Nick waited for Pucinelli to sit down first, then he chose an over-stuffed chair off to the side of the couch where Pucinelli sat. The badass didn't join them, but stayed on the far side of the room. Close enough in case he was needed, but far enough away to make it clear he wasn't part of the conversation.

Pucinelli took a drink, so Nick figured it was safe for him to do so too.

He'd been right. The bourbon was very, very good. He could feel it warming his body as it went down. It might be a hot desert night outside, but in this temperature controlled penthouse, the warmth felt good.

"We've got a few things to get straight, you and me," Pucinelli said. "If we can do that like civilized men, you'll be free to go. With certain restrictions, of course." Those hard eyes, so out of place in the man's face, bored into Nick. "Is that a conversation you're willing to entertain?"

Death or life with restrictions. Whatever Pucinelli had in mind couldn't be worse than the life Nick had been living, which made his answer a no-brainer.

"Yes," he said.

"Good. My niece said you're a smart man."

His niece. He was talking about Stacy. She'd told her uncle about him? That sense of unreality washed over Nick again.

He forced himself to focus on the here and now. He had a feeling whatever was coming next might be the most important few minutes of his life.

"Are you a smart man?" Pucinelli asked.

"I try to be," Nick said.

"I'm told you were cop," Pucinelli said. "That you tried to do the right thing."

No one was supposed to know that. The feds had whisked him away into witness protection. Killed his old name and given him a new one.

"How did you...?" Nick started to ask, but then he knew.

In spite of his looks, Victor Pucinelli was a very, very powerful man. Powerful men got what they wanted. Including, apparently, a peek inside files the feds had sworn would remain confidential. O'Dell's connections in the Vegas police department suddenly seemed penny ante by comparison.

Pucinelli just sat and waited while Nick figured this out.

"Yeah," Nick said after a moment. "I was, and I did."

Pucinelli nodded. "And you tried to do the right thing again the other night."

Nick didn't say anything. He figured he didn't have to.

"Serve and protect, even all these years later." Pucinelli took another drink. "Admirable. Stupid, but admirable."

Nick didn't tell him that he'd done it because Stacy had been nice to him. That he thought Stacy and the old guy she'd been with, the old guy who'd turned out to be her husband, didn't deserve to die in some random act of violence. That the clerk didn't deserve to die, not if Nick could stop it.

Pucinelli turned his head to look out the window. "My brother's an idiot," he said. "He could have come to me, brought his grievances about his son-in-law to me. I would have handled it, neat and clean. But no, he decides he wants to take care of his little girl himself, so he hires the first lowlife he finds for the job."

"Winston Jackson," Nick said, not quite intending to say the name out loud, but his head still hurt and he was concentrating on this conversation so hard his brain felt like mush.

"Is that the name he used?" Pucinelli shook his head. "No imagination, my brother."

The robber's name was an alias, that's what Pucinelli was saying. Winston Jackson was an alias.

Winston. Just like the security guard at the golf course.

Stacy's father had needed an alias for the robber, so he'd picked the first name he thought of. The name of a man he saw every day but probably ignored until it came time to give the man a holiday bonus. Nick felt like an idiot for not seeing the connection sooner. Gino probably didn't know the guard's name. Stacy's father did.

"You never had kids, did you," Pucinelli said.

It wasn't a question, so Nick didn't say anything. He figured Pucinelli already knew the answer anyway.

"I understand my brother's desire to take care of his kid," Pucinelli said. "My own kid, I've been cleaning up after him most of his life. Parents do things like that. Try to set boundaries. Kids push back."

Now he was talking about Gino. Nick guessed one of the boundaries he'd set was forbidding his son from taking up with his beautiful cousin Stacy, husband or no husband.

"My brother made things worse by going to my *son* to clean up the mess he'd made," Pucinelli said. It wasn't hard to see that the insult still didn't sit well with him. "And my son made things even worse by involving the man he'd hired to provide personal security." He shook his head. "I should have nipped that in the bud. But I figured, let my kid make a few of his own mistakes. Let him learn from them, maybe he'd grow up."

His eyes had taken on a faraway look. Nick wondered how many mistakes Pucinelli had made himself along the way. He might even be remembering a few of them now.

"But a disgraced ex-cop, a man who's always going to be out for himself." Pucinelli's eyes focused on Nick. "One who had a rather involved past with you, from what I understand."

Nick took another drink of his very, very good bourbon to give himself time to think. Pucinelli was airing some rather dirty laundry to a virtual stranger. That didn't bode well for Nick's chances on being allowed to walk away from this mess in one piece unless he was very, very careful with what he said.

"That he did," he finally said.

Pucinelli nodded, like he appreciated Nick's honesty.

"None of this is good for the family, so I'm going to take care of it," he said. "Step in. Straighten things out. I'm getting rid of the things that don't work for me. That go off on their own. For vengeance. For revenge. I'm going to clean up this mess once and for all."

He'd already taken care of O'Dell. Nick imagined he'd have his own way of dealing with his son and his brother.

Pucinelli finished the last of his drink, then put the glass down on the nearest occasional table next to a stack of books. All of them were crime thrillers. Nick had seen most of them at the library, had even read a few himself.

When Pucinelli looked back at Nick, it was from beneath lowered brows.

"Are you going to be one of the messes I have to take care of?" he asked.

This was the look a rattlesnake gave you before it struck, or a shark before it bit you in half. This was the look of a dangerous man who'd built a hidden empire in this city of neon and gambling and entertainment. Who'd not only built it, but who thrived in this kind of life.

Nick's blood ran cold. There was only one answer he could give.

"No, sir," he said, meeting the man's gaze and praying that Pucinelli would believe him.

Pucinelli held Nick's gaze for a long moment, then he nodded. When he spoke again, it was to the badass who'd been waiting on the other side of the room.

"Get this man a new shirt," he said. He turned to Nick. "I'm assuming you don't want the old one back."

The old one had come from Jenkins. Nick's clothes, the t-shirt and flannel shirt he'd worn when he'd fled his apartment, were in the trunk of his car.

"No, sir," Nick said again.

"Good." Pucinelli leaned back against the overstuffed cushions and sighed. It was the sound of a man who'd avoided something he would have rather not done. "While he's getting you a shirt, I want to go over those few restrictions I mentioned earlier. They're non-negotiable, but you're smart enough to know that you have no bargaining power here."

No, Nick had known he was in no position to ask for anything from the moment he'd gotten in the back seat of the Escalade.

While he finished his drink, Pucinelli laid out the restrictions, ticking the points off on his fingers.

The first was the most obvious: Nothing had happened at Ace High Pawn other than a computer glitch that meant the store had to close for the night while the glitch was taken care of.

The second was less obvious but understandable: Nick was to have no further contact with anyone in the family, period. That included Stacy. If she somehow managed to contact him, Nick was to disengage immediately.

"I'm going to have her father tell her the same thing," Pucinelli said, "but she's stubborn. I'll keep his secret, even from her. I expect you to do the same."

The third and final restriction was the most harsh, but it didn't come as a surprise. If he'd been in Pucinelli's shoes, Nick would have done the same.

While he was riding down the elevator with the badass, whose name turned out to be Mr. Smith—of course—Nick realized that the thoughts he'd had while riding down the Strip in the back of the Escalade had been eerily accurate. He'd been thinking that he was looking at all the neon and glitz and glamour of the Strip for the last time and noticing, for the first time in a long time, how beautiful it all was.

He'd thought he was going to die, and he'd been saying goodbye to the city.

Mr. Smith had orders to take Nick back to his car. Nick wasn't to go inside the pawn shop. He was never to ask Jenkins for anything again. Pucinelli had given him until tomorrow morning to settle his affairs, and then he was to hit the road.

"I don't care where you go," Pucinelli had said, "as long as I don't hear that you're anywhere near this city. If I do, I'll consider my kind offer rejected. Is that understood?"

Nick had only nodded.

Tomorrow morning he would be saying goodbye to this city for real.

To this city, and to Janine.

42

M r. Smith, Victor Pucinelli's badass fixer—what else
could he be?—took Nick back to Ace High Pawn to pick
up his car. This time Smith did the driving himself and
Nick sat in the front passenger seat.

Unlike the trip downtown to see Pucinelli, Smith took one of the
wide secondary roads that bypassed the Strip. That made the trip
take far less time. Smith was apparently a get in and get it done kinda
guy. Nick would have expected nothing less.

Smith didn't talk during the drive, and that was fine with Nick.
The warmth that had suffused his abused body from the bourbon
Pucinelli had given him was wearing off. Everything hurt, even his
heart. One of the first things he'd have to do once Smith dropped him
off was find a drug store that stocked some heavy-duty over-the-
counter pain relievers.

But it wasn't the very first thing he had to do.

Smith stood next to the Escalade with his arms crossed and
watched while Nick got behind the wheel of his own car and pulled
out of the pawn shop's parking lot. Nick kept one eye on Smith in his
rearview mirror, and he saw Smith go inside the shop.

To check on how the cleanup was coming along? Or to make sure Nick didn't decide to double back and go inside?

It didn't really matter. Nick had no intention of violating any of Victor Pucinelli's restrictions, including setting foot inside Ace High Pawn. He'd been lucky to escape this mess with his life, and he knew it. He wasn't about to jeopardize that now.

After he'd put the pawn shop far behind, Nick rolled down the windows in his car to let the night air in. The sounds of the city came along with it, and he drove for blocks, even up and down the Strip, just enjoying the fact that he was still alive.

Just putting off the call he had to make.

He eventually pulled the burner phone out of his pocket. The number for Janine's burner showed up as his one and only recent call.

In Nevada, the only legal way to talk on a cell while driving was to use a hands-free device. Nick didn't have one. Although the burner had a speaker function, he didn't want to have this conversation over a speaker.

He also didn't want to risk a run-in with the police. He didn't want to have to explain his injuries. To come up with a story that would satisfy the cops and leave him with only a ticket for talking on the phone.

So he pulled into the parking lot for a shopping center anchored by a big-box entertainment store and studded with fast food outlets. The parking lot was less than half full at this time of night, but the fast food restaurants were still open. Enough cars had lined up through the drive-throughs to give him cover. He'd be safe enough just sitting in his car for a few minutes while he talked on the phone.

He had to snort at himself. Safe enough. He'd actually thought that.

He'd spent so many years trying to be invisible, he had a feeling it would take just as many years before he got used to the idea that he no longer had to hide. That no one was out to—what was the phrase he'd heard in some of the afternoon movies he'd watched? Terminate him with extreme prejudice?

He put the phone to his ear and called Janine.

He could hear the relief in her voice when she answered his call. "Jenkins told me you'd be okay if you were smart," she said. "I was hoping you would be."

"Surprised you, didn't I?" he said, then almost immediately regretted it. He was being flippant, and after the night they'd both had, she didn't deserve it. "I'm okay. You?"

Instead of answering immediately, he heard muffled conversation in the background. Janine was talking to someone—Jenkins? Smith? Or one of the cleaners who'd been sent in to take care of the mess?—and she didn't want him to hear.

If she was even still at the pawn shop. Jenkins could have arranged to have someone take her home.

When she came back on the phone, he heard traffic noise in the background. Wherever she was, she'd gone outside to talk to him. Outside, where no one else could overhear.

She was sniffling a little bit, which surprised him. She'd impressed him as someone who could survive anything with her emotions intact. Her fury at O'Dell had been an aberration. Maybe she was one of those people who held things together just fine while a crisis was going on and only let go of their emotions after the crisis was over.

"I'm doing okay," she said. "Where are you?"

He told her.

"Looking to buy a DVD?" she asked. "Or have you upgraded to Blu-ray?"

She was trying to keep the conversation light. Gallows humor, what a great way to let off steam. More than one cop Nick had known back in Jersey used to do the same thing at the end of a tough shift.

"Looking to buy dinner," he said. "Just trying to figure out whether I want Mexican food or something in a burger line."

He was still being flippant, but at least now he knew why. Not gallows humor. He was trying to work up to the real reason for the call.

"I'd go for Chinese food," she said. "I'm starving. I guess almost dying does that to a person. Who knew?"

She was a smart woman. She'd figured out what O'Dell had planned for the three of them, Nick and Jenkins and her. He never doubted that she would.

The ache in his chest grew stronger. He'd put her through so much, and he wasn't done hurting her. Not yet.

When he didn't say anything, she asked "Feel like picking me up and grabbing something to eat?"

"Are you back at your place?" he asked, but he was pretty sure he already knew the answer.

"I'm still at Jenkins' place."

He sighed. He didn't mean to, and she must have heard it.

"What's wrong? Jenkins said you'd be okay. Aren't you okay? You said..." She trailed off.

"I think we should do breakfast instead," he said. He didn't want to tell her that Smith was hanging around the pawn shop specifically to make sure Nick didn't come back.

But she was smart. She caught on.

"That man who took you to see his boss, he's here," she said. "And if he's here, you can't be here, right? Isn't that the deal? That's why your car's gone."

She must have gone out to the parking lot to talk to him.

"I can meet you for breakfast," he said again. "Someplace else, we can get together wherever you want. Just not there."

His head was pounding, and the inside of his car was starting to feel like an oven. He'd rolled up the windows to keep the conversation private. He could roll them down again, but he didn't want to let the world in, to break the illusion that she was in the car with him instead of at the other end of an invisible string attached to a technological tin can.

She stayed quiet for a long time. "You're leaving, aren't you," she finally said. "That was part of the deal, right? And breakfast is the brushoff?"

He rubbed the bridge of his nose between his thumb and forefinger. He'd washed the blood off his face in Victor Pucinelli's opulent bathroom, but his skin felt tight.

"Not until tomorrow," he said. "I'm not leaving until tomorrow. After breakfast." He paused. "I want to see you, and not because I want to brush you off. I want to see you."

He wanted to do more than just see her. He wanted to hold her. To kiss her. To feel her soft skin against his and know that he was no longer alone.

But none of that was going to happen.

After a moment, she gave him the name of a chain restaurant close to her apartment. "I'll meet you there at eight," she said. Her voice had taken on a flat, impersonal tone. "You have someplace to go tonight?"

She might as well have been asking a customer at the strip club if he was sober enough to find his way back to his hotel.

He didn't, but he'd find something. There was always an empty low-rent room somewhere in Vegas. He had a nice shirt now thanks to Victor Pucinelli, a light denim work shirt that actually fit like it was made for him, but his face was too messed up to check into someplace nice.

He supposed he could even go back to his apartment. O'Dell had probably kicked the door in, but Nick could make it work. It was still his apartment, the rent was paid till the end of the month, and no one would be looking for him now.

"I'll be fine," he said. "You?"

"I can get a ride."

"With Jenkins?"

Nick couldn't help the note of jealousy that crept into his voice. If she caught it, she didn't let on.

"One of the guys took him to urgent care," she said, still in that flat, impersonal tone. "He probably broke a couple of ribs, and I'm sure he's got a concussion. His nose won't ever look the same and he's going to have a couple of black eyes to go along with that knot on his forehead. He'll have to stay in the back room for a few days while he heals up."

Nick hoped that Victor Pucinelli wouldn't add to Jenkins' injuries. Jenkins was part of the mess Stacy's father and O'Dell had created, thanks to Jenkins giving his ex Stacy's home address. With any luck, Pucinelli would decide Jenkins had already paid enough for his mistake.

"And you?" he asked her.

"It was just a slap." She sounded impatient now. "I've had worse." After another pause, then she said, "I should probably go. We're eating minutes here, and we didn't have that many to begin with. Just be sure to bring my suitcase with you in the morning."

She disconnected before he could say goodbye.

Nick felt like a door had just been slammed in his face. He rested the burner phone against his aching head and told himself that after everything he'd put her through, he deserved it.

A car drove by with the windows down and such a loud, heavy bass beat coming from the car's speakers that Nick felt the vibrations in his bones. Drunken or stoned laughter from the car's occupants competed with the music. The car had Nevada plates featuring the logo for the Vegas ice hockey team.

Ice hockey in the desert. Vegas had something for everyone.

But not for him. Not anymore.

Only that wasn't quite true. The city did still have one thing for him.

The shopping center had a grocery store at the other end of the parking lot. The store was part of a national chain that he knew had a pharmacy department where he could pick up pain pills and bandages in case any of his wounds opened up.

There'd been six crisp hundred dollar bills in the pocket of the denim shirt when he'd put it on. Smith had given him a look when Nick found the money, a look that told him the money was part of his deal with Victor Pucinelli.

Seed money for starting his life over somewhere else.

It wasn't as much as the feds had given him when they'd put him in witness protection, but it would do.

Nick would use Victor's money to buy the few things he needed for the road as well as some honest-to-God cat food, a new litter box, and the real stuff to fill it with. Maybe even a new cat toy. One with feathers. One she could play with on the road.

Tomorrow after breakfast, after he said his final goodbyes to Janine, he and a fuzzy little girl named Connie were going to put this city far behind them.

43

Nick stopped for food, gas, and a bathroom break in Tonopah, the first of two planned stops on his way to Reno.

The busy minimart had pumps out front, public restrooms in the back, and a sandwich shop on one side and a burger joint on the other. In the middle, shelves full of all sorts of junk food, snack food, and candy shared space with coolers full of all sorts of soda, water, energy drinks in more varieties that he could count, and beer. Your basic middle-of-the-desert one-stop shop.

At least the sandwich shop and burger joint were parts of national chains, so there was a good chance the food would be edible.

He wasn't about to leave Connie in the car. The day was hot and the car's air conditioning had crapped out a mere fifty miles north of Vegas. Leaving the windows open just a crack wouldn't cut it, not in this heat. She was just a little kitten. He didn't think it would take much for her to overheat.

So he strapped on her carrier and took her in the station with him.

She'd been a good kitten, sleeping in her carrier during most of the trip so far. She'd gotten used to the carrier quick for a cat, or so Leon had told him.

"I left it out for her to play in," Leon said when Nick called to let them know he'd be coming to pick her up. "I think she slept in it last night. It probably makes her feel safe, like it's her own little cave."

Feeling safe in her own little cave made Nick think about Jenkins. He wondered if the man would ever feel safe in his dark little lair at the back of the pawn shop again, after everything that had happened. Maybe Victor Pucinelli would set him up in a different business. Nick had no doubt that Pucinelli had his fingers in more pies in Vegas than anyone knew about.

It would take time before Nick would feel safe again, if ever. He finally had to make a conscious effort to keep himself from checking the rearview mirror every few minutes trying to spot a tail. It was a big desert out there, and he was going to be driving through some of the most desolate parts of it.

But O'Dell was dead. No one would be looking for him, not anymore. It was going to take a long time to get used to that fact.

Tonopah wasn't a big town, not by a long shot, but the combination gas station/mini-mart/fast food joints looked like a popular place to stop. The parking lot out front was nearly full, and there'd been lines of cars at the pumps. Most of the people inside the mini-mart looked as road weary as the family he'd seen a couple nights ago getting gas at a mini-mart not all that different from this one.

The exception was a group of about twenty teenage girls.

They must have belonged to a girls' sports team of some sort. A school bus took up four spaces off to one side of the parking lot, and all the girls were dressed in identical green and gold uniforms: short-sleeved shirts, shorts, and bright white tennis shoes. Their legs were tanned, their arms were tanned, and their faces had the healthy glow of teenagers in great physical shape.

Most of them were lined up lined up for sandwiches and salads at the sandwich shop. They were chatting and laughing and just being such high-energy teenagers that he felt sorry for the woman in line with them who was clearly trying to ride herd over her charges.

Nick didn't want to wait as long as it was going to take for the two harried sandwich makers behind the counter to work their way through that many teenagers, so he headed toward the burger joint.

He'd made his way across half of the junk food aisles when two of the girls who'd been shopping for chips spotted Connie.

"Oooo!" one of them cooed. "What a cute little kitty!"

Instead of wearing Connie's carrier like a backpack on his back, Nick had reversed the carry straps so that the carrier rested against his chest. He just felt better when he could see the kitten in front of him. He thought it was probably a form of post-traumatic stress. Or maybe he was just stretching mental muscles, the ones most people used to form connections with other people, that had atrophied over long years of disuse.

The second teenage girl bent down to get a closer look inside the carrier. "A little blue-eyed black kitten," she said. She looked at Nick from beneath thick eyelashes and gave him a mischievous half-grin. "Aren't black cats supposed to be bad luck?"

"She's been pretty lucky so far," he said.

Most people wouldn't call all the things that had happened to him the last few days lucky, but he wasn't most people. He'd been given his life back, even if he had to keep reminding himself of that fact.

A frown creased the teenager's forehead as she noticed the cuts on his face. "Are you sure about that?" she asked.

Her eyes were the same shape as Janine's, and she had the same smattering of freckles across her nose and cheeks. Her hair was ash brown with blonde highlights instead of auburn, but for a moment she reminded him so much of Janine that the two of them could have been sisters.

"I'm kind of clumsy," he said, his voice not quite as casual as he wanted.

The woman in line with the rest of her team at the sandwich shop called the two girls over to get in line "for real food," she said. The girls said goodbye to the kitten.

When they were gone, the kitten tilted her head up to look at him through the mesh at the top of the carrier, almost like she was asking if she'd have to put up with this sort of thing often.

"You'll get used it," he told her.

They both would.

He was going to run into women who reminded him of Janine. That was just the way life worked, and he was going to have to learn how to deal with it. He just hadn't expected to have to deal with it so soon.

Breakfast that morning had not gone well. Janine had appeared in fresh jeans and a plain baby blue t-shirt faded nearly white. The short sleeves of the shirt barely covered the thumb-sized bruise on her inner arm. She had on another wig, this one almost the same color as her real hair but cut in a shaggy style that brushed the top of her shoulders. Her makeup covered any bruises from where O'Dell had slapped her face and she looked rested, not like a woman who'd been holding a loaded gun on a man she was ready to shoot less than twelve hours ago.

She'd smiled at him and let him buy her breakfast—coffee and a danish—but she'd been subdued. After fifteen minutes, after she'd finished one cup of coffee and half the danish, she'd said she had to go.

So he'd left enough money to cover the cost of the meal plus a generous tip next to the uneaten portion of his pancakes and eggs. He was still using Pucinelli's money. He could afford to be generous.

He'd hoped that Janine would go with him to pick up the kitten from Leon, but she'd just asked for her carryon suitcase.

The carryon had been nestled in the trunk of his car against the duffel he'd retrieved from his apartment. It had still been in his living room where he'd left it. Now that old canvas bag carried all the possessions he had left in this world, except for the kitten.

Symbolic? Hopeful? Maybe he'd been feeling those things when he'd chucked it in the trunk after he'd dropped of the key to his apartment with the manager. Once he took Janine's carryon out of the trunk, his duffel just looked lonely.

He'd slammed the trunk lid shut.

They'd stood by his car for a long moment, the sun already beating down out of a cloudless blue sky. It was going to be another hot Vegas day. He hoped the weather would be cooler in Reno. He didn't intend to stay there long—he didn't intend to stay anywhere in Nevada long—but stopping in Reno would give him a chance to regroup and plan what he wanted to do next.

Janine hadn't asked him where he was going. She hadn't asked anything about his future plans.

When the silence became awkward, he held out his hand. "I can't begin to thank you—"

"I lied to you," she said, interrupting him. "Chubs caught me going through his office. Looking in your file for your address."

Nick blinked, surprised. Then he looked at the bruise on her upper arm, a bruise in the shape of an oversized thumb.

"I don't think they followed me," she said. "O'Dell and Gino and the other guy, the one Smith shot. I think Chubs called the number on the card O'Dell threw down on the bar. I think he sold them your address."

That made sense. Chubs was the kind of guy who'd go after the money if he thought there was a deal to be made. He wouldn't have been happy that Janine had been in his office. He'd probably thought she was out to make a deal on her own, so he'd grabbed her and thrown her out, but not before she had a chance to find out where Nick lived.

"You asked me why I stayed, why I kept helping you." She shook her head and looked away from him, her mouth thinned into a tight, hard line. "I didn't lie about that part, but I didn't tell you the whole truth." She took a deep breath and turned toward him. "I stayed because I screwed up. I let them find you."

"No," he said. She was wrong. It hadn't been her fault. "They would have found me anyway. Chubs would have told them where I lived. You gave me time to—"

He was going to say "get away," but she surprised him again, this time by leaning in and kissing him. A long, lingering kiss.

He'd put his hands around her back and pulled her close. He

hadn't kissed anyone in longer than he could remember, and she felt good. She felt more than good. She felt like heaven.

Just when he began to hope that the kiss meant something more than just a kiss, she'd pulled away. Her face was flushed, her eyes deep and dark, her lips still wet and glistening in the sun.

"Justine," she'd said, her voice barely above a whisper.

He'd frowned, not understanding. He'd wanted to kiss her again, keep on kissing her until the world slipped away and only the two of them remained.

She'd cupped the side of his face with a gentle hand. "My real name. Justine. I know Nick's not your real name, but you'll always be Nick to me."

She'd put her burner phone in his hand and walked away from him, her suitcase rolling along after her.

He'd watched as she got in her car and drove away.

She never once looked back.

NICK ATE the burger and fries in his car. A large iced tea sat in the cupholder, and the two-pack of chocolate iced cupcakes he'd purchased on a whim sat on the passenger seat next to Connie's carrier. He'd rolled all the windows down, and it was actually pleasant just sitting in his car thanks to a gentle breeze.

He'd given the kitten half of a ridiculously small can of kitten food, which she'd eaten with gusto. Then she'd used the litterbox he'd set up on the passenger side floorboard, drank some water, and now she was curled up asleep inside her carrier alongside the new toy he'd bought for her last night.

A rainbow flag with crinkly stuff inside and a purple feather on one end. He had a feeling Leon would approve.

The school bus and all the giggling, chatty girls pulled out of the parking lot when he was halfway through the burger. The girl who'd reminded him of Janine had given him a little finger wave when she walked past his car on the way to the bus. He'd raised one hand in response, not really a wave, just an acknowledgment from one traveler to the next.

Justine, he reminded himself. Her real name was Justine. It didn't matter. She would always be Janine to him.

He doubted he would ever see her again except in his memories. She'd given him her burner phone to make sure he didn't call her, and he was pretty sure she wouldn't be going back to work at the strip club. But she was proof that even after nearly half his adult life spent in hiding, avoiding any sort of relationship with another human being, he still had the ability to form a real connection with someone.

It gave him hope that he might be able to do it again wherever this new life took him.

A life where he didn't need to hide. Amazing.

A life where people cared about him.

The thought struck him out of the blue. He did still have people who cared about him. At least, he hoped he did.

He pulled the burner phone out of the pocket of the denim shirt Victor Pucinelli had given him. The rest of the cash that had been in his pocket was now in his wallet, and the empty pocket fit the burner phone like a glove. He might even get used to carrying one again.

The phone actually got a decent signal in Tonopah, which surprised him. But he supposed even people who lived out in the middle of Nevada's unforgiving desert needed cell phones.

He keyed in a number he still remembered by heart.

He listened as the phone rang three, four, *five* times, while his heart beat hard in his chest. His throat felt as dry as the desert.

He could do this. He didn't have to hide anymore.

But would she still be there?

The phone rang three more times before it was answered.

"Hello?" Her voice was timid and small and seemed just a little sad even though she'd spoken a single word.

That one word was enough.

A smile crept over Nick's face. He'd thought he would never hear that voice again, and now his own throat felt tight even as the tension in his chest loosened.

"Hello?" she said again. "Is anyone there?"

He put a hand on the kitten's carrier. His connections, one sleeping on the seat next to him, the other twenty-five hundred miles away.

"Hello, mom," he said. "I think it's time for me to finally come home."

ABOUT THE AUTHOR

A prolific, versatile, and award-winning writer, Annie Reed's written more short fiction than she can count. She's a frequent contributor to *Fiction River, Pulphouse Fiction Magazine,* and *Mystery, Crime and Mayhem.* She's a multiple Derringer awards finalist, and her short mystery fiction has appeared in year's best volumes, including both Year's Best Mysteries for 2023. She's even had her work selected for inclusion in study materials for Japanese college entrance exams. Her *Unexpected* series of short-story collections showcase some of the best of her work.

Annie's a founding member and contributor to the to the innovative Uncollected Anthology series of themed urban and contemporary fantasy anthologies. She writes mystery, science fiction, and fantasy novels under her own name and suspense novels as Kris Sparks. She also writes the Liberty Springs sweet romances under the name Liz McKnight. She can be found on the web at https://anniereed.wordpress.com/.

A Special Request from the author:

Word of mouth is critical for any author to succeed. If you enjoyed this book, please consider leaving a review at the site where you purchased it. Even a line or two would make all the difference in the world and I would greatly appreciate it.

Thank you!

ALSO BY ANNIE REED

ABBY MAXON MYSTERIES

Pretty Little Horses

Paper Bullets

MORETOWN BAY SERIES

Unbroken Familiar

Iris & Ivy

Tales from the Shadows

Not What They Seem

Spells Gone Bad

The Diz & Dee Holiday Mysteries

The Wizard Behind the Curtain

STANDALONE NOVELS

In Dreams

A Death in Cumberland

Faster

Road of No Return

A Christmas Reunion

Gray Lady Rising (co-authored with Robert Jeschonek)

Gray Lady's Revenge (co-authored with Robert Jeschonek)

UNEXPECTED SERIES

Unexpected Aliens

Unexpected Monsters

Unexpected Holidays

Unexpected Criminals

Unexpected Good Guys

Unexpected Futures

Unexpected Encounters

Unexpected Travels

Unexpected Hauntings

Unexpected Family

Unexpected Critters

Unexpected Killers

Unexpected Christmas

Unexpected Cats

COLLECTIONS

Crimes of Yesteryear

Everyday Magic

Life with Cats

Magic of the Heart

Turning the Page

Eight from the Silver State

The Patient Z Files

The Forever Soldier and Other Future Tales

WRITING AS KRIS SPARKS

Shadow Life

WRITING AS LIZ MCKNIGHT

Wedding Belle Blues

Wedding Belle Blues